JAGUAR

JAGUAR

a story of

africans

in america

PAUL STOLLER

The University of Chicago Press
Chicago & London

PAUL STOLLER is professor of anthropology at West Chester University of Pennsylvania. He is the author of six books, including *In Sorcery's Shadow, Fusion of the Worlds,* and *The Cinematic Griot.*

The University of Chicago Press, Chicago 60637
The University of Chicago Press, Ltd., London
© 1999 by The University of Chicago
All rights reserved. Published 1999
Printed in the United States of America

08 07 06 05 04 03 02 01 00 99   1 2 3 4 5

ISBN: 0-226-77527-5 (cloth)
ISBN: 0-226-77528-3 (paper)

Library of Congress Cataloging-in-Publication Data
Stoller, Paul.
        Jaguar : a story of Africans in America / Paul Stoller.
            p.   cm.
        ISBN 0–226–77527–5 (cloth : alk. paper).—ISBN 0–226–77528–3
    (pbk. : alk. paper)
        1. Africans—New York (State)—New York Fiction. 2. Songhai
    (African people) Fiction.   I. Title.
    PS3569.T62277J34   1999   99–35266
    813´.54—dc21   CIP

♾ The paper used in this publication meets the minimum requirements of the American National Standard for Information Sciences—Permanence of Paper for Printed Library Materials, ANSI Z39.48–1992.

For my father, Sidney Stoller
(1920–1998)

Do you think I know what I'm doing?
That for one breath or half-breath I belong to myself?
As much as a pen knows what it's writing,
or the ball can guess where it's going next.

—*Rumi*

HARLEM

Sometimes it's hard to be an African in America—at least Issa Boureima thinks so. He's lived in New York City for more than six years now. Most of the time he feels that Harlem has been sweet for him. His apartment isn't too bad, and most of his neighbors have been kind and generous. They greet him warmly. They even let him use their phones when his service was cut off. What's more, he's made enough money selling baseball caps and handbags on 125th Street to support his wife, Khadija, and his extended family in Niger, West Africa. And yet, he often feels homesick. Sometimes his stomach burns with frustration. The people here don't really understand him, and several times they've made fun of him. No matter how hard he tries to swallow his pride and anger, he cannot forget certain events that have turned his sugar to salt.

There is one New York summer afternoon that Issa will never forget. He had stepped into his battered white Ford Econovan, which he parked daily at his vending space on 125th Street near Lenox Avenue, and pulled out a tattered red prayer rug. Like all practicing Muslims, Issa tried to pray five times a day. As always, he carefully placed his prayer rug on the pavement next to his aluminum vending table. Finding water for prayer ablutions is often a problem for pious Muslims on 125th Street, but for Issa, who prides himself on his pragmatism, "there's always a way." Armed with a plastic bucket and a wrench, he strolled to the nearest fire hydrant, opened the valve, filled the bucket with precious water, and closed the valve again. He then returned to a rickety card chair, took off his shoes and socks, and cleansed himself. Now ready to pray, he faced east, prostrated himself to Allah, and began to recite his prayers.

The intensity of his concentration blocked the blare of a rapping boom box that announced the approach of a group of teenagers, all dressed in baggy jeans and T-shirts. They chattered away and laughed loudly. When they reached Issa's table, several of them sniffed audibly.

"These African brothers smell like animals," one of them said. They all laughed and snorted like pigs.

"Phew," another of them exclaimed. "That's real bad. These brothers don't wash."

When they came upon Issa's prone figure, one of them leaned over him and spat on his head, saying, "He prays like an animal."

They burst out laughing, and one of them sauntered up to Issa's table to snatch a Georgetown Hoyas cap. Nouhou, Issa's partner, ran after him, but was soon outdistanced.

Normally a quiet man, Nouhou screamed after the teenagers. "You will burn in hell! Have you no respect?" The veins in his thick neck swelled and throbbed. Anger creased the smooth black skin of his handsome face. "Worthless creatures."

Resignation soon drained some of the anger from Nouhou's body. Sadness bore down on his face.

Despite the insult, Issa completed his prayers before wiping the spittle from his hair. For once, Issa, who liked to talk, was at a loss for words. He knew that teenagers everywhere harbor some disrespect for, and even hostility toward, adults—traits of that stage of life. But in Niger they are usually outwardly respectful to elders. No matter how hard he tried, he could not make sense of what had happened. His stomach churned.

He realized that there would be no resolution to the problem of disrespectful teenagers, only lingering resentment and a shift in strategy. Whenever he thought about being spit on, he conjured up his father, Boureima, who had taught him much about his religion. "No matter the circumstances," his father told him, "you must try to respect others." That, Issa thought, was a tall order for anyone, anywhere.

"I love this country," Issa told Nouhou later that afternoon. "The police leave me alone, and I like the African Americans in

Harlem. Here I have an opportunity to work. I don't want to be angry at anybody. I just want to work, make money, and provide for my family back home."

On most days, Issa had little time to ponder the difficulties and pressures of his life in New York City. He worked every day from sunup to sundown. Life is hard everywhere, he told himself, so it is best to adapt to one's surroundings.

One week after the teenagers spit on him, he leaned on the shaky aluminum card table he used to sell his wares. Even though it was still rather early in the morning, he had already taken in two hundred dollars—a pleasant surprise, for it was usually only on weekends that he could earn such a large sum of money. Earlier that morning he had put on a pair of baggy black jeans, a black T-shirt emblazoned with "Hugo Boss" in white letters, a leather baseball cap that he wore sideways, and a pair of black Air Jordans. Dressed like the homeboy he would never become, Issa seemed a carefree and prosperous Harlem merchant.

Like many of his compatriots from Niger, Issa was as tall and willowy as the acacias that dotted his homeland. His smooth skin was very black. Continuous exposure to sunlight and New York City's dirty air had reddened the whites of his eyes. That day, he had been at work for two hours, arriving early enough to find a parking spot for his van. Issa, who didn't have a driver's license, bought the van to store his inventory, which exceeded the limited space in his tenement room. "There's always a way." Every day he and Nouhou, who was also from Niger, would pick up the van from a guarded three-story parking lot next to the market and drive it to their spot on the north side of 125th Street. Neither of them had driven in Niger. "I'm learning how to drive in New York," Issa would tell his friends, pointing to several dents and scrapes on the van's side panel. "Fewer accidents, now. Getting better all the time."

Earlier that morning, after a short trip along the traffic-clogged street, they had reached their parking space and unloaded card tables and inventory—handbags made in China, baseball caps with the logos of college and professional sports teams, and leather sacks and purses handcrafted in Niger.

Issa, who loved to talk to his fellow street merchants, searched incessantly for good conversation. As was his custom, he'd set up his table and leave Nouhou, a much quieter man, in charge of the wares so he could greet his comrades, almost all of whom were from West Africa. Conversation and laughter filled his body with good feelings—a zest for life that gave him a sense of well-being. His comrades always welcomed his visits, which made him feel good about himself.

In search of good talk that morning, Issa said hello to Idrissa, one of the market's West African elders, who sold trademarked sweatshirts and T-shirts. A veteran of the street trade, Idrissa now longed for the days of hard work in the sandy millet fields of his rural village in Niger. Issa shook Idrissa's hand and asked in Songhay, the language they shared, if the elder had slept soundly, the customary morning greeting in Niger.

"I slept with peace and tranquillity," the elder responded. Idrissa, whose physique belied his advanced years, had a forehead deeply furrowed by years of hard work. A tribal scar cut across his left cheek like a shallow canal. "I thank God for my health and the health of my wife and children," he said. "My sleep was fine, and I praise God for what he provides."

"Do you think today will bring shoppers?" Issa asked.

"Only God knows," Idrissa answered. "But I hope the day brings me some money. I need to send some to my children in Niger. My younger brother phoned last night; the family needs more food."

"May God lighten your burden, Elder."

Issa enjoyed the ceremonial conversations of his native land. In Niger, a person always preceded a business transaction with elaborate greetings that asked after the health and well-being of families and friends. He found it difficult to get accustomed to the abrupt ways in which Americans talked to one another.

chapter 2

People from Niger started coming to New York City in 1990. Like many of his West African forebears, Issa left his village to travel in search of fortune and adventure. He lived for more than five years in Abidjan, Côte d'Ivoire. At first, he wore scores of cheap wrist-watches on his bare arms as he walked through the bustle of Abidjan's streets in search of sales. Cars whisked by him like bullets; lepers slithered by him like snakes; beggars from the bush blocked his path as they slept on the garbage-strewn sidewalks. Through charm and wit and his ever-present talk, he managed to sell a few watches every day and made enough money to pay for a two small, stuffy rooms in Treichville, one of Abidjan's poorest neighborhoods.

Issa suffered during those first few years in Abidjan. The stifling heat of his rooms made sleep difficult. The high-pitched drone of malaria-ridden mosquitoes woke him from fitful sleep several times a night. To save money, he bought from street vendors poorly prepared *fufu*, a doughy paste made from cassava or plantain. More often than not he felt nauseated. By virtue of his determination, he did save money, but at the expense of losing weight.

Issa's forbearance eventually paid off. After three years he had saved enough money to marry Khadija, a young woman he had met when he was living with his uncle in Niamey, the capital city of Niger. They had fallen in love and pledged themselves to one another, vowing to get married one day. That day came when Issa was able to pay Khadija's widowed mother a two hundred dollar bride-price. Proud to be a man at last, Issa flew to Niamey for the wedding. He paid for several days of requisite parties, at which friends and relatives danced, drank tea, ate mutton brochettes, and chewed kola nuts. He gave his mother-in-law many meters of Ivorian print cloth and more than thirty kilos of kola nuts. As exhaustion set in, an Islamic cleric married them.

Issa remembered the beauty of the nuptial night with his bride. He walked into their bedroom, the walls of which were covered by bright blue, red, and green strips of locally woven blankets—wedding blankets. Wedged against one of the mudbrick walls, the bed stood high off the floor. There was Khadija, lying back on the bed, her small brown body aglow in the flickering lantern light. She said nothing as he slowly took off his clothes. He climbed into the bed and looked at her smooth oval face and clear unblinking eyes.

"I praise the name of God, and of man and woman," he said. "May God protect us and bring us peace."

She smiled and moved toward him. Issa lost himself in pleasure and passion. He was surprised but happy to see that she also moaned in passion and declared her love for him. That first night overwhelmed Issa. He had been with many women prior to his marriage, but had never had such passionate sex. Khadija moved so sensuously and seemed to know how to please him. What good fortune, he said to himself, to have married such a wonderful woman.

"May we always be this way," she said to him. "Let us be only for one another."

"May it be so, my wife."

"I don't want to share you with other women. Even though it is your right as a Muslim, I do not want it."

"Then, that is how it will be with us," Issa declared quickly, wondering if he could adhere to this declaration. He would have to fight his passion, an unaccustomed exercise. He realized that Khadija would have to battle hers also. His life as a merchant might force them to live apart for long periods of time.

They spent several days together in Niamey, after which Issa returned to Abidjan. He wanted Khadija to join him as soon as possible, but not until he could provide her a proper home. He spent the next several weeks preparing for her arrival. By dipping into his savings, he was able to afford a small compound with a three-room house, an outhouse, a separate kitchen, and a spigot connected to the city water supply—and all this in a less crowded section of Treichville. To celebrate his good fortune in the rental market, he bought a bed as well as chairs and tables. He covered the cement floors with machine-made oriental carpets. His work completed, he sent his wife an airline ticket.

Khadija, whose slight build did not diminish her considerable energy, was happy and excited to come and live with Issa in Abidjan. The size of the tropical city impressed her, and she immediately set about to make them a fine home. She bought pots, pans,

"I want to come to New York and share your life there. You must promise to send for me soon."

"I promise, my wife. Let me get established there, and I will send for you, just as I sent for you to come to Abidjan."

Khadija didn't know what to think. Of one thing she was certain: life among Issa's family in Tarma would be unpleasant.

Issa bought Khadija a one-way plane ticket for Niamey. He'd buy his New York ticket after her departure. When he accompanied Khadija to the Abidjan airport to say farewell, his heart ached with sadness. He thought about the exciting two years they had had together and wondered if this would be the sweetest time of their marriage. He tried to be optimistic. "You'll be okay, my wife," he said bravely. "We'll see one another soon." In truth, he did not know how long it might be until they would see one another again. Hard economic times had transformed modern dreams into traditional responsibilities. Normally a woman very much in control of her emotions, Khadija fought back tears, for she also feared the future.

"May God protect you, my husband."

"May God bring you health and well-being, my wife."

One day after his wife's departure, Issa learned that he could only go to America as a tourist and that he needed to buy a round-trip ticket before the American Embassy would issue him a visa. Using funds from the liquidation of his Abidjan inventory, he bought his ticket and procured a three-month tourist visa.

Excitement soon replaced the sadness he felt at his wife's departure. Everyone in Tarma had heard of America. As a child he had seen films of the unimaginably high skyscrapers in New York City. But no one he knew had ever dreamed of going to America. So far away, they'd say, at the other end of the ocean. Even people in Abidjan envied him his adventure. For Issa the prospect of life in America both frightened and excited him.

"Aren't you afraid of living in New York?" one of his Abidjan cronies wondered. "They say there is much loneliness there, that people live alone. They say people don't take time to talk to one another. And there is much crime. They say that people shoot one another on the street for money."

"But there is also much money," Issa would retort. "New York, no problem," he told his friend and anyone else who asked him. "New York, no problem."

Issa considered himself a modern "Jaguar." In search of adventure and fortune, Jaguars were sleek young men who in the 1950s appeared in the market towns of Ghana's colonial Gold Coast. Many migrated to Accra and Kumasi from Mali and Niger. Capitalizing on their adaptability and their market smarts, the Jaguars rapidly integrated themselves into the local economic scene, making themselves aware of fashion trends. In this way, they quickly transformed their knowledge into profits. Like the Jaguars of the past, Issa possessed an indomitably adventurous spirit. He felt that he had succeeded, even thrived, in Abidjan. As a good and daring businessman, he thought that he would succeed in America, a country of unlimited opportunities.

Just before his departure, his more experienced comrades gave him some good advice. They told him to look for any French-speaking African taxi driver as soon as he arrived at the airport. "They'll know where to take you," they told him.

When he reached JFK, Issa thanked God for the advice he had received, for he had never seen anything so big and confusing. He arrived wearing a rumpled brown suit that hung from his shoulders like a loose cape, a white dress shirt with a frayed collar, and a poorly knotted brown tie. When he walked into the cavernous immigration hall, he didn't know which line to stand in. Because he didn't understand English very well, he wandered about the hall in search of Francophones. Had he not been so tired from the trip, he might have become very nervous. Finally, he came upon a French couple.

"Please help me. Which line do I get in? I am confused. My first time to America," he said eagerly.

"You get in same line as us. Follow us."

"Your first time to New York?" the man asked.

"Yes, sir," Issa responded.

"Have you ever been to France?"

"No, this is my first trip outside of Africa. I'm a businessman."

Issa came up to the immigration officer and gave her his Nigerien passport. "How long do you plan to stay in the United States?"

Paul Stoller

Issa stared at the woman dumbfounded.

The officer, a large black woman, sighed, and repeated her question—this time in French.

"Three months," Issa answered.

"You don't look like a tourist," the immigration officer said.

"Yes, madam, I am. I've come to see your country."

"I see. Can I see your return ticket?" she asked.

Issa handed her his return ticket, which indicated a departure date exactly three months in the future. "You see," he said, "I return to Abidjan in three months."

The woman frowned, but said nothing and stamped his passport.

"Where do I go now?"

She pointed toward customs. He gradually found his baggage and made his way through customs without incident. He pushed himself through the doors to the airport and saw crowds of people streaming through the corridors. He had never seen such a diverse array of people: Asians, Europeans, Hispanics, and many black people.

How would he get into New York City? Where would he stay? Following the instructions he received in Abidjan, Issa looked around for the other francophone Africans. The bustle of JFK disoriented him. Heavy, bulky luggage made his arms like tree trunks as he followed the signs to the taxi stand. His head throbbed. Why had he come all the way to America? Concentrating on family concerns, he wondered what Khadija might be doing at that moment. How was she getting along with his mother? How long before she tired of loneliness and took a lover in Tarma? Would her passions overcome her sense of duty to him and his family? He tried not to think about what worried him the most. When he returned home one day—soon he hoped at that moment—he dreamed of going there in triumph. His worst fear would be going home and having to shield himself from the shame of failure.

To his great relief he found a cluster of French-speaking Africans standing next to a line of yellow taxis.

"Excuse me," Issa said. "I've just come here, and I need to get into New York City."

"Welcome, brother," said the men. "Welcome to New York."

One man, tall like Issa, came forward. "Ah, a new arrival . . . from?"

"Abidjan," Issa answered.

The man led him to his cab. Technically, the cabby was supposed to wait in line, but he always made exceptions for newly arrived West Africans. He opened the cab door for Issa.

"But you are not from Côte d'Ivoire, are you?"

"No, I'm from Niger, but I lived and worked in Côte d'Ivoire."

"I am from Mali," the driver said. "Here we Africans must try to help one another. What is your name?"

"Issa."

"Mine is Younoussa. But here I am called Chris. I have an American wife and a beautiful child."

"How long have you been here?"

"Six years. New York has been good to me. Who knows, maybe it will be good for you too. Maybe you will find a wife like mine."

"I don't know," Issa answered hesitantly, though at that moment the idea of a wife sounded very comforting.

"You have a wife at home?"

"Yes. Her name is Khadija."

"I have one in Mali. Her name is Ramatu."

"Does she accept your American wife?" Issa felt compelled to ask, thinking about his late night conversations with Khadija.

"She has no choice. Having wives here and at home is good. How can men live without women? It is impossible, my friend." The taxi driver seemed so confident and comfortable in his skin.

"Doesn't this cause problems?"

"Every marriage has problems, does it not? My problem comes more from my American wife. She doesn't accept Ramatu. She doesn't want me to send money to my family in Bamako. She thinks she owns me. Hah! She gets jealous, and she wants all of my attention. American women are wonderful but also complicated, my friend."

"My wife doesn't get jealous, but she wants all of my attention."

"Really! Is she one of these new African women?"

"I don't know," Issa mumbled. "I guess she is." Issa smiled thinking of Khadija. "Friend, Younouss, . . . Chris, I am very tired. Do you know a place where I can stay?"

"That is no problem, Issa. We'll go to the Gotham Hotel. That's where all the newcomers stay, and you can make contact with your brothers." The taxi driver took him into Midtown Manhattan, but exhaustion prevented Issa from appreciating the wonder of New York City at night. Chris dropped him off at the hotel, wished him luck, and sped away.

Issa moved into the Gotham, a run-down single-room-occupancy hotel on West 28th Street. He immediately found compatriots, Jaguars like him, who taught him the hippest phrases and the latest styles of New York. After they told him what he needed to do to start trading, he sold the return portion of his airline ticket to a student returning to Abidjan. With that money he went downtown with several brother traders to buy baseball caps and handbags from Asians. His new comrades told him that selling these items would be profitable and easy. Issa first sold goods along 34th Street near Times Square. He struggled to learn a little English and started to do business. After a few weeks, just as he began to do well selling handbags, the police asked him for his vendor's permit. He didn't have one. If he didn't pack up and move along, they said, they would fine him and throw him in jail. Other Jaguars advised him to set up a vending table in Harlem. "In Harlem," one of them told him, "the police don't bother you, and the African Americans are friendly and like to buy from Africans." Issa considered this good advice and joined the other Jaguars at the ever-expanding African market on 125th Street. Issa's business there gradually began to thrive. He felt at home on 125th Street and enjoyed talking to the other vendors. He soon made enough money to rent a one-room apartment by himself on 126th Street, close to his work. More important, and much to his satisfaction, his success also enabled him to send money to Khadija and his family every month.

The midday bustle of the market woke Issa from his reveries. As usual, 125th Street was choked with traffic: buses transporting people to appointments uptown or downtown; fleets of large delivery trucks on their rounds; late-model cars, blaring rap music as they cruised down the street; older and more silent clunkers with hand-printed signs in the windows that said "livery" or "taxi," all of which were gas-guzzling gypsy cabs, the main substitute for taxis in the poorer neighborhoods of New York. People streamed along the sidewalks, creating a blur of humanity. Clusters of bow-tied and black-suited young men marched up and down the sidewalks, distributing Nation of Islam pamphlets. Groups of rumpled bureaucrats scurried out of the towering Adam Clayton Powell State Administration Building to enjoy their lunch breaks. A group of three young mothers, dressed in blue jeans, black tops, and brightly colored kente-cloth caps, pushed their respective baby carriages down the sidewalk. Elderly women complimented the mothers on their babies. "Now take good care of those babies," they said.

The young mothers smiled at them and moved on through the African market, a collage of parked vans like Issa's, aluminum tables, incense smoke, and brilliantly colored, imported print cloth. They strolled through the collage, passing here to chat, there to bargain for more Ghanaian kente cloth, Kenyan baskets, Meccan incense, trade beads, or silver jewelry. Perhaps they would buy T-shirts or baseball caps that celebrate Harlem, African American pride, or a hero like Malcolm X, who, a generation earlier, had preached on the very sidewalks they now walked. The young women stopped at Idrissa's table, which was right next to Issa's.

"Hello," they said, greeting Idrissa and Issa.

"What you want today?" Idrissa asked, in almost indecipherable English.

The young mothers did not respond to his halting English. They examined his baseball caps, trying them on and asking one another's opinion. One young mother especially liked a black cap set off with Malcolm's silver "X."

Just then a young man walked by with a giant boom box blaring passages from Malcolm X's most famous speeches.

"Now I *know* that I got to get this hat," the woman announced. "It's a sign, don't ya think?"

"But you better see it on first," her friend suggested.

Idrissa gave her a mirror.

"I like it. I like it."

"It looks good on you, sista," Issa added in an accent affected by West African languages and French.

Idrissa nodded and beamed. "Very nice. Very nice."

The soft smile on the young mother's face hardened into a frown. "How much?"

"Fifteen," Idrissa said. "Very nice. Very nice."

The young mother looked in the mirror once again. "You hear that?" she asked the other women. "Can you believe these prices?"

Issa and Idrissa looked at one another. "But sista," said Issa, "this a good hat."

"Not that good. How about I give you eight?"

Idrissa shook his head no.

"Sorry, fifteen's too much," the young mother said as she put the hat back on the table, and the group of three continued their stroll, pausing here to chat, there to bargain. They pushed their carriages onward. Soon the midday August heat and haze transformed them into amorphous shimmering figures.

"They're just out to amuse themselves," said Idrissa with understanding.

"They will buy nothing today," Issa added.

"There is no doubt about that. May God bring us better clients," said Idrissa, "so we can better feed our families. With patience, we will get by."

"God is great," said Issa, shaking Idrissa's fleshy hand. "I'll be back." Issa knew he would come back to talk to Idrissa that day, but it is impolite to end a conversation by saying "so long" or "goodbye," which implies that the talk is over. It is better to say "I'll be back" or "I will return," which keeps conversation's door open.

Issa walked over to some older men from Niger. For them, the passage of time may have tarnished the sleek image that the younger Jaguars cultivate, but it hadn't diminished their energetic resourcefulness. One of them, Daouda, had made his pilgrimage to Mecca more than fifteen years before his arrival in New York City. Out of respect, the Jaguars called him El Hadj, the traditional name for one who had made that journey. Since his arrival, Daouda's waist had steadily expanded as his hairline had relentlessly receded. El Hadj sold sunglasses. "Thank God for summer sunshine," he would often say.

Issa greeted El Hadj. "El Hadj," he said, pointing at the older man's belly, "you seem to be eating well lately."

"How can I eat well, young brother, without a good woman from Niger to make the good sauces."

"Then why do you look so well fed?" Issa asked.

"Burger King and McDonald's."

Issa nodded with complete understanding.

"Big Macs and Whoppers." El Hadji patted his substantial belly. "If you eat enough of that, your stomach fills up, and you forget for a while about peanut sauce and millet porridge. You forget about the good women who prepare those things. But only for a little while." El Hadj laughed. "One day I'll be back with my two wives in my village, if God wills it."

"How is the market for you today?" El Hadj asked Issa.

"So far, very good for a weekday. And for you?"

"Not so good today. I need to learn more English so I can work better."

Issa had already learned enough colloquial English to get along quite well in Harlem and other parts of New York. "You should study somewhere," he suggested.

"Where?" El Hadj asked.

"Ask around. Someone will know."

"But you need papers to study English, do you not?"

"Not always," Issa answered. "I'll try to find something for you."

"If my English were better, I'd do more business. Maybe I'd be able go home sooner. If I had good English, I'd get papers and go and find some work in the bush."

"Where in the bush is there work?" Issa asked, always seeking new information that might lead to better opportunities.

"They say there is work in Greensboro, North Carolina, a place where there are many fine bushwomen—clean women—who seek African men for sex."

"In God's name," said Issa, "North Carolina is the deep bush, but there can be no such women there."

El Hadj Daouda laughed but disagreed. "Everybody says: Deep bush, good work, good women." For some reason, El Hadj talked incessantly about sex in West Africa and New York—and Greensboro, North Carolina! Besides sunglasses, he also sold pirated videos, maintaining a small table of such cassettes throughout the busy summer months.

Indulging his favorite pastime, making more conversation, Issa asked El Hadj where he got his videos.

El Hadj scratched his head. "I'm trying to remember the word in English." He scratched his chin. "It bothers me," he said, "that I don't remember exactly. Too many days exposed to the hot sun and dirty air." He looked skyward. "Ah, I remember, now. I get them from what they call Mafia. As long as there are no busts, I have an unlimited supply—very cheap. No problem," he said in English.

"No problem? Really?" asked Issa. "But is the quality good?"

"Usually, but that's why I've got the television on the table." El Hadj had placed a television and VCR on his video table and had rigged it to a car battery. "They want to see if the cheap video is good quality. If I could sell sex tapes, I'd do very well. When I sold them before, the Church Ladies complained, and the police came and said not to sell sex tapes anymore—or else. So now I've got kung fu tapes. Not as good. Used to have crowds of young boys playing the sex tapes. Not now."

"The world is patience," Issa chimed in. "Things will get better. Persevere, brother."

"Maybe if I move to Greensboro, North Carolina," El Hadj said, "I can sell sex tapes."

"Yes," said Issa, "sex is always good in the bush."

Issa and El Hadj laughed loudly and for a moment forgot where they were. Issa wondered why El Hadj talked so much about sex. Maybe because he missed the company of women. For his part, after considerable internal struggle, Issa had broken his nuptial night vows to Khadija. After all, how could a man abstain from sex for long periods of time? He still missed Khadija very much, but already had several American girlfriends. These new women both pleased and baffled him. One of his girlfriends, Carmen, had come from Puerto Rico. She said she liked Issa for his considerateness and generosity. Another woman, Angel, who was in her mid-twenties, said she liked to go out with Africans. Still another, a French woman who flew to New York several times a year on business, liked to spend time with him. She found Issa exotic.

Issa couldn't believe his good luck, for the passion of his girlfriends equaled that of his wife. He found these women more open and outspoken than Africans, and this fact excited him a great deal. In time he learned about new and adventurous ways of having sex that made him soar with delight. In Africa, women frowned upon oral sex and unaccustomed positions. Despite these unexpected sexual delights, he struggled to push thoughts of his wife far from his consciousness—especially when he visited his girlfriends. Regardless of his social meandering, his love for Khadija remained strong. To manage the stressful discomfort of his broken promise, he avoided mentioning or daydreaming about their happy time together in Abidjan. To rationalize his infidelities, he told himself that as a Muslim man he had the right to sleep with other women.

Coming back to the present, Issa told El Hadj that he'd be back and strolled westward toward Adam Clayton Powell Boulevard. He had learned about Adam Clayton Powell in the same manner as he had heard about Malcolm X. But he knew little of either man. Adam Clayton Powell, long dead and mostly forgotten, would have no impact on his life. Malcolm X, long dead and energetically remembered, had already brought him an influx of dollars. Issa sold baseball caps marked by Malcolm's "X," which stood for his long-lost African name. As a Jaguar, Issa understood the economic opportunities of the hype generated from Spike Lee's upcoming film, *Malcolm X:* T-shirts, sweatshirts, even potato chips. For him, Spike Lee was an honorary Jaguar.

Issa now approached the table of a tall Rastafarian in dreadlocks who sold perfumes and incense. "Greetings, brother," Issa said in his strange English.

The Rastafarian shook his hand. "Greetings, my brother. You look fine today," he said.

Issa nodded and strutted down the sidewalk, trying to imitate the stuttered gait of the local homeboys. But Issa wasn't a great mimic; he regularly missed a step, and his upper body was out of sync. From the curb, two young homeboys pointed at him and burst out laughing. It didn't bother Issa too much. Like any enterprising Jaguar, he told himself, he would succeed by adapting, by doing.

He strutted on to Seyni, another Nigerien vendor, who had come to New York several months before Issa. Seyni had an enormously round head that overwhelmed his unremarkable physique. More often than not an infectious smile shaped his broad brown face. These welcoming features made him among the most popular street vendors on 125th Street. Conversation and companionship never strayed far from his table. The traders also respected his political know-how, for he had forged many links to the African American community in Harlem and understood better than the others the dynamics of politics in New York City. Seyni, whose English had become quite proficient, sold tailored clothing made from African print cloth.

As Issa came up to greet him, Seyni asked if he had heard the news.

"What news?"

"They say that the mayor is planning to close the market," Seyni said.

"What will they do to us next?" Issa scowled, remembering the spitting incident. "Why can't they leave us alone? We work hard and ask for nothing."

"They say," Seyni continued, "that the merchants and the politics people are tired of us vendors. They think that we are destroying their boutique businesses and that we are dirty and leave trash all over the street. All the merchants and political people are telling the mayor to get rid of us."

"What do you think will happen?" Issa asked.

"They said the same thing last year, did they not?" Seyni responded. "My thinking is that this time the mayor will listen and that he may get rid of us."

"I hope not," said Issa. "They say that Mayor Dinkins was himself a street vendor in Harlem. How could he get rid of us?"

"Well, he could," said Seyni. "He probably doesn't care about us. We don't vote. We have no power. We don't pay taxes. Why shouldn't he get rid of us?"

"You really think so?" Issa wondered.

"I hope not. We are good here. Business is good." Seyni changed the subject. "It's time for lunch, is it not?"

"Indeed, it is. I must be getting back to my table and Nouhou."

"Thank you for your talk," Seyni said.

"Thank you for yours," Issa said. But as he walked back to his table, he worried about what would happen to him if the mayor did close the market. Where would he go? What might he sell? Life presented many possibilities, but also many problems.

chapter 4

By mid-afternoon, car exhaust and humidity mixed with dead air to render the August sky a noxious, dull brown. The Jaguars, however, concentrated on lunch and afternoon prayers rather than the pollution alert that had been announced on the radio. Some of them, like the rotund El Hadj Daouda, patronized Burger King, conveniently located on the south side of 125th Street. Most of the Jaguars, however, preferred African dishes, which they could buy from women who sold prepared food from the supermarket shopping carts that they pushed down the sidewalk. From a Senegalese woman they bought *mafe*, beef cooked in a thick peanut sauce, which she served over heaping mounds of rice. From a Malian woman they bought rice cooked in a spicy leaf sauce. Issa and Nouhou, however, had found a rare treasure of a food source: a young Fulan man from Mali who prepared delicious sauces in his apartment. At the appropriate moment, one of them would go there to pick up food that had been put in plastic containers. Soon thereafter the containers would be distributed to the Jaguars, each of whom found a spot to eat. Most of them sat down behind their tables. Issa and Nouhou usually sat and ate in the bay of their van.

Paul Stoller

Among Nigeriens eating is serious business not to be interrupted with conversation. As the Jaguars completed their silent meals, they washed down the last traces of sauce with iced tea. Issa liked big bottles of AriZona lemon-flavored iced tea. Nouhou usually chose raspberry Snapple.

Mid-afternoon usually meant a brief lull in market action, and so the first afternoon prayer didn't present the Jaguars with too much of an imposition. In the past many of them had prayed on the sidewalk next to their tables. Since the spitting incident with Issa, however, they preferred to return to nearby apartments in the neighborhood to pray, asking one of their compatriots to look after their vending tables—always an easy target for theft.

Early in the afternoon, a tall thin man approached Issa. "Hey, Mr. Africa," he said. "How ya doin'?"

A smile warmed Issa's expression. "Hey, you back again?" Issa asked, walking over to the man.

"Got to come uptown sometime. Things get hot downtown, ya gotta come uptown."

"Yeah," Issa replied with little comprehension. Even if he didn't completely understand someone, he believed it important to act agreeably.

"My brother," the man continued, "can ya let me hold a dollar?" The man had lost much of his hair. A crack pierced the smoothness of one of his eyeglass lenses, the frames of which were held together by adhesive tape. He wore a tattered, blue short-sleeve shirt tucked into a torn and oil-stained pair of pants. He had tightened the over-sized trousers to his body with a belt meant for a much larger man. The belt's unused end hung limply to his side.

"You know I can't do that," Issa replied.

"And you know that I'm too proud to beg. How 'bout I hawk your goods? I'll stand here and give a rap about your product. Ya don't sell nothin' here anyway. I'll rap and you'll see. People gonna come and buy. Then ya pay me my dollar."

"When you hawk, no one buys," Issa observed.

"Okay. Got a better idea." He sat down on the sidewalk and leaned his back against the parking garage wall. He motioned for Issa to come closer. "Looky here," he said, as he pulled from his pocket a stack of credit cards. "I got these downtown. That's where the money is. Look. What ya want, brother?"

Issa leaned over and remained silent.

"We got American Express, Atlantic Richfield, Exxon. Go tell that other brother. You know . . . that tall good-looking one by your table."

"You mean Nouhou?"

"Yeah, Nouhou. Tell him that he can fill up on me. We'll go over to the gas station; I'll give the man this card and tell him to fill her up."

"I don't think so. Nouhou likes to put in his own gas."

The man shrugged. "Well, what else we got here?"

Issa waved for Nouhou to come.

"Why are you showing those cards?" Nouhou asked the man. "If we use one, we will find jail."

The man shook his head. "Every one of these cards is good. Take one and try it." He fanned the cards like a card dealer.

Issa picked up a Medicaid card. "How about this one?"

The man took it back. "Can't have that one. That one's for my girlfriend."

Issa gave him back the card. "What happened to your partner? We haven't seen him." Issa knew the man's story. He and his partner worked downtown and midtown, where they'd break into cars and steal what they could find, especially gasoline credit cards. Their quest for cash and credit cards sometimes took them to Penn Station or Port Authority, where they'd pick people's pockets. On rare, desperate occasions, they'd actually rob people at gunpoint. Robberies violated their moral sensibilities, however. That's why they always tried to treat their victims with courtesy.

"My partner?" the man asked. "He got shot 'bout a month ago. Can't work the way we used to."

"We sorry to hear about him," Nouhou interjected. "We pray for his soul."

"Yeah, they found him in an alley not far from here and they shot him." The man wiped his brow but showed no other emotion. "Well, if ya don't want me to hawk goods for you, I'll be moving on." He got up, straightened his rumpled clothing, and grabbed

Issa's arm. They walked over to his table, "Can ya let me hold a dollar, brother. I'm hungry and I need something to eat."

Feeling pity and sorrow at the loss of a life, Issa fished through his pants pockets, pulled out a ten-dollar bill, and gave it to him.

"Ya playin' with me, brother?"

"No I'm not," said Issa. "Take it and buy a good meal. Take it."

"Ya know I can't take it."

"Look, your friend got shot. You sad now. Take the money. Take it, brother. Get a good meal. Take it and may God be with you."

The man took the money. "Thanks man. God bless you, too. Next time I come up here, I'll hawk some of these hats, and you'll sell a whole lot of them."

"Okay," said Issa.

With that the man walked down the sidewalk and disappeared.

"That man is in a sorry state," Nouhou said to Issa. "How can people live like that?"

"It's not his fault," Issa answered. "He does the best he can, and we as good Muslims should show him our mercy."

Nouhou was tall and muscular, with a face so perfectly smooth and contoured that it seemed carved from black marble. Although his personal modesty rendered him a quiet man, his openness made him a person quick to laugh at life's follies—including his own. He came from the village of Guanga, which played a major role in the political intrigues of the Republic of Niger. From an early age, however, Nouhou immersed himself in religious studies rather than political activities. Although his good looks attracted women to him in both Niger and New York, he paid little attention. After two years in New York, though, he married an African American woman, who made him quite happy. Although many of the marriages between Jaguars and American women were nothing more than a simple way to get immigration papers, Nouhou's grew and prospered. He learned to love his wife, Tamika. She had spirit and a love of life. Tamika also loved Nouhou. Out of respect for his piety, she converted to Islam. She realized quickly that it was the wonder of the Prophet's *hadiths* that truly sparked Nouhou's imagination. Given his moral preoccupations and his stable household, Nouhou always carried himself with reserve and dignity.

"I know that sometimes men like him drink, smoke drugs, steal, father children and then forget the little ones," Issa continued, "but he, too, has his dignity. He didn't want to take our charity. He wanted to work for his money, and I must respect that."

Issa and Nouhou often talked about how Islam protected them from what they considered the moral degradation of America. Their ideal ethic consisted of hard work, humility, generosity; though, like most people, Issa and Nouhou could never follow perfectly these moral prescriptions.

"That's true, but people here often don't work, have sex with too many people, and take drugs."

"Not many people, Nouhou. You can't say that everyone here is like that. But many people have very, very sad lives."

Nouhou agreed.

"You've felt the meanness of life here," said Issa. "Black people especially suffer here. Many of them have to live off the streets. It's different at home. Much different. We have big families that look after us and a religion that guides us."

Just then Nouhou noticed a young man strutting down the sidewalk.

"AT&T, MCI. AT&T, MCI," he chanted.

Issa waved for the young man to come over to the table.

"What you selling today?"

"Just what you brothers need?"

"What you have?" asked Nouhou.

"You give me two dollars, and we'll go over to a public phone. You give me the number over there in Africa that you want to call, and I'll give you the calling card number. Very cheap. All you give me is two dollars, and you talk as long as you like."

"Yeah?" said Nouhou.

"Really?" wondered Issa.

"Yeah. It's simple, brother. Wanna try?"

Nouhou declined.

"I don't wanna try either," Issa said proudly. "I got my own phone and pay my bills."

"Suit yourself," the phone man said, shrugging. "That's your business, not mine." With that, he continued down the sidewalk toward Lenox Avenue. "AT&T, MCI. AT&T, MCI. AT&T, MCI."

Nouhou and Issa continued their favorite topic of conversation: comparing life in New York to that at home. Eventually, a moment of silence settled between them. They sat down in the cargo bay of the van. Like two cats staring at the world, they observed the streams of life passing before them in a peaceful silence.

chapter 5

As the day dragged on, Harlem's dirty, humid summer air weighed heavily against Issa's skin. By late afternoon, sweat had beaded on his brow and had dampened his black T-shirt, leaving white circles of body salt on the fabric under his arms. Shadows cast by the tenements and office buildings stretched over the street. They marked a quiet and peaceful time at the market. Issa had gone home earlier to recite the late afternoon prayer. Now that he was back, he hoped for a surge of business at rush hour, a cool twilight, and a tasty late dinner with Nouhou and Tamika.

Thoughts of cool breezes and an evening with his friends made him miss the camaraderie of life in Africa. There, family and friends would eat together, silently. But after dinner they'd sip strong green tea and talk well into the night. Issa had always liked to talk, but especially after dinner. Whenever he visited Tarma in the past, he recounted to a rapt audience countless stories about his exploits in Abidjan. But he also enjoyed stories told by his father and his father's brothers about the old days, when his ancestors conquered much of West Africa. These stories filled him with royal pride. At home, he had become a hero of sorts. Even his mother softened her criticisms, for her son, a man from a noble lineage, had traveled to the edges of the world. In New York, by contrast, no one knew about his nobility or his adventures in Abidjan. In lonely moments Issa dreamed of sitting with the family elders as they told stories around a crackling cooking fire. They'd talk and talk until sleepiness finally would overcome the will to converse. Then his father, Boureima, would douse the embers. Imagining that scene, he'd hear the hiss of cool water on hot charcoal—the last sound of a long, stimulating day.

The presence of a middle-aged woman leaning over Issa's table woke him from his reverie. Everything about this woman seemed big: a large, round head, covered by an equally large, broad-brimmed straw hat with an assortment of plastic fruit (bananas, apples, grapes, and oranges) on top; black eyes that bulged in their shallow sockets; fleshy arms that stretched the seams of her dress's short sleeves; breasts as large and round as melons; a belly that rose under her dress like a mound. The Jaguars called these heavy-set older women Church Ladies. They usually drove a very hard bargain, and they liked to lecture the Africans about the excesses of sin.

"Excuse me, young man," she said to Issa, "but I am here."

"Yes, my mother," Issa said, out of respect.

The Church Lady's face set in a hard stare. "I'm not your mother, and you're not my son. Don't call me that! Makes me feel too old."

"What do I call you, then?"

"Call me ma'am, or call me Mrs. Jarvis. But you don't call me 'mother.'"

"Yes, ma'am," said Issa.

"Thank you, son," said Mrs. Jarvis. The woman looked at Issa's baseball caps and handbags. She picked up a black cap that had "Fuck Off" printed in large silver letters on its front. Holding the cap, the woman stared at Issa. "Son, do you know what this hat says?"

Issa knew what "fuck off" meant, but feigned ignorance. "No," he said. "You know, my English . . . "

"Son, this hat is downright sinful. We're trying to clean the street of filth. Why can't you get rid of those hats?"

"Sorry, ma'am. People like them."

"I know, son. But God doesn't. You shouldn't be selling filth on the street."

"Sorry."

"It'll be worse than sorry, son. We'll get the police on you if you don't clean up your act."

"I don't want police."

"Then we understand one another," she said, wagging her finger at Issa, "don't we?"

"Yes, ma'am."

"Well good, son," she said, lumbering away down the sidewalk.

Daylight faded slowly into twilight. The contours of old Harlem buildings stood in sharp contrast to the darkening sky. The market had not produced the surge of product-hungry shoppers that Issa and Nouhou had hoped for. The combination of hard work, sun, dirt, heat, and humidity had either exhausted or enervated most of the people walking on the streets. Between 5:00 and 7:00 P.M., Issa sold only one twenty-five-dollar item, but overall, he felt that his day had gone pretty well. Poor Nouhou had sold nothing at all.

As dusk swathed the market in a dim, foggy light, Issa and Nouhou slowly packed up their wares and arranged them in their battered van. Just before sunset, they drove their vehicle into the parking garage, locked it up, and walked to their tenement on 126th Street. After sunset prayers, Issa walked down the hall and shared an evening meal with Nouhou and Tamika. Instead of sitting around his beloved cooking fire to trade stories after dinner, he went for a late-night ride on his bicycle. That night he cycled down as far as the southern end of Central Park. Issa rode where he wanted, for he did not fear Harlem.

That night, before he went to bed, he gave thanks for the previous day and asked God to help him make his way in the world. Then, as always, he thought about his wife, Khadija. Although he had been careful not to mention his girlfriends to her, he wondered if she already knew about his sexual forays. Had she already sought her revenge by openly taking lovers in his home town? Whenever they arranged to talk on the telephone, which was about twice a month, she still asked him when he'd bring her to New York. She'd say that she missed him and wanted to share his adventure. He always said, "Soon, my wife, soon. I'm still getting established here."

"Why does it take so long to get established? You have no trouble sending us money."

"Yes. I thank God that I can send you money every month. But life is hard here. You can't imagine how hard it is."

"Life is hard here with your family," she'd respond. "I cannot live with them much longer. If you don't send for me soon, I will have to go back to my mother's house."

"Soon, my wife. Soon," he'd say reassuringly.

NIGER

As Issa slept in Harlem, the sun pulsed low in the morning sky above the Niger River. By mid-morning the din coming from the river signaled market day in Tarma. Khadija would soon open her store, a small space packed with stacks of canned sardines and mackerel, perfumed soap, bins of chewing gum and hard candy, large cones of sugar, assortments of hardware (nails, screws, screwdrivers, hinges), packages of mosquito netting, mosquito repellent, incense, and boxes of ever-popular perfumes like Bint al Sudan, Bint al Hadash, Six Flowers Oil, and Rose Oil. Large burlap sacks stuffed with dried and fresh dates hugged the whitewashed walls. She also sold Coca-Cola, Fanta, and Sprite but had yet to purchase a kerosene refrigerator. The shop Khadija rented stood in a line of similar businesses that bordered the market plaza, a square space at river's shore. The crude stalls fashioned from tree branches and covered with burlap made the market look like a field of large ant hills.

On the river, scores of dugouts bearing goods had already been anchored and unloaded. Others glided through the shallows guided by long, lanky river pilots who, balanced on their aft perches, skillfully poled their boats into Tarma harbor.

These were the boats of the island people. Like Khadija and Issa, they speak Songhay, but their families had come to the Niger River basin rather recently. Their Songhay has the accent of their northern origins. Known for their thrift and industry, they plant tobacco, sell kola nuts, raise chickens, grow enormous squash, and make butter oil flavored with onion flour and the sweet juice of *burgu* river grass. A generation earlier, many of the island men had gone to the colonial Gold Coast in search of work and adventure, which meant that many of the "old ones" speak English to one another.

As Khadija walked to her shop, she saw the Bella people coming to market. Former slaves to the Sahara desert's Tuareg nomads, the Bella live in isolated regions of the bush, usually near permanent water holes. They sometimes travel by camel or horse; usually they transport themselves on donkey or on foot. In the bush the men herd goats and sheep and the women gather firewood, which they sell at market. One can always pick out a Bella by his or her distinctive "look." The women wear black cotton caftans embroidered with silver threads. They adorn themselves with varied assortments of brightly colored plastic necklaces, charms, and bracelets. Some of them wear these necklaces as headbands. Like their former Tuareg masters, the men wear white or indigo turbans and veils that contrast with bright blue, green, or black dashikis that drape over baggy drawstring trousers.

A hot summer breeze swept across the market, carrying the pungent floral sweetness of perfume. Khadija's nose crinkled. Because Bella live in extremely arid areas where water has to be marshaled carefully, they often use perfume in lieu of soap and water. Perhaps the Bella would make their way to her store?

Khadija's instincts proved correct. Several adolescent Bella girls huddled in front of her shop. She greeted them in what little of their language she knew. They giggled and returned her greetings as she opened the shop's creaky tin door. Khadija entered and waved for them to come inside. More giggles. A short man, perhaps in his early twenties, joined the group. He wore a turban, a fire engine red dashiki, and black trousers. After he said a few words to the girls, they all entered Khadija's shop.

The young man swaggered about Khadija's shop like a big spender. Khadija, who understood his psychology as well as her own, leaned against the counter and enjoyed his performance. Worldly enough to have learned Songhay, he asked Khadija the price of her perfumes, soaps, and mosquito netting.

Paul Stoller

"That is all much too high," he said. "Do you think we are so ignorant not to know the price of goods?"

"I do know that you are knowledgeable enough to have learned my language. I can't say that I've learned yours."

Khadija's humility brought a smile to the young man's face. "I'm sorry," he said. "You are not like many of the others, who make fun of my people. They said that you are a person who respects all people. What they said is true."

"I try to offer a fair price to everyone."

"I believe you. I believe you."

Khadija's oval face softened into a smile. "So, what would you like to buy today?"

"I will ask the girls what they want, and I will buy for them."

He turned to the young women. One of the them pointed to the vials of perfume.

"You know how adolescent girls are, do you not?" he asked Khadija.

"Indeed, I do. It wasn't too long ago that I was one myself." Khadija patiently watched the young girls as they discussed which selections to make. They whispered to the young man, who then approached the counter.

"We'll need ten vials of Bint al Sudan and a dozen vials of Bint al Hadash."

Khadija found the vials and set them on her counter, a four-foot, whitewashed concrete wall, which matched the interior walls. She had long ago arranged her goods on floor-to-ceiling wooden shelves behind the counter as well as on tables set at each end of the rectangular space. "What else would you like?"

"Three cones of sugar, three kilos of dried dates, and one mosquito net."

Khadija placed these items, which in Tarma were in limited supply, on the counter.

The man leaned over the counter.

"What are you looking for?"

"Do you have Coca-Cola?"

"Yes." Khadija bent down, lifted a straw cover from a large clay jar filled with water and pulled out a cool bottle. "Straight from my African refrigerator."

They both laughed.

Khadija took out a piece of paper, wrote down the price of each item, and added the total. "That will be four thousand francs."

The Bella smiled and gave her the money. "Good-bye. We'll come back again."

"May you have a tranquil day," Khadija said.

They left the shop talking excitedly. The sight of young girls giggling impelled Khadija to remember her own adolescence. She thought of the first time she met Issa. She was sixteen; he would have been twenty-two, tall and skinny, with skin as smooth and dark as chocolate. He had started a conversation with her at the market. At that time, she and her longtime friend, Ramatu, sold oranges and lemons. Issa had come by for an orange and ended up talking to her for almost an hour. She had never met someone who talked so much. From the beginning, she knew that she wanted to marry him, but did not think that Issa, a noble from Tarma, would want to marry a common market woman. Ramatu had said that Issa looked good to her. More important, he seemed to her a kind man. "Last thing you need," she said to Khadija, "is one of those wife-beating husbands." Ramatu urged patience.

Day after day he'd come back to buy oranges and talk. One day he asked if he could visit her family compound. Thereafter, he became a regular evening visitor and would talk and talk to Khadija and Ramatu and Khadija's mother. Khadija liked listening to Issa's endless stories. His stories made Khadija's mother laugh with much pleasure. Ramatu, who liked to study people and give advice about their characters, observed him like a desert hawk, probing for hidden signs.

"He may be good looking," she cautioned her friend, "but don't sleep with him."

After more than one month of visits, Issa said he had to leave for Abidjan, but that when he had made enough money, he'd like to come back, marry Khadija, and then move to Abidjan. For Khadija, the prospect of moving with Issa to Abidjan seemed too good to be true. Her heart fluttered with joy; sparks streaked through her body.

Ramatu remained skeptical. "Why would that good-looking

Paul Stoller

noble want to marry you? You are a wonderful woman, Khadija, but do you know what those nobles think of people like you and me?"

"It will be different with Issa and his family," Khadija said. "I know it."

"I know these people better than you," Ramatu said. "They can be very mean. Besides, I think it's just a line. He'll come back and want to sleep with you, but I'll be surprised if he goes through with it. Don't set your heart on going to Abidjan. Noble families almost always insist that their sons and daughters marry kin."

"The world is changing, and my case is different," Khadija persisted, wanting to believe that a happy life with Issa was possible.

Khadija's mother, Fatima, seemed even more troubled than Ramatu. She liked Issa's visits and found him a decent and entertaining young man, but had difficulty imagining him as her son-in-law. "The nobles don't marry people like us, my daughter. They might talk to us, sleep with us, even trade with us, but I've never ever heard about a noble marrying a trader. Even if he did marry you, I'd worry about his family. They will not like you. And they might try to scare you or even make you sick. I'd worry too much about you if you married Issa."

"Issa would never let anything happen to me."

"Issa," Fatima retorted, "would have little or no control over those matters. His family can spoil an unapproved marriage."

"Not in my case," Khadija again responded with confidence to her mother's arguments.

"And where would you live?" her mother asked. "Abidjan?"

"Maybe."

"And what would become of me? I depend on your work in the market. Would you leave me alone to follow your romantic dreams?"

"We'd make arrangements, my mother. You shouldn't worry."

"That's right, mother of Khadija," Ramatu chimed in. "Don't worry because nothing will happen. Nothing."

Ramatu's prediction, of course, had been quite wrong, Khadija thought to herself as she listened to the din of the market.

The previous day, a Peugeot 505 truck had chugged up the mesa leaving thick clouds of brown dust in its wake. Khadija sat next to the driver in the bush taxi's cabin—the place reserved for someone who could pay a bit more for a comfortable ride. The driver had stuffed the other travelers into the truck's carrier, which had been refitted for passenger service: two benches were bolted to the floor. People squeezed together along the benches and sat on the floor tangled like so many knots. Road dust streamed in through the open windows, sullying them with copper-colored grit.

When the taxi reached the mesa's flat top, the driver stopped the vehicle. Issa's village, Tarma, where Khadija now lived with great reluctance, was a two kilometer walk down the mesa. She thanked the driver for giving her a comfortable seat and stepped out of the taxi. The driver's apprentice, a young wiry boy of perhaps sixteen years, climbed up to the taxi's roof and untied Khadija's things. She had been to the big market in Niamey and had bought supplies for Issa's family and her small business: several cast iron pots, some print cloth, many bars of lye soap, onions, spices, two one-hundred-kilo sacks of millet, three cases of Coca-Cola, three boxes filled with mosquito nets, and a case of Chinese green tea.

Early that day she had received word from Niamey that she had a telegram from Issa, which meant that she needed to go to the Niamey post office to cash Issa's international money order. Khadija enjoyed these visits to Niamey. She usually visited her mother, who made sure she ate a delicious afternoon meal. In the market she'd see her friend, Ramatu, whose company she always enjoyed. She liked Ramatu's zest for life, her resilience. Even several miscarriages and two divorces hadn't dampened her spirit. Her stories still made Khadija's body rock with laughter. Skeptical of marriage in general and especially ones involving nobles, Ramatu had never learned to trust Issa, especially now that he was in New York. "I'm sure that man is having the time of his life in America," she'd say. "He's probably making more money than you can imagine."

"He sends two hundred dollars every month to help support me and his family," Khadija stated proudly.

"True. But how much does he make every month? He probably spends much more on his girlfriends."

"Do you trust any man?"

"No. I've never met a trustworthy man, Khadija."

Khadija would also visit Yusef, an Arab shopkeeper who, besides being her principal supplier, had become a good friend. Although she had heard that Arabs often dealt badly with women, Yusef treated her with the utmost respect. He gave her good prices, served her tea, and engaged her in conversations about politics, social customs, and history. A prosperous merchant, he had two wives and several servants.

Filled with these pleasant expectations, Khadija had nestled into the back of a bush taxi and headed for Niamey. By noon, she had cashed Issa's money order. In the afternoon, she ate rice and fish sauce at her mother's compound and then bought provisions from Yusef. She expected to return to Tarma in the late afternoon after visiting Ramatu in the market and buying food for Issa's large family.

Issa's family, which numbered more than fifty people, lived in one very large compound that bordered the Niger River. Descended from the great fifteenth-century Songhay king, Sonni Ali Ber, people respected their genealogy and their reputed prowess as sorcerers. At one time Issa's family had been rich, but during the past few generations, they had fallen on hard times. Although his relatives worked from time to time, they did not earn enough money or work hard enough to support themselves. Instead, they depended on Issa's regular contributions sent all the way from New York City. While the quality of life for most people in Niger had steadily decreased over the years, families that included Jaguars like Issa could expect regular infusions of foreign capital, making them relatively prosperous. Life was sweeter still for Issa's family. They not only enjoyed regular infusions of cash, but could rely upon the industrious Khadija to look after all of their domestic needs.

The taxi that returned Khadija to Tarma zipped through the dusty light of late afternoon, making very good time, indeed; they reached Tarma in only thirty minutes. In his haste to move on, the driver's apprentice left Khadija's things in a heap at the edge of the mesa.

As the taxi disappeared into a cloud of dust, one of Khadija's neighbors arrived on a donkey-driven cart. Age had withered his body into what seemed a carcass covered with cracked black leather, but activity brightened his eyes and gave him sufficient energy to work hard every day. A group of young boys suddenly materialized out of nowhere. They would help the man load the heavy millet sacks onto the cart. In return, he would give them a portion of his fee.

The driver directed the loading operation. "Hey, Khadija, hey," he said. "Come sit on the cart. The boys will run down to your compound to help unload."

"Thank you," said Khadija, whose bearing commanded great respect among the people of Tarma. Her black oval face seemed almost malleable. From one minute to the next, her expression could change from a warm, engaging smile that would charm any person to a piercing stare that would bring discomfort to someone of great self-assurance. Above all, people in Tarma respected Khadija for her resoluteness. A person of many deeds, she provided for her husband's family, ignoring their all too frequent verbal slights. What's more, she had transformed some of the foreign cash sent by Issa into a relatively successful dry goods business.

In Niger it is still rare for women to assume so much responsibility. In the past, brothers had always lived together with their wives and children. They pooled resources to care for their families. In recent times, however, economic hardship had compelled many men to leave their families in the countryside, which often meant that, like Khadija, wives sometimes became family providers. True grit, energy, and commitment to family graced Khadija's life, and for that she was thankful. So was Issa. Even though he lived far away in New York, he had gained great respect as a son who looks after his family. People in Issa's family did not feel the same way about their daughter-in-law, however. Even as they enjoyed the leisure that Khadija's good works afforded them, they resented her competence and industry.

From her seat on the cart, Khadija gazed at the quiet emptiness that filled the vastness of the Niger River basin. A shroud of unrelenting dust made it seem all the more inspiring. Bathed in the golden light of late afternoon, the mesa walls framed a peaceful scene: a hawk rode an updraft between hazy spires of jagged sandstone, all caressed by wind-furrowed, reddish-brown rivers of sand. Below, at the river's shore, stone and sand met mud and water; variations of rusty brown gave way to the dull, dark green of the burgu river grass that hugs the Niger's shores and the vibrant light green of rice grasses that spread across the shallows. No hawks at river's edge, only egrets basking under the hazy sky.

The Niger River basin blazed in the intense heat of the Nigerien summer. Through the haze, Khadija could see where clusters of green—trees planted years ago—marked off the village compounds. The rounded contours of the houses shimmered in the languorous heat. People often talked about the persistent harshness of the desert wind, the Harmattan. Despite its powerful and provocative presence, the Harmattan was a minor concern when compared to the Nigerien sun, which rose high and fiery in the humid summer air above Tarma. The unwavering strength of the sun deserved the fear and respect that the Songhay people accorded it.

"Let's go," Khadija said to the driver, focusing on what needed to be done. "Lets get this unloaded before sunset. There's still a meal to serve."

"Yes, we go with God's blessing," the old man said. He patted Khadija on the shoulder. "You, too, are one of God's blessings," he added fondly.

Saying nothing in response to such a compliment, Khadija fixed her gaze on Issa's compound. She wondered if Ramatu had been correct about Issa. Did he have girlfriends? And if so, did he care about them? More practically, she wondered how much money he spent on them. Ramatu said that the behavior of Nigerien men was inexcusable. Issa no doubt shared many traits with the typical Nigerien male. But in Abidjan he had supported her, made wonderful love to her, and allowed her to start a small business. And he said that he was proud of her success in Tarma, for no woman had ever owned and operated a dry goods shop in that river town. Despite the doubts triggered by Ramatu's comments, Khadija loved and missed Issa very much. She missed the intimacy of marriage:

Jaguar   **43** the conversation, the sex . . . She dreamed about joining Issa in America. Going to America! Thinking of America made her picture Issa's face; she wondered what he might be doing at that very moment. Self-discipline, however, kept her from dwelling too long—or longingly—on her distant husband. There was too much to do. She'd do her dreaming at bedtime, the most peaceful moment of her long, exhausting day, the time when she'd think of Issa and pleasure herself.

The cart rolled over a boulder, jolting Khadija into the present. Experience had made her driver a prudent and careful man. He drove his cart defensively. Ruts and rocks made the descent to Tarma treacherous. To make vehicular matters even more dangerous, he had to contend with the cows, sheep, and goats that had wandered onto the path. There were so many animals that the old man had to weave his wobbly cart through the herds, making sure to remain on a narrow path rived with fissures, deep holes, and crumbling shoulders.

But the driver had much experience in these matters and maneuvered his cart effortlessly down the mesa. Smoke from cooking fires mixed with dust kicked up by the returning herds to form a thick cloud above Tarma. Khadija heard the distant din of a dozen conversations and the familiar beat of pestles thumping mortars. She had returned to the family compound after a very long day and dreaded what might lay ahead.

The walled compound of Issa's family had been built on a small hill overlooking the Niger River—prime real estate in a village like Tarma. Only the oldest noble families, like Issa's, lived along the river. Khadija's mother's fear of Issa's family had deep cultural roots. Songhay believed that people in families like Issa's could fly, kill their enemies with words, and defy death itself. Although fear of these noble sorcerers had diminished with time, most Nigeriens, like Khadija's mother, thought it prudent to respect them. One didn't want to thoughtlessly insult someone from such a family, for that person might carry an amulet or possess a power that could sicken, maim, or kill. Khadija, however, felt protected from these curses, for no one in Issa's family, she reasoned, would dare to kill the wife of their most prosperous son.

The eight-foot walls of the rectangular compound marked off an area the size of a soccer field. There were eight identical mud-brick dwellings in the compound. They each had two rooms, front and back; six windows—shuttered holes in the mudbrick—two in front, two in back, and one on each side; and one door, made of cor-rugated tin, in the front. Four of the houses had been built in the compound's corners. The remaining four stood near the center points of the longer compound walls, which ran north and south. This spatial arrangement left enough room in the compound's cen-ter to tether the family animals, build a square, mudbrick cooking house, and construct three granaries, two mudbrick spherical ones for rice and a thatched conical one for millet.

Adults usually sat in small groups and talked in front of their houses. When the children saw Khadija that evening, they sur-rounded the cart and jumped up and down. "Bonbon, bonbon. Give us candy!" Khadija, always prepared, threw handfuls of hard candy at them; the children ran after their treats, screeching and scream-ing with delight.

The young boys who had loaded the cart had already arrived in eager expectation of collecting their fees. Khadija paid the cart dri-ver and watched as the boys struggled to carry their heavy loads to the granaries. Streams of smoke curling skyward from the cooking house meant that the women had started a fire there in preparation for the evening meal. Several young boys, Issa's nephews, tethered returning goats and sheep. An older boy secured one of the family's three cows to a post. Khadija poked her head into the cooking house and found one of Issa's nieces and a neighbor whom she had hired as a cook. The niece, a ten-year-old, was short, plump, and sweet—one of the relatives who helped Khadija in the compound. The neighbor was tall, lean, and middle-aged, one of several peo-ple that Khadija paid to help prepare lunches and dinners for the large compound.

"Welcome, welcome, Khadija. Was your trip a safe one?" the neighbor asked.

"Without incident. And the market was sweet with bargains today. My friend Ramatu there gave me breaks on the price of mil-let. For that, I am thankful."

"Any trouble at the post office?" the neighbor asked her, referring obliquely to previous difficulties Khadija had had cashing Issa's money orders.

"None. The people at the post office now know that my faraway husband in New York City wires me money every month. No trouble now. You know how the bureaucrats are in Niamey—all distant and snotty. But once they get to know you a little bit, they too can be pleasant and gracious. I then saw my mother briefly and ate and ate and ate. And then I drank tea with my friend, Yusef, and bought provisions from him," she said almost longingly, remembering how much she enjoyed Yusef's company.

"You must be exhausted."

"A little tired. That's all."

The greetings completed, Khadija sat and rested. The helper brought her a glass of tea. Another of Khadija's employees, a short plump woman in her thirties, arrived and greeted her. She watched them as they as they worked. The girl stirred her vat of viscous green gumbo sauce. The short woman cleaned the serving pots. The tall woman used both hands to mix the millet paste. As the mixture thickened, her burden increased. Large droplets of sweat dropped from her brow. "Hey, hey, heey," she chanted as a way to give her the extra strength to churn the mixture. "Hey, hey, heey." The woman continued to stir. "The spoon stands on its own," she said, breathless from her considerable efforts.

"Good," said Khadija in an energetic voice, even though exhaustion burdened her body. "Divide the millet and sauce into smaller pots and then take it to the people." She addressed Issa's niece. "Little one. Find small water bowls, fill them, and bring them to everybody."

In the compound the dull glow of kerosene lamps offset the utter darkness of a moonless night. While Khadija tried to rest, the women in her employ began their rounds of food deliveries. They first took food to Issa's mother's people, who lived on the north side of the compound. They walked to the oldest male's dwelling at the northwest end of the compound. Codes of respect dictated that he receive food before anyone else. Sitting in front of his house with his younger brothers, he watched passively as the women put the food down in front of him.

Paul Stoller

They then took food to Issa's mother's house, which stood directly across from her older brother's dwelling. Hampsa sat on a canvas director's chair in front of her house. The wives of her brothers sat on the ground around her. With the exception of her swollen belly, which made her look pregnant, Hampsa was a thin woman of medium height. Her skin was dried and wrinkled like tooled leather. Maintaining her superior status, she neither looked at nor spoke to the women who so dutifully delivered her food. When they became elders, Nigerien women happily relinquished their domestic duties to their younger in-laws. In their view, years of hard work give them the right and privilege to be waited on.

Khadija's group returned to the cooking house, loaded up, and made food deliveries to Issa's father's family, which lived on the compound's south side. This time Khadija accompanied her helpers. Her relations with the paternal side of the family were much more cordial than those with Issa's mother's people. She enjoyed talking to Issa's elderly uncles, but she reserved her greatest fondness and sadness for her next-door neighbor, Abdu, Issa's youngest uncle, a man in his early forties.

Years before, Abdu's wife had died. Destitution forced him to send his children away to live with his wife's people. Despite the tragedy of his life, music periodically infused Abdu with great pleasure. He thoroughly enjoyed playing the one-stringed violin, the *godji,* for the Tarma spirit possession troupe. There were spirit possession priests, musicians, and mediums in most Songhay towns, and Tarma was no exception. Most Songhay believed that a variety of spirits, most of which periodically took the bodies of mediums, controlled natural and social destiny. Many of the spirits represented powerful personages in Songhay history. The chief of all spirits, Za Beri, had been one of the greatest Songhay kings in the fifteenth century. Many Songhay towns organized yearly ceremonies to ask the spirits to bring rain and a good millet harvest. Abdu believed that the spirits gave him the gift of music and that it was his burden to play the godji. Despite his relative youth, serious illness had forced him to curtail his music. Even so, he sometimes managed to visit Khadija in the evenings and play sweet spirit rhythms for her.

Khadija's serving women eventually brought food to the elderly uncles and their wives and children. She told the women to put any extra pieces of meat in a special pot for Abdu, who usually ate alone. He needed these extras to combat his sickness. That evening he asked her to return later to listen to his music.

When Khadija arrived after her work was completed, Abdu smiled weakly and managed to limply shake her hand.

"Thank God for this moment, Khadija. It is through your energy that I manage to live."

"I thank God for your resolve, Abdu."

Abdu sat on pillows in the corner of his house. Determined to play his music for Khadija, he removed his godji from its sack. As he rubbed his bow with rosin, his brow furrowed with concentration. He picked up his bow and tried to play, but his arm, trembling with weakness, couldn't steady the bow. He sadly shook his head.

"I don't have the concentration."

"Abdu," Khadija replied with great sadness, "I know that the godji is your life."

"That, my sister, is the white truth," he said.

Abdu rested a few moments and concentrated all his energy on his instrument. Then he played the godji with such sweetness that it sent cries into the night air. He played Tooru (the noble spirit) airs. He played praise songs in remembrance of the great sorcerers of the Songhay past. He played airs for all the spirit families of the Songhay pantheon.

Moments before, pain had pinched Abdu's brow; now the melodious music of the ancestors—his ancestors—brought the softness of serenity to his face. The sacred sounds lifted Abdu's eyes to a distant place known only to those whom the spirits have touched. He played and swayed, voyaging deeper and deeper into his spirit-touched world. Such intensity didn't last long, though, for Abdu had soon exhausted himself. Reluctantly, he put down the violin and rubbed his face with his palms.

"Abdu," Khadija said, "it is enough."

Abdu nodded with resignation. They sat together silently for a few peaceful moments.

Khadija reluctantly said good-bye and returned to her own house. She wondered about the fate of people like Abdu. He was kind and blessed with talent but had suffered terribly. How remarkable, she thought, that someone like Abdu didn't complain about his fate. Instead, he sought and found happiness in music and song, providing much pleasure for others. As she lay in bed, the sound Abdu's music lingered in her mind, filling her with life and sensual energy.

chapter 8

That night the gurgle of river water rushing over rocks in the Niger's shallows gradually lulled Khadija into a deep, dreamless slumber. A rare sound in the middle of the night startled her awake, but the river's rush gently coaxed her back to sleep. When the glow of the impending dawn settled into the compound, Khadija opened her eyes—another long and exhausting day ahead. She would at least enjoy herself at Tarma's weekly market, the most economically important day for her shop, which was open for business every day.

The cock's crow sounded the compound's wake-up alarm, but few people stirred—only Khadija and Issa's niece stumbled simultaneously into the compound's open space. Khadija rubbed sleep from her eyes. They had both wrapped cotton blankets around themselves—protection from the early morning chill at river's edge.

They greeted each other briefly and moved toward the rapping of knuckles on the corrugated tin door. The niece pried open the compound door to find three women, all Khadija's employees, shivering in the doorway.

"Welcome," said Khadija. "How was your sleep?"

"We slept in good health," they replied in unison.

"Good, wonderful," Khadija replied. "Are we ready to work?

The women smiled and nodded, grateful that Khadija paid them to help prepare meals for Issa's family. They liked her cheerfulness and respected her resourcefulness.

The first woman went to build a fire in the cooking house. Khadija asked the second woman and the niece to collect the leftovers from the previous evening and heat them up for breakfast.

Jaguar

Like clockwork a group of water haulers entered the compound, carrying their charge in two, ten-liter zinc buckets, which they had tied to each end of a thick stick. Khadija's workers delivered the reheated leftovers to various family members in the compound. One of the family cows provided a bowl of fresh milk, which Khadija sent over to Issa's mother. Two young girls, large brass platters balanced on their heads, entered the compound to sell fried millet and bean cakes. Khadija bought a dozen and asked Issa's niece to distribute them.

Amid this swirl of chaotic activity, a young girl, the daughter of one of Issa's mother's brothers, walked up to Khadija.

"My mother."

"Yes?"

"Hampsa is calling for you."

Khadija nodded. Her brow furrowed and stomach tightened as she followed the girl to Issa's mother's corner house. Hampsa usually ignored her daughter-in-law unless she felt like berating her about the declining quality of the food. Khadija dreaded these summonses, but according to custom, could not refuse.

Sitting in her director's chair, the old woman sipped milk from the bowl Khadija had sent over.

"Sit down, in-law," she commanded.

Khadija looked around for a chair to sit on but found nothing. She did not want to sit on the ground, which was fit only for children, beggars, and people of servile status.

"Why don't you sit down, in-law?" Hampsa repeated.

"Because there is no place to sit, in-law," Khadija answered.

Hampsa spat on the sand. "Hey, hey," she cried to someone in her house. "Bring out the straw mat."

A young girl brought out a palm frond mat and unrolled it next to the old woman's chair. Khadija sat down.

"In-law," Hampsa began, "I am very disturbed. My son, Issa, sends word of his life in New York, but you never tell us anything."

"You never ask me, in-law. I'd be happy to tell you about Issa's life in Harlem and his business there. I could tell you all about his comrades there and his dealings with the Blacks in America."

"Yes, yes," Hampsa said, waving her arms in frustration. "That, we know about."

"Then what do you want to know about, in-law?"

"You know, in-law, in our families we have always preferred to marry from within, marry our cousins. Issa's father was my father's brother's son, my first cousin. Such marriages bond families tightly."

"You have told me this many times," Khadija stated.

"That was our Songhay way in the past. But all that has changed. Cousins no longer marry very much anymore, and families have lost the feeling of trust. Sometimes your blood kin may disappoint you, but you can always depend on them. You can trust them."

"Yes, in-law."

"Do you know our proverb about the snake hole? If you have confidence and trust, you step over the snake hole without fear. If you lack confidence, you sidestep it."

"What are you trying to say, in-law?"

"I am saying, young in-law, that the confidence of past families has escaped this one. I am saying that we are all sidestepping the snake hole."

"And whose fault is that, in-law?" Khadija could not restrain herself from asking.

The wrinkles in Hampsa's dried-out face deepened. "We want to know about Issa's money. Where is it? Why do we see so little of it? He has sent it for us."

"Do you eat, in-law?"

"Yes."

"Do you drink milk?"

"Sometimes."

"Do any of the children lack food, clothes, or school supplies?"

Hampsa remained silent.

"Do you or any of your brothers work to provide for your family?"

"You meet your obligations to us in-law, but we also know that there is more money and that you are keeping it. God will punish you for your lack of generosity. I will write my son and tell him that you are stealing from him," Hampsa threatened.

"You should write him more often! He would like to hear from you. But if you say these things, he will not believe you. Issa knows where his money goes."

Khadija stood up and walked away. She had the same argument with the old woman whenever she received one of Issa's monthly money orders. Before coming to Tarma, she knew that Issa's mother, a woman of noble birth and great pride, would be difficult. When Khadija married Issa, she became a convenient target for her mother-in-law's resentments and frustrations. By now she felt more sorrow than anger toward an old woman so locked into the past that she could not enjoy her life. Her pity and sense of duty enabled her to interact with Hampsa with a measure of respect. And yet, she didn't know how long her patience would hold. The burden of catering to the needs of Issa's family was beginning to sap her spirit. As long as she lived in the compound, custom dictated that she, as the wife of the oldest son, should manage its domestic affairs. She liked managing the chores. But in most families the younger wives and female kin would help the wife of the eldest son. In the Tarma compound, however, most of Issa's relatives, taking their cue from his mother, refused to demonstrate even a modicum of respect for Khadija. One day, perhaps soon, she'd have to leave. As she prepared to go to the weekly market, she wondered how the family had managed before she arrived. She also began not to care what would become of them when she left.

chapter 9

By midday, dust and smoke settled over Tarma market; the space had filled up with merchants and shoppers. From above, the sun seared the marketplace, forcing the merchants to conduct business in the shade of their canopies. Many shoppers opened umbrellas as they strolled among the market stalls. The aroma of roasting mutton wafted through the air, mixing with the smell of fried fish. Peanut oil crackled and meat sizzled. Donkey's brayed and camels grunted. Babies cried and people criticized, cajoled, and conversed.

A short man strolled into Khadija's dry goods store. Three vertical scars that identified him as a Yoruba cut into his fleshy cheeks.

His expansive stomach bulged under an untucked white shirt that was two sizes too small.

"Sister, how are you today?" he said in accented Songhay.

"Fine, brother," Khadija responded. The man, a trader from Nigeria, lived in Niamey but circulated among river markets, selling enamel pans and cast iron pots. Tarma's market was an important one, so he came every week. Since it would be inefficient to transport his entire inventory from market to market, he arranged to store his things at each market with merchants like Khadija.

"How is your family? And your husband in New York City?"

"God is with him." Khadija bent down and pulled out several of the man's enamel pans. "You want these, no?"

"It is good that we can find people to trust," he said, taking his pots. Far from home in Nigeria, the man often complained to Khadija about his difficulties. He found the Songhay people distant, stubborn, argumentative, and very suspicious of strangers. He had been in Songhay country for more than twenty years but had few Songhay friends. Like Issa and the other Jaguars in New York, he bided his time in a foreign land, saved his money, and waited for the not so distant day when he would return to his village to live out his time as an honored elder. He gave Khadija his storage fee of one thousand francs, the equivalent of four dollars, and turned toward the door.

"Come to my stall," he said to her as he departed. "I want to give you a special market gift today."

Two tall, thin women entered the shop. Dressed in indigo tops and skirts fashioned from homespun cotton, they smiled at one another and at Khadija.

"Good afternoon. Market greetings to you," they said in Fulani, the language of Fulan cattle herders.

Khadija knew the greetings in their language, but that was all. "Good afternoon," she said.

The women had tattoos on their foreheads—blue lines that spread like vines from a base between the eyes. Like many of the Fulan, they had copper-colored rather than black skin. Their earlobes drooped under the weight of the heavy silver earrings that framed their thin, finely chiseled faces. Unlike the Songhay, these women lived a nomadic life. The Fulan accord as much respect to their cows as to one another, for they consider cows to be their ancestors. They also consider cow's milk to be the essence of life—their most powerful medicine. Although men possess most of the Fulan cows, women, who do the milking each morning, maintain rights to the milk. Throughout the week they ferment the milk or churn it into butter. Then on market day, they bring to market gourds filled with butter floating in sour milk. Because the modest sums the women receive for the milk and butter is the result of their own labor, their husbands have no claim to it.

The women pointed to the perfumed soap arranged on the shop counter. Khadija picked up a bar and smelled it. She gestured for the Fulan women to do the same.

The women sampled several brands and settled on lavender soap. Between them, they bought ten bars.

Although many Bella, Fulan, and a few Yoruba people sold goods at Tarma market, the majority of the traders there were Hausa people from the east of Niger. The Hausa had a well-established reputation as long-distance traders in West Africa. They supplied the Niger River basin with kola nuts, oranges, mangoes, and papayas. They also sold beads and leather goods and were the local butchers. Although some of them traveled the market circuit, many of them lived in Tarma's *zongo*, the neighborhood of newly arrived strangers.

By far, though, the greatest number of people at Tarma market were Songhay. The women usually sold dried spices such as ginger, hot pepper, garlic, and onion flour. Some of them sold dried leaves for use in preparing millet and rice sauces. Others bought fish to fry and then resell. Still others prepared large vats of rice and sauce. The men sometimes sold livestock. A few of the men owned dry goods shops like Khadija's. Most of the Songhay at market, however, were shoppers. Although the haughty Songhay considered shopping at markets a necessary activity, they usually looked down upon their brothers and sisters who made a living by trading.

This attitude had made life difficult for Issa, whose family members never missed an opportunity to tell him how unthinkable it was for a man of noble birth to buy and sell goods in the market. Noble men, they reminded him, should farm and run large households. When Issa's monthly checks arrived, though, no one complained about his trading activities.

These traditional attitudes at home also made life more unpleasant for Khadija. But trading energized her. She loved market days, and this day was no exception. By midday, people clogged the passages between the rows of market stalls. Shoppers streamed into Khadija's shop, buying soap, perfume, dates, and mosquito nets. They bought so much that she would soon have to return to Niamey to buy more inventory.

In the mid-afternoon heat she heard her name being called from a distance. The sound of her name grew louder and louder until a short chubby man with a scraggly beard whooshed into her shop.

"Kareem?"

"Me, indeed," he responded in Songhay.

"Are you here again?"

"I've returned to buy Nigerien leather, and Issa asked me to come and visit you. Here I am!"

"When were you last in Niger?"

"Three months ago. Don't you remember? We saw one another in Niamey."

"Yes, I remember. God is great! God is great!" Khadija cried. "Welcome. You will stay with us tonight. You will eat dinner and stay with us tonight."

"With pleasure Khadija."

"Have you seen Issa?" she asked him.

"Oh yes," he replied. "Just the other day. He says that business is good in Harlem and that the summer heat rivals that of Niger."

"There's no place that gets as hot as Niger," Khadija stated.

"True. But it does get really hot in New York City in the summer, especially with all the people and cars."

"That's what Issa says." Khadija said. "He says that sometimes the air is so dirty, he coughs when he breathes. He also says that summer there is good for business. He's selling many handbags and hats."

"I know. I saw his table two days ago. He sells shirts and hats, each marked with a big 'X.'" Kareem drew the design on a piece of paper. "It's like this."

"What does it mean?" Khadija asked.

"The 'X' represents Malcolm X, a hero among American Blacks. There will be a film about him, and so his symbol, the 'X,' has become popular. You put it on a T-shirt, handbag, or hat, and people will buy it."

Khadija nodded. "Yes. Issa is a true Jaguar. He understands such things."

"That, he is," Kareem said. "But you are some trader, Khadija," he said with affection and respect. "You, too, are a Jaguar."

"Thank you for your kind words, Kareem." His words struck Khadija. In the past, only men had been Jaguars. But Khadija did not see why women could not travel and trade.

Khadija had always felt a fondness for Kareem. She'd known him in Niamey, a fellow trader at the market. He left for Abidjan years before Issa and had done well in New York City. By now he had been married to an American woman for more than five years, which meant that he had families in both New York and Niger. At first he sold inventory on the street. His success there led to a thriving import-export business. He supplied the New York street merchants with West African crafts and Turkish textiles. Because his affairs required continuous travel between New York and Niger, Kareem also offered his services as a private courier. For a small fee, he'd transport letters and money between the continents.

Although he was still young, Kareem had grown fat in America. His life was sweet, but, as always, drawbacks presented themselves. When he visited his family in Niamey, his wife and mother insisted that he eat copious amounts of rich food: sauces heavy with meat and butter oil flavored with onion flour. In New York his American wife, not to be outdone, prepared him sumptuous meals: food so rich that at least an inch of oil—butter, palm, or peanut—floated delectably on the surface of the sauce, rendering it irresistible to Kareem's palate. To refuse such loving efforts, as he knew well, would amount to a grievous insult. And so with few regrets, Kareem resigned himself to a daily regime of overeating.

Kareem gave Khadija an envelope.

"Open it," he said.

Inside was a wad of money and a smaller envelope. "What is this?"

"Issa asked me to give it to you."

Khadija counted it. "There's 250,000 francs here. In the name of God!"

Kareem touched her hand. "Yes. Issa wanted you to have it. He gave me a thousand dollars American, and I changed it yesterday at a bank in Niamey. I promised to deliver it to you. He said you must use it to make your business grow and to feed the family. He also knows how much trouble it is to cash the money orders."

"That's easier now."

"Yes, but everyone knows that money has arrived. Issa says that you are not to tell the family about this money. Use most of it for your business, he says, and save some of it to open a bank account in Niamey."

"A bank account?"

"Yes. He will continue to send money orders, but will also try to send money this way with people like me. You know, sending cash by money order is slow and costly. You have to pay the U.S. post office, and then when the money order gets here, you have to pay the Nigerien post office." Kareem went on to explain how the conversion process from dollars to West African francs depended upon the monetary exchange rate, which was rarely favorable to the West African franc.

"This is a good idea," Khadija confirmed.

"Khadija, I have business in the market, but I will come for the evening meal."

"Inshallah."

Alone in the store, she opened the sealed envelope and read the letter Issa had sent her.

Dear Khadija,

I am writing this letter on a hot summer day. I ask after your health. I pray to God that you are in good health and that your spirit is light and happy. I ask after the health of my mother and her people and the health of my father's people. I recite a special prayer for Uncle Abdu's health. May God grant him the strength to soon play the godji again.

The market is good. We are selling many hats and

handbags. We are saving as much money as possible from the profits. I thank God that I can send this money to you by way of Kareem. I asked him to explain how to open a bank account for you and me. I will not dismiss my family responsibilities, but I will not forget about your welfare. I will send money this way whenever it is possible to do so.

After our life in Abidjan, I know Tarma is difficult. I think about you every day. I want us to be together again soon. Maybe when I get my papers, I will come home for a visit.

May God grant you and the family peace and well-being.

Issa

Like all of Issa's letters, this one brought tears and frustration; it also reflected his love and kindness. Khadija liked the idea of a bank account. The money Issa sent demonstrated his respect for her abilities as a trader. And yet, this letter did not mention when they might resume their marriage. She had not seen her husband in more than two years now and did not know when she would see him again. She longed for the intimacy and conversation of married life; the lack of it frustrated her. First Issa said he'd send for her when he had established himself. Now he said that he'd send for her when he got papers. What did that mean? After two years, she found herself thinking a great deal about the many men in Tarma and Niamey who had demonstrated an interest in her. She thought Issa a fine husband and tried not to dwell on his likely infidelities. Even if her patience had worn thin, her love for him remained. At the same time she had also enjoyed the financial and emotional independence gained from running her own business. But was it necessary for independence to come with the considerable cost of being separated from her husband and being denied the pleasure of sexual intimacy?

Later that day Kareem joined Khadija for dinner. After a fine meal of rice in zesty fish sauce, they sat on canvas director's chairs in front of Khadija's house. As the air gradually cooled, he patiently answered Khadija's questions.

"Kareem, what does Issa mean by 'papers?'"

Paul Stoller

"It means that you get a card that allows you to work for a wage. It also means that you can leave and return. If Issa left New York without papers, he would not be able to return. With papers, he can go wherever he wants without fear of the police."

"And how long with it take to get papers?"

"It can take a long time, unless . . ."

"What?"

"Because you have to fill out so many forms, and the Americans make mistakes, it can take years to get your papers."

"You got one quickly."

"Yes, but I married an American woman to get papers, and we now have a good family."

"I don't understand."

"At first, I paid her money to get married. Then I got papers. I never thought it would work out, but it did."

"And Issa?"

Kareem laughed, a bit nervously. "Issa told me he didn't want to get married for papers. He'll try to apply for political asylum, which takes longer."

"How long?"

"No one knows."

Khadija showed Kareem to his sleeping quarters and returned to her chair to think a bit about their conversation. If she and Issa were to remain apart for years, she would have to think about the possibility of a lover, if not a new husband. She needed sex in her life; she wanted to bear children. She entered her house, undressed, and got into her bed. She blew out the lantern and fell into a fitful sleep.

HARLEM

At dusk the wind kicked up dust and dirt along Lenox Avenue, which was under repair—one southbound lane closed down. During rush hour, taxis, trucks, and cars clogged the intersection at 125th Street. Horns blared. Frustrated drivers rolled down their windows and stuck their heads out into the cold January air.

Traffic posed only a minor problem for Issa and his fellow Jaguars. Most of them did not own cars. Those who did used them strictly for inventory storage. Issa's commute from the parking garage was a short, usually uneventful trip. The biting cold did not change Issa's daily routine. As always, he enjoyed morning conversations with the other Jaguars at the market. Some mornings he took a short trip downtown to buy more handbags from his Asian suppliers. In the afternoons, he used his considerable charm to convince any number of reluctant shoppers to buy hats and bags—no small achievement in the winter market.

As he walked down the sidewalk, Issa reflected on the benefits of simplifying his life. He did most of his traveling in New York either on his bicycle or on the subway. His motto of "no problem, anytime," fit his mode of transportation. He had purchased a few luxury items like Air Jordan shoes and a warm leather jacket, but he usually dressed in nondescript, inexpensive clothes and refused to wear the gold jewelry he coveted. Flashy dressing, he knew, invited trouble. Like the other Jaguars on 125th Street, he didn't want to attract the attention of petty thieves. One never knew what they might resort to. He simply wanted to conduct his business quietly, socialize with his friends, flirt with his female customers, enjoy good food, and occasionally ride his bicycle. Not that his life had become completely carefree. He worried a great deal about getting immigration papers. Papers would give him the freedom to travel between Niger and New York. The idea of seeing other regions of America also appealed to him. With papers he could travel freely and trade anywhere.

The traffic on Lenox at 125th had ground down to gridlock. Nothing moved. People got out of their taxies, preferring to walk or take the subway to their destinations. Amid the wind, noxious car exhaust, and blaring horns, Issa meandered through the stalled traffic, crossing to the east side of Lenox. He walked north to 126th Street and turned right—to the east. He knocked on the basement door of his building.

Henry, the super, a big and round African American man of perhaps sixty years, opened the door.

"You want your mail, don't ya?" The building had no mailboxes, which meant that Henry distributed the mail to residents.

"Yes, Yes," Issa said eagerly.

"Same thing every day, isn't it?"

"Yes, maybe I get letter from my wife and maybe one from immigration."

"Well . . . " Henry sorted through the day's mail. "Let's see if . . . "

Issa inched closer. "Do I get something today?"

"Yeah." The super gave Issa three letters.

Issa beamed in expectation, for along with a bank statement and a piece of junk mail, he had received an envelope from the Immigration and Naturalization Service. Perhaps it contained his papers. "I want . . . read the letter," he said nervously. "You help me if I don't understand?"

"I'll do what I can, brother," Henry said. He was a kind and helpful man who felt sorry for the lonely Africans who often rented space in the building. "Why don't you step inside out of the cold?"

Issa came into the dimly lit basement room, which served as Henry's work space: several wooden tables covered with plumbing parts and tools; a grimy floor; and bare plaster walls cracked by the stresses of weight and age. He gave the envelope to the super, who put on his reading glasses.

Henry read the two-page letter and looked up at Issa. "I'm sorry brother, but they've rejected your application."

"But why?" Issa wondered.

"Says here that you didn't send in your fingerprint card, FD-258."

"But I did," Issa protested. "I sent it! Went down to the police, and they printed me on special cards. I did!"

The super shook his head. "Hell if I understand these things."

"What is the other page?"

"Let's see . . . How 'bout if I read it to you?"

"Okay."

"Here goes . . . 'On October 18, 1992, you filed an I-765 Application for Employment Authorization pursuant to Section 274a.12(a), Title 8, Code of Federal Regulations. This application for employment authorization is based on your pending Form I-589, Request for Asylum in the United States . . . which provides that any alien who has filed a non-frivolous application for asylum . . . may be granted employment authorization. "Frivolous" is defined as manifestly unfounded or abusive. Following a review of your asylum application and any attachments, it has been determined that your Request for Asylum in the United States is frivolous.' "

"Excuse me, sir?"

"Yes, brother?"

"What means 'frivolous'?"

"Says here 'unfounded' or 'abusive,' but it don't make any sense to me . . ."

"I don't understand," Issa said impatiently.

The super held up his hand. "Slow down, brother." He studied the page and shook his head. "Okay . . . says here that you didn't answer most of the questions on the asylum application. You know, stuff about political problems you have in your country, which is . . . ?"

"Niger."

"Right. So many countries. Have a hard time remembering them all."

"Go on."

"Right. They say that you didn't give any info about whether people in your family had been persecuted, arrested, sentenced, or imprisoned in your country. They say that . . . I'll read this part: 'Request for Asylum in the United States must be based on your fear of persecution on account of race, religion, nationality, membership in a particular social group, or political opinion.' That's why they rejected you, brother. They say that you can't appeal the decision, but you can file another application."

Issa shook his head. "I'll did all the papers and fingerprints and photos. I don't understand. Other people did this and got papers."

"You fill that thing out yourself?"

"Yes."

"You best find someone who understands the program, you know what I mean?"

"Yes. Thanks. Thanks."

"No problem, brother," the super said, feeling sorry for Issa and his plight. At least the super could work where he wanted, though jobs hadn't been easy for him to get. All sorts of black folks, he thought, suffered in America. "You have a nice evening, now."

Issa turned and walked up the steps to the street, pain gripping his stomach. It had taken him so long to fill out the forms. So much effort for nothing! He sent in his fingerprints. How could they not have received them? Trying to fight back his disappointment, he focused on more immediate and pleasant matters. He envisioned the thick frame of the super, whom he liked. Henry always took a few extra minutes to answer his questions or give him advice. When Issa thanked him, the super always responded, "It's the Christian thing to do, brother." Unfortunately, the Christian generosity of his neighbors, however wonderful it might be, wouldn't get him papers. He shook his head. If only he had papers, the larger world of America would open up to him. With papers he'd be able to make a great deal of money. He might be able to operate a thriving import-export business and travel between Africa and America.

A wind gust jolted Issa from his self-consumed thoughts. Parked cars lined both sides of the street. Several older men, wrapped for warmth in their wool overcoats, huddled on the opposite side of the street. A man wearing a bow tie and black suit shepherded a flock of small children down the street. Issa turned, skipped up the tenement's steps, and walked inside.

Deep cracks cut through the plaster walls of the narrow hallway. The walls, which had originally been painted a green that reassembled slime, were mottled with gray craters—places where chunks of plaster had fallen out. A bare bulb cast a dim light in the windowless space. The stairwell smelled of cooked onions.

Issa walked up the creaky stairs and unlocked the door to his second-floor room. Light from a single ceiling bulb illuminated a narrow, rectangular space. A window in the back wall gave him a view of an alley cutting through fenced-off backyards. It was littered with the refuse of urban life: rusting carcasses of gutted cars and decaying remains of refrigerators, stoves, and bicycles. The shards of hundreds of broken bottles glistened in the street light.

Issa had furnished the room with modest simplicity. Two single beds lined the long side opposite his door. Along the parallel wall next to the hallway was a four-drawer white dresser. Scores of compact disks, mostly by rap artists, rose in uneven piles on the dresser, which served as the perch for a boom box and a platform for a table lamp.

His sitting area consisted of two plastic lawn chairs on either side of a small, round, wooden coffee table—all along the door wall. A phone rested on the table. Months earlier, he had hammered nails into his walls to hang his clothes: one black suit, two leather jackets, a leather vest, one white shirt, an assortment of long-sleeved bright print polyester shirts, and several pairs of classic and baggy black jeans.

Issa stored food in a small refrigerator, which stood at the front end of the room, and prepared meals on a hotplate placed on a nearby kitchen counter. Even though he paid four hundred dollars a month plus utilities, he had neither a toilet nor a shower. These amenities were down the hall, and he shared them with the other second-floor residents. He found it quite cumbersome to leave his room every time he wanted to bathe or relieve himself. Sometimes the walk to the far end of the second-floor landing seemed interminable.

Issa hung his leather jacket on a nail and sat down in one of his lawn chairs. He picked up his phone and dialed Seyni, his politically savvy compatriot, who had received papers the previous year.

Seyni picked up the phone. "Hello?"

"Hello, Seyni. It's Issa," he said in Songhay. "How is your evening?"

"Very good. Thank you. It is good of you to call, Issa."

"I'm calling for a reason. I need your advice about immigration papers. My application was rejected."

"It happens. I received five rejection notices. Have patience my friend," the practical Seyni said.

"I have the letter here," Issa said in frustration. "I don't know what to do. I really want papers so I can see my family."

"Slow, slow, Issa," Seyni said. "I need to see the letter before I can advise you."

"I'll bring them to the market tomorrow. Enjoy your evening," Issa said.

"Inshallah."

chapter 11

Issa put down the phone, got up, and opened the refrigerator. He found some lemon-flavored AriZona iced tea, opened it, and drank a huge gulp. He felt too restless to remain in his apartment, and he didn't feel like visiting anyone. Even though it was quite cold outside, he decided to ride his bicycle—always a tonic for his bad moods. Later on, he'd go down the hall to Nouhou and Tamika's and eat dinner with them.

He zipped up his leather jacket, tied a scarf around his neck, put on his Timberland ski cap and his leather gloves, and grabbed his bike. He scurried down the stairs, unlocked his bike from the banister, and was out the tenement door in a flash. A blast of cold air fueled him with energy. He got on his bike and was off.

In warm weather Issa liked to explore Harlem's little nooks and crannies. He'd been everywhere in central, west, and east Harlem.

He especially liked the boisterous street life in Spanish Harlem. When he rode or walked through Harlem streets at night, he carried himself with quiet confidence. People left him alone. In the cold of a December night, he wanted to vent his frustration by riding as far and as fast as he could, and so he turned on Lenox and headed south toward 125th Street. The end of the rush hour had diminished the traffic flow. Issa crossed to the opposite side of Lenox at 125th Street and continued south toward the Masjid Malcolm Shabazz. He whizzed by a crowd of men crouched over a fire they'd lit in a trash can. He passed 123rd Street and 122nd, noticing dwellings he knew to be crack houses. They stood dark and looming in cold night shadows. He passed a smoke shop that Seyni, who knew about such things, said was the most dangerous spot in Harlem. Issa had heard that the people who owned it supplied guns to local thieves.

He made very good time and before long found himself at 116th Street and Lenox, the site of Malcolm X's old Nation of Islam Temple. Just as his pilgrimage to Mecca had transformed the religious beliefs of Malcolm X toward the end of his life, so time had transformed the original temple. Once a week or so, Issa would buy meat from the Muslim butcher located on the Mosque's ground floor. As a practicing Muslim, Issa approved of the religious rites held at the Mosque; he went there every Friday for Sabbath services. Out of curiosity, he once went to the Nation of Islam Temple near 125th Street and Lenox, but found the services there "too much like church."

The relentless cold night wind that knifed through his leather jacket made his body shudder. He peddled faster down Lenox and, in the distance, saw the north end of Central Park. The fast pace brought warmth to his body. He peddled up to 110th Street and the residence hotel that French-speaking African immigrants called "Le Cent Dix" (the 110th). He had heard that hundreds of West Africans, mostly Senegalese, lived there along with an assortment hard-working African Americans, as well as prostitutes, crack dealers, and crack addicts. When he decided to leave the Gotham Hotel his first year in New York, he had contemplated a move to Le Cent Dix, but his compatriots dissuaded him. "Too many drugs," they told him, "which means too many guns and too much theft." Issa didn't regret his decision to move to the 126th Street tenement, but he sometimes wondered if he should have moved into Le Cent Dix. The Senegalese he knew there often complained about the grimy walls and the stench of urine in the hallways, but also spoke of the warm camaraderie of living among hundreds of West Africans. "We help one another," one of the Senegalese residents told him. "We prepare communal meals and collect money for brothers who are in the hospital. Le Cent Dix has become for us a village."

Issa turned east on 110th Street. After streaking past Central Park, he turned south on 5th Avenue. He planned to bike down to 59th Street and rest a bit near the Plaza Hotel. With the park on his right, he raced toward Midtown. Hunched over the handle bars, he took in the long line of luxury apartments that towered over 5th Avenue. Blurred images of uniformed doormen pacing about ornate foyers flashed by his peripheral vision. What kind of people lived in such buildings? How did they make their money? What kind of life did they lead? The wind whipped up yet again, and Issa marshaled his physical energy. He needed to peddle faster to keep warm. He wanted coffee but did not want to go all the way to Lexington Avenue to find a take-out grocery. And so he peddled on, maintaining a racer's pace past the Guggenheim, which reminded him of an eroding termite hill, and the Metropolitan Museum of Art, with its steps and fountains, and its huge, brightly colored flags that whipped in the wind. Why would someone erect a building that looked like an anthill? And those flags? Maybe flags are good for a country, but a museum? He sometimes wondered how they hung those flags and what they did with them after they had taken them down. Some things in America never ceased to amaze him. Who paid for the flags, anyway?

The Plaza soon came into his view. He dismounted and walked his bike across 59th Street. No one strolled the sidewalk. His blood ran strong and warm through his body, overpowering his desire for coffee. He breathed in deep gulps of cold night air and stared at the Plaza, which looked to him like an ornate fortress. Although he had many times walked by the entrance, he never had dared to walk inside. Seyni had told him that when the President of Niger came to New York, his party always stayed at the Plaza. How much, he wondered, would it cost to stay there? Probably a lot more than the

Paul Stoller

Gotham. He snickered at the thought and at the excessive waste of luxury—not a way to simplify one's life.

By now Issa had grown hungry, and his weariness had driven away much of his anger and frustration. Despite his problems with "papers," he had rediscovered his Jaguar's sense of optimism. With Seyni's help, he'd send off another letter to immigration to reapply for asylum. Issa smiled to himself and walked to the 59th Street curb. A Medallion Cab pulled over to the corner. The African driver rolled down the passenger window.

"Good evening, brother," he said in French. "Why are you down here on a bike on such a cold night?"

"I'm out for a little fresh air," Issa said.

"Fresh air is sometimes good," the driver confessed.

"Yes, it is," Issa replied beaming.

"Are you going uptown?"

Issa nodded.

"Well, you take care, brother. It's cold out there. You look out for yourself." The cabbie drove off.

Issa mounted his bicycle and headed west on 59th Street. He'd ride up Central Park West just to see that wonderful apartment building with majestic towers rising from three corners of its roof. And he wanted to ride by the American Museum of Natural History. How many flags would be displayed there? Would they be as big and as colorful as those at the art museum? As he peddled ever northward, he watched the neighborhoods change. Fortress apartments and doormen soon disappeared. Before long he saw the northern extreme of Central Park, and when he got to 110th Street, he turned east and made his way to Lenox, coming upon Le Cent Dix once again. A group of West Africans had gathered in front of its entrance.

"Good evening," several of them chanted in French, smiling broadly. One of them wore a long, white damask robe, a *boubou*, embroidered with swirls of gold thread. He waved for Issa to approach the group. "I miss riding my bicycle," he said. "Back home in Senegal, I rode every day. I'd ride to work. I'd ride along the beach. I'd ride to visit my friends."

"I used to ride a great deal at home, both in Niger and especially in Abidjan. It's good to ride," Issa said.

The man in the white boubou nodded. "I pray to God that I can soon buy myself a bicycle."

The cold sent visible shivers through Issa's body.

"Brother, it is cold out here," the man said. "You must continue your journey, and may God be with you."

Issa shook the man's hand and headed north on Lenox, which had become quite empty and quiet: a few cars, a lonely pedestrian, and an occasional group of men huddled around fires. The city never ceased to dazzle him: the massive buildings glowing in the street light; rich people dressed in black, stepping out of limousines, and walking into the Plaza; the twinkle of Christmas lights in the cold night air—all so different from the dunes and dust of his country. By now heaviness in his limbs and a strong head wind had slackened Issa's pace. Hunger gnawed at him, but he was nearly home. He turned onto 126th Street, dismounted, and walked his bike up the stairs into his tenement. West African Highlife music filled the hallway with sweet sounds, and the aromas of one of Nouhou's sauces, maybe a stew with mafe, permeated the stairwell. Knowing he'd soon eat a fine meal, Issa locked up his bike, strode up the stairs, and entered his apartment to change for dinner.

chapter 12

In Niger men don't cook—not at home at least. Several of them might cook at a restaurant, but never at home. In New York City, Nigerien men who once expected their women to shop, cook, wash, and clean house for them learn to fend for themselves. They buy food at supermarkets, vacuum their apartments, and take their clothes to the Laundromat. Some of the Jaguars like El Hadj Daouda eat at McDonald's or Burger King; others buy sandwiches at carry-outs; others eat in the apartments of compatriots who have discovered the joys of fine cooking.

Such was the case with Nouhou, Issa's quiet and studious business partner. When he first came to New York, Nouhou so longed

Paul Stoller

for his homeland that he started to cook the foods that he ate as a child. To his surprise, he discovered that he thoroughly enjoyed this new avocation. Although married to an African American woman, Nouhou now spent a considerable amount of time thinking about cooking—much to his wife's delight. How might he increase the zestiness of his peanut sauce with American spices? And how might he reproduce the flavor of free-range chicken in New York City? And where could he find large quantities of *halal* (pure) mutton? Tamika relished that her husband made her delicious African meals. Her girlfriends envied her good luck, but not the extra pounds that such indulgence produced. Nouhou didn't mind. He told Tamika that he liked big women. In Niger, heavy women are considered beautiful, which meant that for Nouhou, Tamika's increasing girth made her even more appealing. As for Tamika, she told him there'd be hell to pay if he stopped cooking!

With quiet determination, Nouhou resolved most of the problems of cooking African dishes in New York City. Even if he could find the right amount of mutton in the supermarket, it would not have been purified according to Muslim standards. And so, like Issa, he bought beef and small quantities of mutton at the Shabazz Halal Butcher at Malcolm X's Mosque. For larger quantities, he and Issa would occasionally go to a New Jersey mutton farm, the owner of which employed a halal butcher, an Arab from Jordan, who would prepare for him a side of mutton. Nouhou kept much of it in his refrigerator's freezer and asked the other Jaguars to keep what remained in their freezers.

But the question of American chickens seemed a more difficult matter. The blandness of the fat, force-fed American chickens made Nouhou wince. Besides, the meat was too soft. In Niger, people called some chickens *"poulet cycliste,"* which meant that the muscles in the bird's legs were as hard as those of a bicycle racer. Although there wasn't much fat on those chickens, they had flavor. "In America," Nouhou often wondered, "who would buy a poulet cycliste?" The absence of fine-tasting chicken remained a culinary problem.

Nouhou had much less trouble making his sauces zesty. A short trip to a bodega in Spanish Harlem or the South Bronx produced rich rewards: Scotch Bonnet peppers, assorted chilies from

Mexico, plantains, palm oil. Besides, couriers like Kareem provided a continuous supply of Nigerien ingredients. When Kareem periodically announced his imminent departure for Niger, Nouhou would place his order. Several weeks later he'd receive the spices he had asked for. Kareem's recent trip to Niger yielded a five-kilo sack of dried baobab leaves as well as *gebu*, a spice made from onion flour, sesame, and hot peppers sautéed in butter oil. The pungency of these spices filled Nouhou's apartment with the smells of his homeland.

After Issa's bike ride in the cold, the aromas of Nigerien cooking led him to Nouhou's door. When he opened the door, the aromatic odors plunged him into a dreamy state. For the briefest of moments, he closed his eyes and envisioned dusk in the family compound. Seated around a common bowl of millet and sauce, he saw himself eating a silent meal with his father's brothers. Such moments had always been special for Issa. For him, the silent communal consumption of food spoke of a bonding that was inexpressible. When he finished eating, he would share a common water bowl that had been passed around. He would hear his uncles burp with satisfaction and say: "Alahumdu Lilahi." After dinner the children would often gather in front of Issa's house to listen to his oldest uncle, who liked to talk as much as Issa, recount a story.

Feeling much better after his emotionally exhausting day, Issa brought his attention back to the present and stepped into the apartment. Nouhou and Tamika lived in a space larger than Issa's. They had a small salon/dining room with a rectangular wooden table that comfortably seated four people. A large refrigerator/freezer overwhelmed their kitchen, which was located at the end of the sitting room. Standing tall and majestic, the master chef chopped onions and meat on the kitchen counter, next to the sink. Beyond the kitchen, toward the front of the apartment building, were two windowed rooms, each perhaps ten by fourteen feet in dimension. Nouhou and Tamika had filled them with king-size beds and bulky dressers, whose chipped surfaces suggested their long history.

"Older brother," Issa said in Songhay to Nouhou, "what is that slightly sour aroma that I smell? Could it be mafe sauce?"

"You almost guessed correctly, younger brother," said a beaming Nouhou. "There is baobab leaf in this sauce, which accounts for the acrid smell. But it is not pure baobab sauce. I mixed it with tomato paste, some gebu, and added some American butter oil."

Tamika strolled into the kitchen from one of the bedrooms. "Ah," she said, "baobab sauce!" Tamika was one who took great pride in her appearance. She always seemed to wear new clothes: blended wool tights—never jeans—matched by bright, cotton print blouses that fit snugly over her large body. This particularly cold night, she had put on a tight black and gray fisherman's sweater over a pair of black tights. Nouhou wanted her to dress more modestly, but she refused. She'd dress anyway she wanted, she told him. Many Nigerien men might be upset with such female independence, but Nouhou liked her spunk.

"It has been some time since I had good baobab sauce," she said.

"What you mean, Tamika? You eat good baobab sauce every week."

"No. They've gotten less tasty lately."

Nouhou looked at Issa. "Can you believe this woman?"

"I'm used to her by now, Nouhou."

Nouhou shook his head. "Maybe the sauce smells better tonight because Kareem brought me the dried leaves just the other day."

"Well, that explains it," Tamika said, winking at Nouhou. She was a tall fleshy woman, whose frown lines suggested that she knew much of the world. She had come to Harlem ten years earlier, having grown up in Beaufort, South Carolina. From an early age, Africa had fascinated her. As a child and teenager, she had read all she could about African peoples. She dreamed that one day she'd travel to the land of her ancestors. After graduation from high school, she went to business school and learned how to type, compute, and manage. When she first came to New York, she managed small offices. She now managed more than fifty office workers at a large Midtown law firm. When she wasn't with Nouhou, she spent as much time as possible learning about Niger. She took French lessons and hired a Songhay tutor. Her industry made Nouhou quite proud; her commitment to his culture and religion made him feel very much loved. She enjoyed the regular dinner visits of Nouhou's friends and always treated them with grace and good cheer. Despite their generosity, they tried to save as much money as possible, hoping one day to raise a family in a spacious house outside the city.

As Issa greeted Tamika and got settled in his chair, Ayel, who was a tailor, walked in.

"Ah, baobab sauce. God bless you, Nouhou." Ayel worked in an African-owned fabric shop on 125th Street, where he created contemporary fashions from African print cloth.

"Amen to that," Tamika said.

Nouhou laughed. "Can you imagine that Issa thought that I was making mafe!"

Ayel nodded. "Oh yes, I can imagine. Issa is such a young man. And young men have no noses; they can't smell anything." Ayel scratched his head. "What do they say here? 'He can't smell fo' shit.'"

Issa tapped Ayel on the arm. "Oh yeah," he said playfully in English. "I can to smell fo' shit." He switched back to Songhay. "You old men can't smell anything at all. I pity you all."

Tamika asked Nouhou for a translation. She smiled. "Listen to the empty words that come from that young man's mouth. It makes me want to cry. Really, it does."

Meanwhile Nouhou put out a large bowl of rice and poured his baobab sauce over it. Four large, white pasta bowls, one on each of the four place mats, gleamed in the bright kitchen light. The master chef gave his guests soup spoons, which they used to serve themselves heaping portions of food. In silence they ate and ate and ate until they could eat no more. Nouhou filled a large bowl with water and passed it around the table. Usually the Jaguars drank water from glasses, but sometimes they liked to drink water the Nigerien way. Tamika preferred to drink from her own glass.

Issa raised his hands above his head. "Praise be to God, we have eaten well tonight. I give thanks, older brother."

Ayel and Tamika echoed Issa's sentiments.

Nouhou beamed.

Having dispensed with the after-dinner formalities, the time had come for conversation. Normally, Issa sparked the evening's talk, but that night silence gripped his being. His frustration had returned.

Nouhou talked about his latest foray to the halal butcher at 116th Street. Ayel talked about cantankerous clients. "Some of the women," he complained, "never like what I do." Out of respect for Tamika, who was still learning Songhay, they stopped often to translate what had been said. Issa said nothing.

"Issa, you look glum," Ayel proclaimed. "For a man who loves to talk, why don't you have anything to say?"

Issa shook his head and said nothing.

"You must get it out," said Tamika, who, like most Americans, believed that one should talk openly about problems. "We are your family here. Tell us your news."

Issa pulled out the envelope he had received that afternoon. "I've been turned down for papers," he announced. "I don't know what to do. I want to go home to Niger, but I can't without papers."

"We know how you feel, Issa," said Ayel. "I haven't seen my family in three years. And I could be making more money. Getting papers is a difficult thing."

"You're an American, Tamika," Issa stated in English. "What you think?"

"I'll tell you the truth, Issa. Americans sometimes don't like black people, and if you're a black immigrant, they like you even less. They'll try to keep you out. It's getting harder all the time."

"But what do I do?"

"You need to reapply," Nouhou said.

"I agree," Ayel chimed in.

"Isn't it easier to find an immigration wife?" Issa asked.

"Fill out the forms again and get your papers that way," Nouhou stated flatly. "I was lucky to find Tamika; she is a wonderful woman. But chances are that if you marry a woman just for immigration, it will be very difficult for you. I know so many African brothers who have suffered because of these marriages."

"Older brother, you know I want asylum, not marriage."

Tamika urged Issa to be patient. "Get yourself a good broker who knows the system. That way, you'll get your papers. Maybe Seyni knows a good person? Be patient," she urged.

"Patience is only so good," Ayel told her in English. "If you wait too long, the world goes away, no?"

"Does your letter say anything about a hearing?" Nouhou

asked, returning the conversation to Songhay. "Sometimes you can go to the immigration office for a hearing. They can tell you what you need to do to get papers."

Issa looked carefully at his rejection notice. "It says, I think, that the decision is final, but that I can go for hearing and that I can apply again."

"Where does one go for a hearing?" Nouhou asked.

"Is it downtown?" Ayel wondered.

"It says that hearings are in Newark."

"Newark!" Nouhou moaned. "Do you have to go to Newark?"

"I went to Newark once," said Ayel. "I never want to go back."

"What's so bad about Newark?" Issa asked.

"No one smiles there," Nouhou said.

"It's dirty," Ayel remarked. "And the people are rude and sometimes mean—especially to us Africans," Ayel said.

Having understood the gist of the conversation, Tamika waved them off. "You all are full of it. What do you all know about Newark? Nothing!"

Nouhou and Ayel laughed.

"Should I go there?" Issa asked Ayel in Songhay.

"I think you should see Seyni," Ayel counseled. "Maybe you can arrange to go there with him. He has papers, and he knows his way in America. With him around, they might treat you correctly."

Issa's face lit up. "Good idea. He's already agreed to look at my letter from Immigration tomorrow. Maybe he will be willing to go to a hearing also." After this conversation he again felt more optimistic. He decided to ask Seyni to accompany him to an immigration hearing in Newark as soon as possible. When he got back to his apartment, he phoned Seyni, and they arranged to meet the next day at Penn Station.

chapter 13

The next morning Issa waited for Seyni just under the Amtrak announcement board at Penn Station. Seyni had agreed to go to Newark that morning in effort to get an immediate resolution to Issa's case. Seyni knew that if immigrants were willing to wait, they could show up anytime during business hours to talk with an immigration official about their cases. If anyone could help him, Issa thought to himself, it was Seyni, a person who knew the ins and outs of getting papers.

Issa knew Penn Station well from his early days in New York and liked the feeling of anonymity he got when standing amid the continuous flow of business-suited commuters, unwashed homeless people, and clusters of tall, wiry Senegalese, who idled near the station's phone banks seeking phone credit-card numbers. Their particular scam impressed Issa greatly. From an unobtrusive distance, they'd observe someone punching in his or her telephone code and figure out the numbers, which they would discretely record in a small notebook. Then they'd go to places like Harlem, Brooklyn, or Queens and rent the numbers to immigrants intent on making cheap international calls to Bangladesh, Nigeria, or El Salvador. Although Issa possessed a telephone credit card, he never thought of using it—especially at Penn Station! He knew that, for his Senegalese brothers, business was business and that if he, a brother African, exposed his number to them, they would be happy to record it and rent it out. Although Issa did not like such "getting over," he admired the creative industry of these young men. And yet he had to agree with Nouhou, who once told him: "You won't be so impressed if you get a bill that charges you four hundred dollars in international calls to Bangladesh."

The clatter of the Amtrak announcement board grabbed Issa's attention. A crowd gathered at the center of the arrival hall. People strained to read changing arrival and departure times. Issa and Seyni had agreed to meet at the announcement board at 9:00 A.M. Before long Issa recognized Seyni's beaming expression amid a crowd of dour faces.

"Hey, brother," Issa said in Songhay. "How has your morning passed?"

"In peace and tranquillity," Seyni responded, even though he had gotten out of bed early in the morning after a restless night. It is a Songhay custom to respond to greetings in a pleasant manner, even if one is miserable.

They took in the scene at the arrival hall. Red Caps deftly maneuvered carts of baggage through the motley crowd.

"Let's be on our way, Issa," Seyni suggested, after looking around briefly.

"I've never been to Newark," Issa declared. "Will they arrest me and put me in detention there? I've heard that detention is very, very bad."

"Sometimes immigrants get put in detention. But you're a businessman," Seyni said strongly. "There's no reason for them to treat you badly or put you in detention."

They walked down the steps toward the subway to make their way to the New Jersey Path Station, the departure point for Newark. They passed the Long Island Railroad ticket booths, walking at a pace so brisk that Issa had trouble taking in the subterranean sights. On such walks it was Issa's custom to observe the vendors for future business possibilities, but at Seyni's pace that morning, he found himself so harried that his vision blurred.

In short order they pushed through the turnstiles and found a seat on the next train leaving for Newark. As they sat waiting in silence, Issa wondered what might happen in Newark. A sudden jerk marked the train's departure.

"Sorry, Issa," Seyni said. "I've been so preoccupied with business matters that I haven't asked you the details of your case."

"That's okay," Issa said. "I am very grateful to you for coming along with me. I don't know what to expect."

"Hard to know. It takes patience to be granted political asylum. Did you bring copies of your application?"

Issa opened his valise and thumbed through a sheath of papers. "This," he said, handing the papers to Seyni, "is what I brought."

Seyni looked through the papers. They had crossed under the Hudson and now glided through Jersey City's decay: gutted warehouses; the rusting frames of pillaged cars and trucks; the motionless parts of abandoned machinery; dumpsters overflowing with the trash and garbage of urban life. "Do you have your application?" Seyni asked, still perusing.

"I think so."

The train rolled over a rusty bridge spanning a waterway. Smelly smoke formed clouds above the oil refineries that lined the northern New Jersey shoreline. Seyni's face crinkled. "It really does stink here." The train rounded a curve, and they saw the Newark skyline.

"They've done a lot with Newark," Seyni remarked. "People have told me that it used to be a very, very bad place."

Issa nodded. "I've heard that the place is mean and that the people are also mean."

The train pulled to a stop at Pennsylvania Station/Newark, a drab structure, whose walls had taken on the dull gray sheen of ingrained soot. They descended an escalator, made their way to the street, and hailed a taxi driven by a Haitian, who, upon seeing Issa and Seyni, spoke French.

"Where to?"

"Federal Building."

He looked back at Issa and Seyni. "You going for a hearing?" he finally asked them.

Issa nodded.

"I take people there every day. Africans, Indians, my Haitian brothers and sisters, Latinos. Every day, they come and I take them. Me, I've been here for twenty years. One day soon, I'll go back to Haiti—God willing."

After a short drive, the taxi driver stopped in front of the Federal Building, a six-story structure with imposing columns. "Good luck," he said, "and may God be with you."

Issa nodded his thanks and caught up to Seyni, who had already entered the building.

They walked through a metal detector and approached the uniformed, middle-aged African American man who guarded the elevator. He wore a holstered gun and a brass badge.

"Excuse me, sir," Issa said. "I want Immigration Office. Where do I find it?"

"Look at the directory," the man sneered. "You can read, can't ya?" He shook his head. "Get a million of these people comin' here, and not one of them reads the damn directory."

"Sir?" Seyni interjected. "He asked you politely. There's no need to be rude."

The man frowned. "You got attitude, young man," he said to Seyni. "Attitude don't cut it with me. As far as I'm concerned, you can take that attitude and move on out the door."

Seyni knew better than to lose his temper. He said nothing, stepped toward the directory, and saw that the Immigration Office was on the sixth floor.

After letting a few strategic minutes pass to give the guard time to cool down, they approached him a second time. "Sir, we'd like to go up to the sixth floor."

"That would be Immigration," the man said officially, responding a bit to Seyni's respectful overtures.

"Yes, sir."

"Sign the ledger. You don't sign, you don't go."

They signed the ledger and took the elevator to the sixth floor. There they followed signs to the Immigration Office. They had both expected long lines, but there were no crowds. They came upon a glass partition, behind which a young African American immigration officer stood.

"I received this for hearing," Issa announced.

"Let's see it," the woman said.

"Do I get hearing?" Issa asked.

The woman read the form. "You get a number," she said curtly. "Go through the door and wait until I call your number."

A large conference table took up most of the space in the waiting room. Three people sat at the table. Several other people sat in chairs that lined the room's walls. Seyni and Issa sat down and waited quietly.

"I've been here for four hours already," one woman said. "I came from one hundred miles away for a hearing, and they give me a number."

"That's nothing," another man responded. "They said I had to be here today. I came from two hundred miles away, from near Washington D.C. Don't know why they sent me all the way up here. They said my case is complicated." He paused and sighed.

Paul Stoller

"They might not get to me today."

"When I go into the hallway and look to see what they are doing," the woman said, "they seem to be joking around and having a good time. If you want to know something, they act like you're ruining their fun. It's just not right."

The immigration officer called Issa's number, and he and Seyni presented themselves.

"I looked up your case," she began. "You application was judged frivolous. That's why it was denied."

"What does that mean?" asked Seyni, whose English was better than Issa's.

The woman frowned and arched her back. "It means . . . that he presented no valid reasons for seeking asylum in the United States. That's what it means."

"I see," Seyni said. He knew that it would not help to question her further.

"Excuse me, ma'am?" Seyni asked.

"Yes?" she replied, relaxing her back.

"Can he reapply?"

"Yes, there's nothing stopping him from reapplying." The woman shrugged her shoulders. "He can apply as many times as he wants."

"That's good."

"It's hard to be granted asylum in the United States," she stated smiling.

"Thanks." Seyni took Issa by the arm. "Let's get out of here."

They walked toward the elevator. "I will reapply," Issa stated. "I will apply as many times as it takes to get papers."

"It *is* difficult to get political asylum in the United States," Seyni stated. "You have to make sure to answer all the questions on the application. Maybe you should hire a broker. I know a Malian who is very, very good. You give him two hundred dollars, and he'll fill out the application for you. He gets excellent results. He's the reason I got papers last year."

Issa nodded and slipped into silence as they descended the elevator and walked out of the Federal Building. No clouds appeared in the winter blue sky; no taxis appeared on the street. And so they walked in silence toward the train station. Eventually, Issa flagged down a taxi, and they sped off to the train station, where Issa bought tickets. After a short wait at the station, their train came and took them toward Manhattan. Issa felt that the trip had been a waste of time.

They sat in an uncomfortable silence as the train lurched forward. Issa commented on the clear sky. "It is so beautiful that it even makes Newark look good."

Seyni nodded with resignation. The rude insensitivity of the officials at the Immigration Office had made him angry. "Those immigration people treated you like a number," he remarked, "like an animal."

Issa stared out the window at Jersey City's urbanscape. Other passengers stared at Seyni and Issa as they spoke in Songhay. Both wore black jeans and black leather jackets. Issa sported one of the Malcolm X caps that he sold.

"I will reapply. I will get papers," Issa said, trying to convince himself.

Seyni faced his compatriot. "I think you will get asylum, but if you want papers quickly, why not marry an American woman?"

Issa shook his head. "That is not what I want to do. You didn't. The African brothers who married Americans just for papers are mostly miserable. You must give the woman a thousand dollars or more to get married," he said. "But then after you get your papers, sometimes the woman wants more money. If she doesn't get it, she might turn you in, and you get deported. This," he reiterated, "I do not want."

"I'll introduce you to the Malian broker," Seyni said, patting Issa on the shoulder. "You'll get your papers, Issa. I filled out an application just like yours, and I got papers. So did some of the other Jaguars."

"So why didn't I get papers this time?"

Seyni cleared his throat. "If they judged your application 'frivolous,' it means that they think you don't qualify for political asylum. Did you write about your political problems in Niger?"

"I don't have political problems there. I'm a merchant, not a politician."

"How about your family?"

"Some of them have been in jail for politics."

"Did you mention them?"

"No."

"Ahah. The Malian will be able to help you, Issa. I'm certain you can get asylum."

"You think so?"

"Yes. No doubt."

Issa face brightened. "I will contact the Malian and reapply at once."

"That's the Jaguar spirit," Seyni said, playfully hitting Issa in the arm. "That's the spirit."

The train reached Penn Station, and the two friends walked to the subway. Seyni had business on Canal Street. Issa was headed uptown. After thanking Seyni for his time and help, Issa suggested that they meet for dinner the next week.

chapter 14

Issa entered an uptown subway. As he settled down next to a young white woman, her body visibly stiffened. She arched her shoulders and shifted her handbag away from him. When Issa glanced at her, her face froze into a pale mask with pursed lips.

Why do so many white people think that all young black men are criminals, Issa wondered. America's racism presented a dilemma for him. If white people knew that he was an African, and a French-speaking businessman, it might be different. But people, he concluded, are locked into stereotypes. At 72nd Street, the white woman hurriedly gathered her things and left. At 110th Street, an old black man sat next to Issa and looked him over.

"You're one of those African brothers, aren't you?"

"Yes, sir," Issa said respectfully.

"Where you goin'?"

"125th Street."

"Me too."

The incident amused Issa. Most white people lumped him in

the category of "young black man." Most black people lumped him in the category of "the African," thinking him incomprehensibly exotic.

"Do you sell up there?"

"Yes, sir."

The screech of the train's brakes ended the conversation. Issa helped the old man to his feet.

"Thank you, son."

Issa strolled along the north side of 125th Street, greeting his comrades. His smile concealed much anxiety. He had worked hard lately, buying inventory downtown and selling it here. But winters are mean seasons for street vendors. No matter how charmingly he talked to prospective customers, they often refused to buy his handbags. His income dwindled; he worried about paying his bills.

When he arrived at the market, he greeted Nouhou and Idrissa. No one asked him about his morning. Among the Songhay, one is joyously forthcoming about good news and discretely silent about bad news.

Nouhou motioned to Issa. "Issa, you know that young girl, Charlene? She was here today asking after you."

"You mean the tall one with the brown eyes who has been coming around the last few weeks and talking to everybody?"

"That's the one," Ayel said.

"She seems very nice."

Because of his charm and good looks, there was no shortage of young woman interested in Issa. Charlene, Issa had noticed, had an alluring walk and had been pleasant and respectful.

Nouhou handed him a slip of paper.

"What's this?" Issa asked.

"It's Charlene's phone number. She wanted you to phone her. She likes you, Issa. I think she wants you."

Issa shook his head and walked back to his table. Why not call Charlene? She was attractive and interested in him. Whenever he thought lustily about women, he pondered the same issues. He recognized that extramarital sex was as common in America as it was in Niger. In Niger, in fact, he knew that it was quite common for men of even modest means to have several casual lovers and perhaps a concubine, in addition to one or more wives. One of his own friends back home had three wives, two concubines, and who knows how many casual partners. Women also took multiple lovers, some already married, some not, but usually before or between their own marriages. In rare circumstances women even had affairs while married. So far, he didn't feel too guilty about his relationships with several American women. And yet, he hadn't met anyone who had held his desire or interest. Maybe an evening with Charlene might be the beginning of something better.

NIGER

As Issa pondered a relationship with Charlene, Khadija clambered
up the hill behind Tarma to the depot and climbed into the first
bush taxi headed for Niamey. As usual, she intended to buy provisions for her shop and visit her mother and friends. The cloudless
sky forecast another dry day in Niger. For three months it hadn't
rained, and even though the air felt cool, the dreaded Nigerien sun
had already baked the bush to a dull brown. Only the acacias that
dotted the flat plains like so many pin pricks remained green.

Dust kicked up by passing vehicles hung like fog above the
road. Khadija liked the cool, dry season. During the day, the sun
warmed the air to a soothing temperature; at night breezes cooled
the air—wonderful sleeping weather. Cool air also meant that there
was much to eat in Tarma: assortments of vegetables grown by the
island people, much millet—harvested two months earlier, and
many varieties of fish caught in the shallows of the Niger River. But
there was also a downside to the cool season for Khadija, for the dry
air always cracked her skin, especially the heels of her feet.

If all went well in Niamey, she hoped to return to Tarma in the
evening. That morning she had flagged down a Mille Kilo, which
was more of a bus than a taxi. Nigeriens relished the irony of calling these slow, lumbering hulks "Le Rapide." Anything but. The
one Khadija had chosen was particularly old and prone to backfir-
ing down and sputtering up the many hills between Tarma and
Niamey. The driver was skilled, though. Squealing brakes didn't
faze him, and he knew how to adjust for the steering that had been

out of sync for months. He also knew how to load his vehicle to maintain a precarious balance. On downhill sections he often coasted, switching off the engine to conserve precious fuel—especially if, trying to cut corners, he hadn't filled up his tank. His frequent miscalculations produced regular delays. Such are the vicissitudes of travel in Niger. On this day the driver hadn't miscalculated his gasoline levels, for Le Rapide made its way to the outskirts of Niamey without incident. Once there, however, he was forced to stop at a newly erected roadblock.

Still five kilometers from Niamey, they had come upon what looked to be a serious inspection. Several young police officers, thin and tall as millet stalks, strutted among the vehicles, inspecting cargo and checking papers. One young policeman strode toward Khadija's group. His oversized camouflage fatigues hung limply from his willowy frame. Age had not yet left its traces on his round black face nor had it deepened his young voice. In an inauthoratively high, shallow tenor, he shouted at the people in the bus.

"Everybody out . . . now!"

Because the passengers had been literally stuffed into the bus's every nook and cranny, they reacted slowly to the young man's order.

"Out, people. Fast!"

Normally the commands of such a young man would not be taken seriously among the Songhay, but this officer carried a machine gun. Slowly, the passengers squeezed out of the overloaded bus. Using his gun as a pointer, the police officer directed people to stand in a line at the edge of the road.

Ever the cool and competent professional, the driver greeted the young policeman with obsequious respect—the only way to interact with Songhay people rendered arrogant by excessive authority. "How is your morning?" he asked.

"The morning goes," the policeman responded blandly.

"What goes on here? Yesterday there were no such stops and searches."

"Tell your passengers to get their papers out for inspection."

"It's been a long time since this has happened."

"You must unload all of your cargo. We must inspect everything."

"Everything? You've got to be joking."

The policeman scowled.

"I'll tell them," the driver said, "but why?"

The policeman pointed his gun toward the cone-shaped straw hut. "See the sergeant. Show him your papers. Don't talk to me."

The driver stalked off to see the sergeant. Meanwhile, a cold mid-morning wind had risen, and the passengers, all clad in thin cotton wraps, shivered as they stood in line. As the bus's two apprentices unloaded cargo, the policeman slung his gun over his shoulder and began his inspection of papers. The papers of the first few people were in order. He then came upon a tall Fulan man dressed in a filthy tunic; he was little more than skin and bone.

"Papers?" the officer asked in Songhay.

The Fulan man, who didn't understand Songhay, shook his head.

"No identity card?"

The man, terrified, stood motionless, the wind flapping his tunic.

"No card of the Party?"

The man shook his head.

The young policeman slapped the man's face. "How can you travel without papers? Worthless peasant!" He shoved him in the direction of the sergeant's hut. When the man tried to turn back toward him, the policeman waved his gun at him, motioning him toward the hut.

The policeman came up to Khadija, who like everyone else in the line, felt the nervous tingle of being inspected by a machine gun-toting teenager. She presented her identity card.

He read it slowly. "And your Party card?"

"I don't have one."

"You don't? How do you expect to travel without a Party card?"

"I came here two weeks ago without one."

"Silence!" the young policeman thundered. "Even women need Party cards." He pointed to the sergeant's hut. "Go there and talk to the sergeant."

Enraged at such treatment, but powerless to protest, Khadija tried to hold her head high as she walked briskly to the sergeant's office. A sentry allowed her inside. Even though it was cool outside, the presence of bodies and absence of windows made the hut a hot, stuffy vault.

The sergeant was talking to the driver. He was a massive man, big and thick, who sat like a mountain behind a rickety desk fashioned from scrap wood. "I'm sorry, Hassan, your insurance is now insufficient, and the fine for this infraction has been doubled to five thousand francs. Of all people, drivers especially must have their papers in order. We've had trouble in Niamey."

"But how can I pay it?"

The sergeant shrugged his shoulders. "I'm sure you can find a way."

"Impossible, sergeant."

The sergeant smiled. "If you can't pay, we will take your bus and confiscate the goods of your passengers."

"I'll pay. I'll pay," the driver said with resignation, reluctantly handing the sergeant a five-thousand-franc note. Previously, the driver had given the sergeant periodic small bribes to avoid such hassles.

"Hassan, our old arrangement is no good anymore. It's not my fault that some junior officers in the army attempted a coup d'état last night. Since then, we've had to enforce all regulations, including inspection of Party cards."

The driver shook his head sadly.

"By the way," the sergeant asked, "do you have your Party card?"

"No."

"You cannot travel without it. Better pay up for that also."

"How much is it?"

"Two thousand francs."

"What!"

"As I said, there is no choice."

Shaking his head, the driver handed over another two thousand francs and left the hut muttering.

The sergeant swatted at several flies that dive-bombed onto his flat nose. He looked at the Fulan man and spat in his direction.

The Songhay and the Fulan have never liked one another. For

Paul   Stoller

centuries the Songhay had been farmers and warriors. In the six-teenth century their armies controlled much of West Africa. They believed in force, will, and obedience to princely authority, unlike the Fulan, who respected no national or ethnic boundary. The Fulan considered themselves superior to "enslaved" farming peo-ples. Fulan herds would frequently trespass and trample Songhay fields. A mutually felt contempt expresses itself to this day in a va-riety of contexts—especially at roadblocks at the outskirts of Niamey.

"Put him in the holding cell. We'll decide later what to do with him." The sergeant cracked a kola nut and chewed it. Slowly, he fixed his gaze at Khadija. "Hmm. What brings you here, woman?"

Khadija shook her head. "I don't know, Mr. Sergeant."

The sergeant looked at the tall young policeman who had silently entered the hut.

"What's the problem with her?" the sergeant asked the young man.

"No Party card, Mr. Sergeant."

"Aha!" the sergeant uttered. He stared at Khadija's round face. "No Party card?"

"That's correct, Mr. Sergeant. When I came to Niamey two weeks ago, I didn't need a Party card. I don't understand."

"Women," the sergeant stated, "are not expected to seek un-derstanding."

Khadija stared at him in silence.

"Do you obey your husband, or are you one of these women who do what they want?"

"I have a fine husband, Mr. Sergeant, and I'm a good wife to him."

The sergeant studied her papers. "I see that you are from Tarma."

"Yes."

"Is your husband there?"

Khadija didn't want to answer but felt powerless. "He is a mer-chant in America."

"How can such a good man leave such a beautiful woman alone in Tarma?"

Khadija remained silent.

Jaguar

"You know these fines can become very, very steep indeed. I do hope you can afford to pay for your transgression."

Khadija maintained her composure.

"I am sure, however," the sergeant continued, "that we can find a way for you to reduce the financial burden of your fine."

Khadija's eyes narrowed; her face stiffened. She stood straight and took a step toward the sergeant's desk. "I'll pay the fine," she said.

The sergeant avoided Khadija's stare. "Very well, woman from Tarma. Pay me three thousand francs."

"The driver just paid two thousand francs. That's what I'll pay."

The sergeant pounded his fist on his desk. "How dare you challenge my authority here! I'll have you locked up."

Khadija fought to keep her composure. "Mr. Sergeant, I run a dry goods store in Tarma, and I am from a family of Niamey merchants. I understand how business is conducted in this country." She took two thousand francs from her purse and nonchalantly gave it to the sergeant. After a few tense moments of contemplation, he accepted it, gave Khadija a Party card, and dismissed her. She quickly slipped out of the hut and nodded to the other passengers waiting in line to pay their fines.

The entire cargo of the Mille Kilo lay spread out on the ground. More gun-wielding teenagers rifled through every suitcase, opening every box, package, or container—no matter how small. One of them grimaced as he opened a bottle of cold cream and tasted it. Another rushed off to the hut, carrying a small cloth satchel. "Drugs! I found drugs!" he cried excitedly. He emerged a few moments later, dejected, and walked back to the inspection. In his eagerness he had mistaken medicinal tree bark for controlled substances and had been scolded by the sergeant.

Knowing that the inspection would take much longer, Khadija sat next to an old man under a tree. A young girl, carrying a tray of cooked greens stuffed with peanut paste, approached them. "Leaves. Cooked leaves."

"How much?" Khadija asked.

"Ten francs each."

Khadija bought six of them and offered three to the old man next to her. He was slight, and his bearded face had been creased by a lifetime of farming millet under the hot sun. He wore a turban around his cap. A dusty, long white billowing robe covered his dirty white drawstring pants. "I give thanks, my child."

"God is strong," Khadija said.

"God is strong," the old man agreed, "but sometimes I wonder why we mortals have to suffer so much."

"What do you mean, Baba?" Khadija asked, addressing the old man as "father" out of respect for his advanced age.

"Look at the way those owners of power treat us. They prevent us from traveling. They look through our things. They treat us contemptuously."

"It is difficult," Khadija acknowledged. "But it seems much worse now. When I was a child, people treated one another with more respect."

"Do you think so, daughter?"

"Yes, I do."

"I'm not so sure. Old men like me like to say that if we adhered to our Songhay traditions, life would again be sweet. In truth, my daughter, the peasant's life has always been hard. It was no different in the time of my grandfather. The only difference has been in who rules us. In the old times, it was the kings of Songhay who pummeled us. Yesterday, the French broke our backs. And now it's the iron-fisted soldiers and the rich merchants who steal from us and make us suffer."

"It is sad that you feel that way."

"How else can I feel? I am a simple old man. I wanted to travel to Niamey today, and some young boy with a gun insults me. They throw my things on the ground and soil my clothes. Is this the way to treat an elder?"

"No, it is not."

"As our ancestors said: Our only strength is patience. Patience is the world."

The old man's talk stirred Khadija's emotions. She began to contemplate her current circumstances. She considered herself a strong and patient woman. But to what avail? Her considerable patience hadn't affected the tension between herself and Issa's mother. It hadn't brought Issa back to Niger. Perhaps he didn't want to come back? She sometimes wondered if she wanted him to return.

In his absence, she had begun to question their marriage. Their differences were great. Could patience change the fate of her birth? Like the old man, she was of common birth, a fact that carried social stigma in Niger. Shaking herself, she resumed her conversation with the old man.

"But Baba," she said, "how have you made your way in the world? Patience is not enough, is it?"

"No, it is not. In the past, we learned to disappear."

"Disappear?"

"Yes. Vanish. If the owners of power didn't see us, we were safe."

"But how do you disappear?"

"You walk slowly, say little, and live quietly in the bush. In that way, you disappear. This way you are free and at peace."

"But . . ."

"Yes, sometimes they beat you or extort money from you. This you must accept as an annoyance and no more."

What the old man didn't know, of course, was that Khadija could not disappear. She had to live among Songhay nobles who looked down upon her common status. How does one disappear when one is oppressed by ones in-laws? How can one be patient when one is seen by those in-laws as a worthless common woman? Khadija's pride battled against her deep sense of responsibility to Issa and her marriage. Her departure from his family would surely disappoint her husband. Would her unsteady marriage survive such a departure? She had been quite happy with Issa in Abidjan, but knew that, even in the best circumstances, a life as the woman in the compound would never satisfy her craving to be a trader.

As they talked, the tall young police officer left the Mille Kilo and sauntered over to a Toyota van. Perhaps he would find drugs in the baggage of one of its passengers. The Mille Kilo driver's two apprentices climbed up the ladder to the bus's roof and began the arduous process of arranging and securing cargo to the bus's roof. They made rapid work of a time-consuming task, and soon enough, the driver signaled for the passengers to board. Slowly, they filed in and found their seats. The driver started the engine, the tall young policeman lowered the roadblock—a chain pulled taught across the road—and the bus at last chugged into Niamey.

chapter 16

As the bus resumed its course, Khadija thought about her day. Because of the time lost at the roadblock, she would have to alter her plans. She wondered if she'd have enough the time to buy all the provisions her shop required. She decided to start at the central market first and then rush over to Yusef's shop. If she was efficient, she'd have time to visit her mother briefly. She might even have enough time to see Ramatu. The need to rush so much disappointed her because she enjoyed her time in Niamey, especially her visits with Yusef and with her mother.

As the bus puttered into Niamey's neighborhoods, Khadija watched the landscape change. Men led burden-laden donkeys and camels toward the capital's center. In the distance, towering cranes and tall stockpiles of cinder blocks marked partially completed government construction projects. Closer to central Niamey, the bustle of a minor makeshift market produced a swirl of taxis, trucks, mopeds, cows, camels, and pedestrians that brought traffic to a crawl. At a traffic light, children converged on the bush taxi, platters piled with offerings of fruit and grilled meat balanced precariously on their heads. The light turned green, and the taxi lurched forward. Two-story luxury villas, partially hidden by walls covered with bougainvillea, lined both sides of the road. The expressive splendor of Niger's leisure class soon gave way to urban grit, however: the putrid odor of open sewers; flies swarming over soapy pools of dishwater; children playing hide-and-seek amid heaps of rotting garbage. Close to the central market, Khadija's destination, toothless lepers hobbled toward the Mille Kilo. One man thrust his stump hand into Khadija's window. She gave him twenty francs. Young boys and girls led their blind parents into the din of the market, a huge square enclosed by concrete walls. Like the lepers, they, too, sought the charity of pious Muslims. Finally, Le Rapide rounded a bend in the road and entered the bus depot, a large square blacktop at the edge of the market.

After some effort, Khadija managed to slip out of the bus and walk toward the market. Badly in need of refreshment, she found a young boy pushing a wooden cart.

"Coca, Esprit. Coca, Esprit."

"I'll have one Coca," she said.

The young boy opened the cart's lid and lifted off the burlap that covered his iced soda bottles. "You pick the coldest," he said.

Khadija made her selection, paid the boy, and walked on. The depot was filled with small Toyota vans and Peugeot pick-up trucks (the notorious bush taxi) as well as large buses and trucks (long-distance carriers). Scores of small food stalls offering coffee, tea, bread, and rice ringed the depot. The aromas of roasting meat filled the air. Eager to get started, Khadija ignored her hunger and entered the market.

The old market had been a maze of market stalls constructed of corrugated tin or scrap wood. At the old market most merchants sold their wares from crudely fashioned tables or from palm-frond mats. When the rains came, the market's winding dirt pathways became large lakes. That market's vibrant life came to an abrupt fiery end. No one knows how it burned to the ground. Some people said it was a merchant's carelessness. Others said the government torched the market to rid the capital city of an embarrassing eyesore. As a child, Khadija spent many happy hours in the market working in her mother's spice stall. She remembered the strong aromas of ground hot peppers, dried garlic, and dried onions. She missed the old market, but like most people in Niamey, did not mourn its passing.

The new, partially enclosed market was a vast improvement. The open-air structures had been built to capture refreshing Sahelian breezes and offer protection from the sun. The market authority assigned each merchant a numbered stall in one of five concrete enclosures. By hosing down the concrete walkways every evening, the authorities kept the market reasonably clean. At the market's center stood a police tower and a holding cell, a stern warning to would-be thieves.

Khadija made her way to the food section, housed at the back of the market under a tall rectangular structure that looked like a huge tent. The food merchants arranged their various offerings on

Paul Stoller

large wooden tables. She went immediately to Ramatu, who was selling sun-dried tomatoes that week.

"Hey, Khadija, hey," Ramatu chanted. Awash in bright sunlight, Ramatu's round face looked like a large melon. "Are you still among the living?"

"Indeed I am, older sister. I'm happy to see you. I thought I might miss you today." After a few moments of holding hands and smiling at one another, Khadija shook her head and said, "Life is becoming more and more difficult."

"This I know well," Ramatu answered with a sigh. She liked to talk about the many problems in the world.

"This morning they stopped our Rapide, inspected our things, and demanded to see our papers." Feeling the need to unload her frustrations, Khadija described in detail what had happened that morning at the police stop.

"I know it already," Ramatu said, nodding her head. "They want to see your ID and your Party card. Imagine! A Party card. Hah! What a band of thieves. They've been stopping us on the street asking for them. I had to pay a one-thousand-franc fine for not having a Party card. Can you imagine?"

"Imagine this—I had to pay two thousand francs."

"You swear it?"

"In the name of Allah. And you know what? The fat police sergeant offered me a reduced fine in exchange for sex. What a hideously fat donkey he was!"

Ramatu laughed. "There are too many of those old, fat, limp Songhay men around, younger sister. I should know, I've been married to two of them. What will they want next?"

"Who knows?" Khadija wondered.

"I hear they want to come to the market and increase the tax we pay on our stall rents."

"Do you pay less rent if you have sex with the market police?"

Ramatu doubled over in laughter. "You always make me laugh, younger sister. Today you get a special price on my tomatoes."

Beginning to feel better already, Khadija thought about how much she liked being in Niamey. Living in Tarma had narrowed Khadija's outlets for fun. She had learned to control her emotions in Issa's family's taciturn compound. Among merchants one was expected to express oneself vigorously. In her own family she had been taught to enjoy language and humor. Her kin considered the capacity to make another laugh the greatest of personal gifts. What a loss she felt by restraining these aspects of her self in Tarma. It was only with the women in the central market that she felt the full measure of life pulsing through her veins. There she felt free enough to express herself completely. There she made people like Ramatu double over in laughter.

"How much, older sister?"

"One large sack for one thousand francs. You will make a large profit on that."

Khadija smiled. "I'll take two sacks." She turned toward the flow of people and cried out, "Djéjé. Djéjé!" looking for someone to haul her provisions. Within moments, a teenage boy appeared with his cart, offering his services. "Put the tomato sacks on the cart and follow me. I have many more purchases to make."

The boy put the relatively light sacks on the cart and followed his patron to the northern end of the food hall. She stopped in front of a peanut oil vendor who was also her cousin, the son of her mother's sister.

"Greetings, big cousin," Khadija said.

"And greetings to you little cousin," Harouna replied, beaming at his relative. "Have you yet seen your mother?"

"No, I haven't yet. The bush taxi I took this morning was stopped outside of Niamey for a long inspection. They looked at everything, every container in every suitcase. And they checked all papers, including Party cards. I'll have to cut short my visit with my mother."

"Were you badly treated at the roadblock?"

"The young police officers were very rude."

"Where is the spirit of the past when we Songhay were one nation, when people helped one another? Now we steal from each other. This is not our way, Khadija. Not our way."

Khadija remembered her earlier conversation with the old man at the roadblock. "But, Harouna, it was always bad for the poor person, then as well as now. Is it not so?"

"You think so?" Harouna scratched his scraggly chin. He was a tall thin man with stooped shoulders. His prominently rounded cheekbones made his face appear gaunt. "Perhaps you are right. One thing I know for sure is that things are bad for us today. There is no money here, and what money one earns is taken away by the government."

"Times are difficult," Khadija said.

"Yes, they are," Harouna responded.

"But today let me ease your burden," Khadija offered. "I want to buy fifteen liters of peanut oil."

"You've never wanted it before. Why the change?"

"I want to expand my offerings at my shop in Tarma."

"Ahh. Delighted to sell to you at a very good price."

"How much?"

"How about twenty-five hundred francs for a ten-liter can?"

"But cousin, that is too little."

"Yes, but that is my introductory offer so that you'll continue to buy from me. Next time, I will charge you the going rate, no?" He smiled. "Besides, it is our custom to help a family member who is trying to expand a business. You know that!"

Khadija face beamed. "You are a good man. Your heart is no less than pure." She turned to the cart pusher. "Put three, ten-liter cans of oil on the cart." She gave her cousin seventy-five hundred francs and bade him a fond farewell.

"Come again soon," he called after her.

Khadija, boy, and cart rolled into the hardware section of the market, which was run by Yoruba immigrants who also sold enamel plates, pots, and dishes.

Khadija spoke to an enormous woman with a round face prominently marked by three vertical scars that ran from her cheekbones halfway to her jaw. She stood behind a large makeshift table covered with nails, hinges, mousetraps, screws, nuts, and bolts. Hundreds of porcelain pots and plates were piled high behind her.

"Madame, I bid you hello." Although Khadija bought regularly from this woman, she did not know her name.

"Ah, the woman from Tarma," the Yoruba replied. "Back again?"

"Yes, madame. I've already sold the pots I bought here two weeks ago."

"Really! How wonderful. You want more?"

"Indeed." Khadija ordered sets of white plates and bowls with the same red flower pattern as those she had already sold. She also bought three, ten-liter cast-iron cooking pots.

After the boy loaded these onto the cart, they continued their market stroll through the strip-woven blanket section and through batteries, radios, and televisions. Toward the southern edge of the market, she came to the print cloth merchants and went immediately to her cousin Moussa's stall.

A small man with a square face and scraggly beard, Moussa had been selling print cloth since he was a teenager. Because they had always liked one another and were age-mates, people in both families thought that one day they would be married. But Khadija didn't feel that way about Moussa, and Moussa had never expressed his feelings about his cousin. After Khadija had married Issa, Moussa wed a woman outside the family.

"Ah, cousin," Moussa said, beaming and taking Khadija's outstretched hand. "How is your family?"

"They thank God for their health, cousin. And yours?"

"God be praised."

"Moussa, we are family and have known one another for such a long time." She watched Moussa's face break into a warm smile, which encouraged her to continue her talk. "I need to discuss an important matter with you about Issa's family."

Moussa frowned. "These nobles can be very bad."

"They are, Moussa. I don't want to complain, but they bear me much ill will. I help to feed them and look after their well-being. In exchange, they often insult me and treat me as if I don't exist."

"These are powerful and spiteful people. You should be among people who love you."

"I want to leave, but I have my business and my obligations— no matter how stressful."

"You are a remarkable woman, Khadija. In your place I would leave immediately."

"My business is doing very well. I do not want to leave it. Yet, if they continue to beat down my soul, I may one day start another business, perhaps in Niamey. Do you think I should try to persist until Issa returns?"

"I don't know what you should do, but I would leave if I were in your place," Moussa replied with empathy.

Khadija sighed and then focused her attention on business. She fingered Moussa's bolts of cloth. "I'll buy some cloth for myself. Maybe it will cheer me up."

"No," Moussa interrupted. "I will make you a gift of cloth. First you will take eight meters of cloth for yourself. Then select the cloth you want to sell in your shop. I will only accept money for the shop cloth."

Khadija selected her cloth and paid Moussa. "Thank you, cousin. You are a good man," Khadija said, moved by Moussa's concern and generosity. "I must take my leave now. I hope to return to Tarma this afternoon," she said quickly.

"Do not forget what I said. Think about coming home," Moussa called after her.

Khadija nodded and waved to the hired boy to move on. As they made their way toward the street, two young teenagers dressed in tattered rags ran past them and snatched Khadija's cloth. Running after the boys, Khadija screamed, "Thief! Thief!" Moussa ran with her.

People in the market stared passively at the screaming woman. Unbeknownst to Khadija, theft had become a common occurrence in the market. "They stole my cloth! They stole my cloth!" she cried, running after the culprits, but she was quickly outdistanced. By the time Khadija and Moussa reached the police tower at the market's center, the boys and the cloth had vanished—forever. A tall police officer, who was an older version of the youth who had inspected her papers that very morning, slowly walked toward them.

"Did someone steal something from you, woman?" he asked, rubbing sleep from his eyes.

"Yes, two young boys in rags stole my new cloth," she said between breaths.

The policeman nodded. "Ah, but you know this happens every day at the market. You are not from Niamey, are you?"

"I grew up here, but I live in Tarma now."

"Then you should know that Niamey is different now. Many young boys have no work. So, they steal. These petty thefts happen every day. Next time, you will be more vigilant, no?"

"Can you report this theft?" Moussa asked. "I will describe the cloth."

The policeman laughed. "Come now. We can't waste our time on such petty matters. Did the boys injure you in any way?" he asked Khadija.

"No."

"Did they stab you?"

"No."

"Then it is not worth a complaint. Consider the theft," he said patronizingly, "a lesson in life."

Khadija's face froze. "My complaint is that this country employs policemen like you who don't care about people. My complaint is that you do nothing and thieves operate with complete freedom."

The policeman pursed his lips, performed a stiff about-face, and returned to his tower. Khadija's anger gave way to sadness. Her arms hung limply to her sides as she and Moussa returned to the cloth stall. Why had no one, save Moussa, helped in her attempt to catch the thieves? Why had people in the market become so callous, so uncaring? She realized with great disappointment that even in the market the credo had become Look out for yourself.

"Cousin, I am so sorry for your loss," Moussa said as they reached his place of business. "Please take another eight yards of cloth."

"No, I cannot. My day is spoiled."

Moussa shook his head. "The little thieves strut through the market every day. Some of them are children who work for the thief bosses. Some are teenagers, and some, the most dangerous, are young men armed with knives. They steal vegetables, cloth, radios, cassettes—anything they can get their hands on. Before, you could yell 'thief' just like you did, and the whole market would run after the culprit until he was caught. Now with the tower up there, no one pays attention, least of all the young policemen who watch over us. They are paid off by the thief bosses."

"It is a sad time," Khadija said, getting depressed about the calamities of a very long day.

"And then you have the big thieves—the government," Moussa continued. "They are so bad, they steal from their own warehouses and then sell back to us the stolen merchandise—at very high prices. And for this," Moussa sighed, "we pay taxes! May God deal with them justly."

Khadija said good-bye and turned to the cart pusher. "Let's go on to the Arab boutiques." She turned back to Moussa. "Good-bye, cousin. I hope to see you again soon."

chapter 17

Following the cart boy, Khadija crossed the always bustling Boulevard Charles de Gaulle, the busiest street in Niamey. Although she liked the air-conditioning in the Lebanese-owned Uniprix supermarket that stood like a square fortress just across from the one of the gates of the market, the high prices and the surly attitudes of the employees dissuaded her from shopping there.

"Where to, madame?" the young man asked.

"To my friend's store. To Yusef's. Follow me."

Khadija looked out for thieves as they walked down a paved road, moving west past Uniprix and following a wide, open sewer. How sad, she thought, to feel the need to follow the callous policeman's advice. And yet, she couldn't afford to lose more inventory to theft. At the third intersection, they turned onto a rutted dirt road lined with mudbrick houses. The street teemed with children at play. The early afternoon sun pounded Khadija's head, impelling her to walk slowly. She thought again about her life. Did she have the courage to leave Issa's family? She thought about living in New York City. These thoughts of escape were fleeting, however. At that moment her life was very much in Niamey and Tarma. Family difficulties and social problems could not be ignored. Besides, she had a business to run, which meant she had little time to reflect on the imponderables of life. She had always felt proud of her business skill. Taking a deep breath, she headed to the shop of her Arab supplier and friend, Yusef ibn Muhammed.

Yusef's shop stood in the middle of a line of walled mudbrick compounds that bordered a dirt road. The corrugated tin door had been propped open, revealing part of a counter and a whitewashed wall. His space was much larger and more diversified that Khadija's shop in Tarma. She had been doing business with Yusef for more than a year now. Her mother had told her about him, and when they met, Khadija immediately felt that they'd become good friends. Khadija's initial feeling turned out to be accurate. Yusef went out of his way to extend her credit. When she asked him to find particular goods, he did so with quickness and diligence. Khadija particularly liked the afternoons she spent in his shop drinking tea and talking about business, religion, and politics. Even so, she knew little about this man of perhaps forty years. She knew that he came from Mauritania and had two wives, but she had never met them, for they never set foot in the store. In the store the only female she had seen had been a servant woman, usually dressed in homespun indigo cloth. Several times a day, the servant hauled water to Yusef's compound, a spacious villa one street away. She also brewed tea for her patron.

Yusef had several older children back in Mauritania. His younger children were here in Niamey, however, and they sometimes wandered into the store. Though Yusef had not mentioned how long he had been in Niamey or when he'd like to return to Mauritania, if ever, Khadija sensed that the better they got to know one another, the more he would want to tell her about himself. How surprising, Khadija thought, for an Arab to befriend and talk seriously to a woman. From the beginning of their relationship, though, Yusef had been impressed with her energy, intelligence, and business acumen. When they talked, he unexpectedly found himself attracted to her.

Khadija slipped into the cool air of Yusef's shop. He leaned against his counter. For a tall man he had a surprisingly small round head, which was usually clean shaven. A large nose drooped over his smooth copper face. Yusef had stuffed the tall shelves of his shop with the goods Khadija sold: laundry detergent, soap, hardware, mosquito netting, batteries, dates, hard candies and chewing gum, kola, tobacco, soft drinks, tea, and aspirin.

"Ah, Khadija," he said. "You bring such freshness to the stale air of my shop. Welcome. Welcome." As always, he held out his hand

Paul Stoller

and smiled warmly at her. Motioning to a small table in the corner, he invited her to sit down. "You've had a long journey. Sit, and we shall drink tea." He turned toward the opening that led to a courtyard behind his shop and in Arabic called for his servant to bring them tea. "The tea will be here in a moment," he said eagerly.

Looking at Yusef, she found herself attracted to this man who was so different from Issa. When in recent weeks she tried to satisfy herself sexually, her thoughts had sometimes shifted from Issa to Yusef's less familiar but more exotic image. As Yusef looked intensely at her, she felt her pulse racing.

"I imagine you had a long trip," he said, resuming their polite conversation.

"Very long, Yusef," she said with a measure of relief. "They are inspecting baggage at the entrances to the city. They made me pay a fine for not having a Party card. Worse yet, thieves stole cloth from me in the market, and no one ran after them. They steal without fear."

Yusef nodded. "What has become of the world? If only we would follow Islamic principles, we would have peaceful world."

Yusef's servant brought a round platter with a teapot and several shot glasses. "The tea will energize you," he said, searching for a way to help her and hoping that she would stay for the second and third pots. "How is your business?" he asked, knowing that business talk usually animated Khadija.

"It is doing well. People seem to like the products I carry—thanks to you."

Yusef smiled and leaned very close to her. "You are a kind and able woman, Khadija." After moment of uncomfortable silence, he asked after her family.

For some reason Khadija did not respond in the formulaic "they are fine" manner. It wasn't customary for a Songhay person to vent her or his soul to a stranger, let alone a foreigner. Somehow, though, Khadija felt safe in Yusef's shop. Although he was an Arab, she felt free to express herself. "My in-laws are nobles, so they look down on traders like me."

"Ah," he said looking intently at her. "And they treat you poorly."

"Yes. They cannot accept that the fact that their son married a merchant's daughter. Worse yet, they resent that I run their compound so well, keeping them well-fed and clothed, and think that I steal the money my husband sends."

"These things happen in families, especially when the husband is away." Yusef sipped his tea. "And your husband, how long has he been away?" Yusef had wanted to ask her this question for some time.

"A long time," Khadija said sadly.

Yusef shook his head. "It is not right for a husband to leave his wife for so long. I can understand going on a journey of even six months. My ancestors took goods on caravans for months at a time. But years? That, that is too long."

"He is a good man, though," she said. "He sends money for his family and for my business. He says he wants me to visit New York."

"And will you go? Do you want to go?"

Khadija was not certain how to answer this question. What would await her in New York? She did not speak English and knew nothing of American ways of living. Her sense of adventure made her want to go, but she didn't know what to expect. In his letters and phone conversations, Issa had not talked about what life was like in America. She also wondered how she would feel about life there with Issa. Would she experience the joys that she felt in Abidjan? And what would happen to her business? Her independence?

"I do not know," she replied, finally. "My husband first needs some kind authorization from America. So far, they have not given it to him. Perhaps I will go there for a visit if they give him these papers." She took a deep breath. "In truth, Yusef, I don't know if I want to go there anymore."

"Forgive my boldness, Khadija, but a great sadness grips you right now, does it not?"

"Yes," she said weakly. "It loosens its grip only when I'm in my shop, in the market, or talking to clients, family, or friends like you." She paused. "Even so, the grip tightens."

"Perhaps, then, we should talk business to lighten your spirit."

For a man, Khadija thought, Yusef was an exceptionally sensitive person. He had said exactly the right thing. Once again, she wondered about him, about how he treated his wives. She mused about what life would be like with him. Could she ever marry an Arab? Would he insist on cloistering her? Would he require her to wear a veil? Such a life was unthinkable to an independent daughter of the market. She felt that Yusef was interested in her. His prices were just a little bit too good, his talk just a little bit too sweet. If she married him, a relatively prosperous merchant far from his family, many of her present worries would dissipate. She tried to push these adulterous thoughts out of her mind. Besides, she still cared deeply for Issa. She didn't think she wanted to divorce him. Maybe there was another way to squeeze a little sweetness from life?

Concentrating on business, Khadija rattled off her order to Yusef, who made a list: a carton of small-size laundry detergent, a case of sardines in soy oil, one half-case of mackerel in tomato sauce, two cartons of cubed sugar, one carton of mosquito nets, two cases each of Coke and Sprite, a large box of Chinese green tea, and one large sack of dried dates.

"That is all I need today," she said.

"It is a large order, Khadija. It comes to twenty-five thousand francs. Do you want to pay it all today?"

"I have more than enough money to pay the entire bill today," she said with no small amount of pride, "and that is what I choose to do."

"Very well. Do you want to check my figures?"

"No, Yusef. There is much confidence between us." She counted out and handed him the correct sum and then turned to find her cart boy. "Hey, young man, hey," she called. "Come and load the cart. It is time to go." She turned back to Yusef. "Thank you for your kindness. With God's blessing, perhaps I will have time for a short visit with my mother, catch a late afternoon Rapide, and make it back to Tarma by sunset."

Khadija and the cart boy made their way to her mother's house, where they snacked on bean cakes. Over tea, she recounted the adventures of a very trying day to her ever-supportive mother. Hesitant to leave, she lingered in the emotional comfort of her natal compound. She knew that she wouldn't make it back to Tarma until well after sunset, but that was just as well.

chapter 18

By the time Khadija had returned to the compound in Tarma, the night wind sliced through her body. The moonless night made the descent from the taxi depot quite treacherous. But the old cart driver, who had heard the Rapide stop at the depot, came to Khadija's aid. He and several village teenagers put Khadija's considerable load on the old man's rickety cart. Their eventless descent brought them into the eerie silence of Tarma at sleep. Since it was such a cold night, most people had retired early. Soon enough, they came upon Khadija's compound, opened the tin door, and drove the cart inside to unload.

As soon as she opened the compound's door, Khadija saw the bent figure of Hampsa, her mother-in-law. Wrapped in three cotton shawls, the old woman appeared to have been waiting a long time. She greeted neither her daughter-in-law nor any of the men, who slowly unloaded the cart. Instead, she stood silently and stared at Khadija and her entourage.

Khadija felt too tired to deal with yet another disagreeable incident in what had been a long and tiring day. Why was the old woman waiting for her, watching her, judging her? Her confrontations with the swaggering young police officers and their ridiculous inspections had exhausted her. The fat sergeant's thinly veiled proposition and the fines had infuriated her. The theft of cloth had repelled her. Even thinking about the considerable pleasures of her conversations with Ramatu, Yusef, and her mother would not sustain her through another argument.

Khadija watched Hampsa scrutinizing the cart driver's assistants. They quickly completed their work, accepted a small payment, and slipped into the darkness outside the compound's gate.

When they were finally alone, silence filled the space between the two women. Hampsa lifted the scarves from her head and wrapped them around her shoulders. "I've been waiting for you, in-law," she said softly.

"I can see that," Khadija responded reluctantly.

The old woman pointed to the boxes and cartons that had been stacked in the compound's center. "Why do you come so late and with so many things?"

Khadija took a deep breath but did not answer.

"I already know the answer, in-law," Hampsa continued. "You came late to avoid us. You came late so we would not see your precious things. These are things that belong to us. I know what you do when you go to Niamey and buy things. You steal our money that Issa has sent, and you buy things for your worthless store."

"Excuse me, in-law, but I did not receive a telegram from Issa and did not get one franc in Niamey."

"Hah. How can I believe you? You are nothing more than a merchant's daughter, a peasant. We know very well that you and your kind steal from the likes of us at every opportunity. It has been this way for centuries. You can't help the way you act; it is in your blood."

Khadija felt that blood raging through her body. "I bought these goods for my business! The money comes from the business and not from Issa. It has nothing to do with you."

Hampsa wagged her finger at Khadija. "You and your business. In the past we hired slaves to tend to our affairs. We had people to plant, weed, and harvest for us. We had people to trade for us. We maintained our distance from your kind of people. We have no use for you. I mourn the day that Issa became a trader. I curse the day he married you. We still do not welcome you here. We accept you only because of Issa; it is his wish."

At that moment, Khadija decided that she had had enough of this treatment. Even though it would be difficult to pack up the goods in her shop, gather the things in her house, and leave, she could no longer bear life with Issa's family. When she left, she wanted to leave very noisily, openly—all to humiliate this spiteful women and her hateful, outmoded thinking. But Khadija's soft side gradually subdued her anger. She worried that the innocent children in the compound would eat poorly in her absence. She also wondered how Issa might react to her departure. He'd probably be disappointed, if not angry, and she didn't know how she might respond to his anger.

"Well, in-law, maybe you should be freed of your burden," Khadija responded, overcoming her worries. "I am thinking about leaving here. See how well you get along without me!"

"I will tell Issa of your betrayal!" Hampsa snapped, somewhat surprised at Khadija's answer.

"Go right ahead, in-law. I also will inform him. I will be overjoyed to inform him! Goodnight." Slowly, she turned away from her mother-in-law and walked toward her house.

The next day nothing much had changed in the compound. If Hampsa was worried about Khadija's departure, she didn't show it. Khadija knew that she had discussed the confrontation with other people in the family, but no one mentioned it. If anything, the compound's aura of formal politeness became more pronounced, making family relations even more distant. Hampsa still didn't think that Khadija had the temerity to leave the compound. At first Khadija wavered about leaving. She didn't want to quit her business and didn't want to disappoint Issa. More important, leaving would be an admission of failure. Eventually, though, a deepening frustration undermined her considerable pride. She harbored no anger toward Issa's family. Like many nobles in Niger, they lived in a long-departed past. She even felt sorry for them. But she vowed to live where people loved her and would give her moral and economic support. She would live with her mother, eat well, and see her friends and family in Niamey. She could sell her wares in Tarma and use the proceeds to start over again in Niamey. Ramatu and Yusef would help. She'd regain her independence and attempt to reaffirm her pledge to be an equal partner in a modern marriage. She counted on Issa's reasonableness. If he turned out to be unreasonable, she'd explore other ways of living and find another man who would appreciate her. She tried not to think too much about Yusef.

HARLEM

The dusty air of the Nigerien hot season had never bothered Issa, but in Harlem the summer haze, brought on by the mix of automobile exhaust and sunshine, made his lungs burn. He coughed as he inhaled the polluted air, but discomfort did not diminish his hopes for a windfall during the warm weather. He stood behind his two card tables on the north sidewalk of 125th Street and hoped that the summer would be profitable. As always, the winter market had been slow. But after the long gray days of the cold season, Issa believed that clear sunny days would compel Harlemites to come out, stroll through the market, smile—and buy. A good thing, too, because he hadn't been able to send much money to Niger throughout the winter.

The winter had been difficult not only in Harlem, but in Niger as well. His family had been in an uproar about Khadija's departure. He himself had mixed feelings about Khadija's exit from his family's compound. He knew that life had been difficult for her there and that his mother was not easy to live with—even for him. Although he didn't want his wife to suffer, he also felt that family responsibilities were more important than individual needs. If he had not been a "modern" man, Issa would have been furious rather than confused. How could any man, he wondered, maintain a long-distance marriage?

A few months earlier, a telephone call from Issa's mother had brought him the first news of Khadija's departure. Khadija had often expressed her desire to leave but had never mentioned that she had made a definitive decision. Had she done so, Issa, given his persuasive capacities, might have convinced her to remain. His mother had called him immediately after Khadija left. It was the first time she had called since he'd come to New York.

After they exchanged traditional greetings, Hampsa started in on Khadija. "She left," Hampsa had told him, "because we caught her stealing from us. Besides, she has never been one of us. How could you have married such peasant, my son?" she had asked him.

Talking to his mother made Issa realize that he had underestimated the depth of Hampsa's bitterness toward his wife. Hadn't the family appreciated his regular infusions of money? Why hadn't they come to appreciate Khadija's resourcefulness as he himself had? His mother's malice had gradually overpowered her reasonableness, it seemed. And yet, his sense of family loyalty still burdened him. Assuming that Khadija was staying with her mother, he immediately phoned her to discuss the possibility of her return to compound—for the sake of the family.

"No," Khadija had responded firmly, but without losing her temper. Having expected this kind of reaction from Issa, she braced herself. "I don't want to go back there. I will not live where I am not wanted." She paused a moment, the crackle of the phone connection breaking the silence between them. "As you know," she continued, "it took me a long time to decide to leave, and I think it was the right decision."

"But I thought that they would come to appreciate you, Khadija," Issa could not help adding.

"They are lost in the past. My only regret," she said, "is having left Uncle Abdu. I fear that his days are short."

"I'm afraid so."

"I have no other regrets about leaving. I'll stay with my mother and start another business here. I'll work here until I join you in New York."

Issa felt guilty about his family, but also about Khadija. Her words reminded him of how long he had been away, how long they had been apart. He thought of their early years together and remembered their pledges to one another.

"How will the family manage in Tarma?" he finally asked, not wanting to express his other feelings.

"I will continue to help them when I can. They will have to cash your money orders and sort things out for themselves," Khadija added.

In some ways it was as if Issa was talking to Khadija for the first time. Did he really know this strong-willed woman? He was suddenly fully aware of her toughness and decisiveness and wondered if he wanted such a woman in his life. Perhaps living among relatives and friends in Niamey would calm her a little? He hoped so. He had always loved her energy and resourcefulness, but their separation had changed her. She seemed more sure of herself, and tougher—a new element in Khadija's personality. Issa didn't know what more to say right then. "Please give my greetings to Uncle Abdu and to your people," he had managed to mutter. "I'll talk to you soon."

He wondered how well Khadija would get on, but eventually he began to think of other things. The heat of politics in Harlem now rivaled that of Issa's family in Niger. Many of the Jaguars worried about whether City Hall would disperse the "illegal" and "unregistered" market on 125th Street. Many people in Harlem liked the African market, but just as many wanted to see it disbanded. No one knew what would happen.

As usual, business was slow on a Tuesday morning, meaning that the Jaguars had time to daydream or talk. Nouhou interrupted Issa's daydream by asking him about his family.

"Khadija has moved in with her mother in Niamey. She feels she can't live with my family anymore."

"It is very sad when a family cannot remain together, is it not?"

"That, dear friend, is the way of today's world, no?"

Nouhou agreed. "The way of the world, brother, is that men like you and me have no peace. If it is not money that ruins the wholeness of families, then it is the greed of the power people."

"That is the white truth," Issa admitted.

"Seyni told me last night," Nouhou continued, changing the subject, "that they want to close down the market. The politicians and the merchants say we are dirty, that we pay no taxes, that we take business away from real Americans, and that we make no contributions to the community."

"Yes, but many merchants like us, don't you think?"

"Yes, but just as many don't want us here."

"What will we do if they chase us away from here?"

Issa already knew one possible answer to the question: return to Niger. El Hadj Daouda had declared several months before that he had eaten his last Big Mac: "I am tired of this place. I am tired of being shoved around by people who will never know me or care for me. I am returning to Niger." Idrissa, the elder who loved to farm, had left the previous month: "I must sow, weed, and harvest my fields. I don't know if I will come back. I am weary of their politics. One day they say we can stay here. The next day they say we must go. They don't care about us." Going back to Niger, however, wasn't yet an option for Issa. He hadn't made enough money and was too young a Jaguar to shoulder the social burden of failure. El Hadj Daouda and Idrissa, after all, had made much money and had provided well for their families. No matter how little they brought back from America, their relatives and friends would receive them well. Younger men would seek their advice. They'd be much beloved Jaguars. If Issa returned without substantial amounts of money and goods, he'd be laughed at and humiliated. How could such a young Jaguar, his neighbors would say, return from the land of plenty with next to nothing?

Issa had also learned to like his life in New York City. Although the Jaguars often complained about the economic and social privations of the city, such talk had become their "party line." Many of them enjoyed themselves in New York. They liked the frequent attention they received from beautiful African American and Hispanic women. Drawn to the seemingly carefree life of exotic traders far from the soil of the motherland, these women often gave the Jaguars their addresses and phone numbers. No exception to this pattern, Issa had filled his little black book, and he went out frequently. Although Issa felt the burden of his personal and social responsibilities in Niger, the thought of leaving New York had no current appeal for him.

"We will find a way," Nouhou responded to Issa's question, focusing attention upon the immediate problem.

Paul Stoller

"There is always a way," Issa said, trying to convince himself as well as Nouhou.

"Yes. We can go to the suburbs and sell in the malls. We can go downtown and sell on Canal Street. We can travel. We can find laboring jobs in the bush."

Issa nodded. He knew that Nouhou's list of possibilities were reasonable alternatives. But none of them would be as profitable as the 125th Street setup.

"Yes. But we are much better off here. Even though it is slow during the week, there are always people around to talk with, and we don't have to pay for space."

Nouhou nodded. "We should be grateful for what we have and pray that our good fortune continues."

Just then Dabé approached them. He was a Jaguar who, like Nouhou, came from Guanga in the northwest of Niger. The Jaguars called him the "Chauffeur." As he was always restless for the road, they saw little of him in Harlem. Since he was such an itinerant, Dabé maintained an address at the Bendix Hotel, an infamous establishment on the Upper West Side of Manhattan. The ramshackle hotel's cheap accommodations had long attracted legions of West African art traders eager for business excursions into the American bush. Dabé transported them willingly. A slight man with a delicate face and long thin nose, he looked diminutive behind the wheel of his dented Econovan. But he was a fearless and tireless driver. The Jaguars said that they had never seen anyone who could drive as far as fast and as safely as Dabé. Immodesty reinforced Dabé's vanity. He boasted frequently about his vehicular fortitude, crowing that he had visited more of America than any other Jaguar. He incautiously bragged about his three passports and four driver's licenses. When discussion turned to money, however, he remained curiously silent.

He now greeted Nouhou and Issa and shook their hands.

"Since when have you been here?" Issa asked.

"Yesterday," Dabé answered. "I've been to New Orleans, Kentucky, and Indiana." He patted Nouhou's shoulder. "Business is good. I packed up my van full of African things. I came back yesterday, and the van, God be praised, was empty."

"That is very good," Issa and Nouhou both said with admiration.

"Well, you know how it works for us in the bush. You go to Black American events: conventions, celebrations, sometimes a Black Expo, USA. Black Americans like their brothers from Africa. They are very kind to us. We go to festivals, and they buy from us. We wear our boubous and tell little stories about Niger or Mali or Burkina. They smile and bring out money. They call us 'brother;' we say 'brother' and 'sister.' Although they know little about us, it is very nice to be appreciated." Dabé looked at shoppers strolling through the market. "I guess we've learned a little bit about them." He paused and looked up and down the sidewalk. "We have to, don't we? That's how we make our way here. You know, it's good to keep alive the mystery of the 'motherland'—what they call Africa. Mystery sells very well in the bush—even better than here. We tell them we live in Harlem. Their eyes light up. 'Really?' they say. 'You brothers live in Harlem!' All of this is good for business."

"You're very much the businessman," Nouhou observed. "Is business the only reason to talk to people in the bush?"

"No. I've met some very kind Black Americans, some very nice people. I have some good Black American friends. In truth, I respect their attempts to understand us and their own history," he said seriously, "but that doesn't diminish the business opportunities their ideas present us."

"Sounds like business is very good in the bush," Issa said.

"Why don't you try it?"

Nouhou shook his head. "I've too much to do here. I don't want to leave my wife for weeks at a time."

"And you, Issa?"

"The costs seem high, no? You have to pay for gas, food, hotel, and a vendor's fee, don't you?"

"True, but I know the best places to stay—for cheap. With me, you save much money on food on the road. The vendor's fee runs between two and five hundred dollars, but we always sell and make a lot of money."

Issa and Nouhou considered the possibilities.

"I go to Chicago next week. Why don't you join me and try it out once? There is a Black Expo, USA, there next Friday. The stalls cost $350 each."

"We will get back in time for the Saturday market?" Nouhou asked.

"No, you'll miss Saturday. Doesn't matter. Thousands of Black Americans come to the Black Expo. They want to spend."

"What about the Sunday market?"

"You'll miss that, too. We'll leave Chicago late Sunday afternoon and drive all day and night. You'll be back Monday."

"I don't like missing Sunday market, but I'll think about going," said Issa. "I'll see if I can arrange for it and let you know in a few days."

"And so will I," Nouhou stated. "The market here is very slow now."

"If you want to come, leave a message for me on my phone machine. If you come, bring your goods here next Thursday at 7:00 A.M. We'll load up and go, God willing."

"We'll let you know," said Issa. "Thank you for the information."

"If you do come, don't forget your clothes from Niger. We want to look like real Africans," Dabé said as he left them to visit with other Jaguars.

chapter 20

One week later, Dabé parked his van next to Issa's space on 125th Street. The Chauffeur had already stocked his vehicle with bolts of green-and-black striped homespun Mali cloth and the white-on-black *bokolanfini* cloth with geometrical motifs—both big sellers in the bush. He had also packed away beads, kente-cloth hats, and pieces of sculpture. Issa and Nouhou complemented Dabé's cargo with large round straw hats from Burkina Faso and pointy-topped leather and straw Fulan hats from Niger. They also crammed in a variety of Nigerien leather bags, embroidered robes, Tuareg silver necklaces, rings, bracelets, and boxes covered with tooled leather dyed red and black.

Ever the experienced voyager, Dabé came around to inspect how they had arranged the merchandise. "I see you are new to this," he said to Issa and Nouhou.

Nouhou and Issa had rarely left Harlem and had never been outside of New York City. They looked at him warily.

"You need to balance the load and secure the packages. That's what I use spare tires for." Dabé positioned the five spare tires in the back of the van to secure the various boxes, sacks, and cartons of goods.

"Is that all you use the spare tires for?" Nouhou asked, looking skeptically at the tires on Dabé's van.

Nouhou and Issa said nothing more as they got into the truck. Dabé started the engine and grinned at them. They headed down Broadway and then over to West End Avenue. Before long they entered the Lincoln Tunnel, emerging after several minutes into the beginning of the bush—New Jersey. Driving infused the Chauffeur with so much energy that he talked incessantly—more even than Issa. "Take those kente-cloth hats," he said. "You know about them?"

"We don't sell them," said Nouhou.

"Black Americans like them very much," Issa observed.

"Do you know why?" Dabé asked, eager to educate them.

"My wife says it's because the cloth comes from Africa," Nouhou stated.

"That's what most people think. But it's not African, really."

"Some of the cloth is printed here in America," Issa professed.

"Yes. Some of it is made right here in New Jersey." As they turned onto Interstate 80 and headed west toward Pennsylvania, Dabé continued his story. "First, Black Americans liked to wear kente strips. These came from Ghana."

"Those were silk, no?" Issa wondered.

"That's right. Strips from larger pieces of cloth."

"The kind that the kings in Ghana wore," Nouhou said.

"Right. These strips were old. Hard to get. Very expensive. All the famous Blacks started to wear them."

"To demonstrate their pride in Africa," Issa said, smiling.

"Yes," Dabé continued. "They wanted to do that, but so did

other Blacks—even poor people. People in Chinatown, who are very smart, realized this, and they began to copy the kente patterns in cotton. They produced copies in their New Jersey factories and shipped them to Chinatown. Our Malian brothers found out about it and went downtown to buy cheaper kente. They took it uptown and sold it to people in Harlem, who began to buy lots of it. Then they'd take it to African or Black American tailors to make shirts, skirts, dresses, and hats." Dabé paused a moment to adjust his rear-view mirror. "In Ghana," he continued, "they found out about the China kente cloth and printed their own cotton copies—very, very cheap. Soon bolts of new cloth showed up in Harlem. Chinese people then came up to Harlem to buy the new Ghanaian copies of Ghanaian kente. With it they made many hats and bags."

"They left the trade in shirts, trousers, and dresses to African tailors?" Nouhou wondered.

"Yes, because you can make a hat or bag without measuring the person who will wear it."

"So, many of the kente hats and bags are sewn by China people?" Issa asked.

"Yes. The Malian brothers now go to Chinatown and buy their hats and bags—for very cheap. I bought my kente hats just off Canal Street."

"The Chinese are very, very smart," Issa said, admiringly.

They stopped mid-morning at a rest stop/restaurant in the Pocono Mountains of Pennsylvania. When Issa stepped out of the van and took a deep breath, he exclaimed, "The air is so clean here! I can breath and my lungs don't burn."

"That's right," Dabé said. "The air is clean in the deep bush." He walked toward the rest-stop buildings. "Let's change into our African clothes."

"I can't," Issa said. He had dressed in his usual baggy black jeans, plain white T-shirt, black baseball cap, and Air Jordans.

"Why?" Dabé asked.

"Because I don't have any. Even in Niger, I don't wear African clothes."

"Here in the American bush," Dabé proclaimed, "it's good if we look foreign."

"In Harlem," Nouhou observed, "the Africans dress like American Blacks and the American Blacks dress like Africans. My wife thinks it's very strange."

"Out here," Dabé said, "a black man who is dressed like . . . um . . . what do they call it, ah, . . . 'homeboy,' they usually think that he's going to steal, rob, or even kill them. Some Americans are very isolated; they only see Black people on television. So they get nervous and call the police, who come and give you many problems. Bush police are much meaner than the Harlem police."

"Do you have something I can wear?" Issa asked nervously.

"I always have extra clothes. And you, Nouhou?"

"I have something. Let's go and change, right now."

They slipped into the rest room and changed. Dabé and Issa wore white damask drawstring pants and matching long shirts with wide three-quarter sleeves. Gold curlicue embroidery swirled around the shirts' round necks. Nouhou wore a similar unembroidered outfit in canary yellow. All three put on sandals.

Properly dressed, they went to a McDonald's to buy road food. People stared at their strange dress, but not in a hostile way. While the three waited in line, Nouhou heard a group of older white people whispering.

"I bet they're all the way from Africa."

"Why would they be all the way out here?"

"Don't know. Maybe they're traveling somewhere."

"No kidding."

An old black man tugged at Dabé's sleeve. "You from Africa?"

"Yes, sir," said Dabé. "I am from Niger."

"Is that near South Africa? Kenya?"

"No sir," Dabé replied with great patience. "It is western Africa."

"Never heard of it, but I'm proud to shake your hand."

After vigorously shaking Dabé's hand, the man returned to his companions.

This interchange made Nouhou and Issa uncomfortable. In Harlem curiosity brought them attention, but only at the market. They were, after all, selling Africa, and so they sometimes fielded questions about Niger. But the African presence in Harlem had been of such long standing that, outside the market, most people left them alone.

Paul Stoller

Nouhou, who had finally reached the front of the line, faced a young plump teenager dressed in her McDonald's uniform. She had beady blue eyes and a round, moonlike face marred by acne. "Hi," she said with a trained enthusiasm. "Whaddya want?"

"Hello. Can I get food with rice?" Nouhou asked in his accented English. He had been in McDonald's only once during his time in New York City. Because he was so wedded to cooking and eating African food, he had never been attracted to a McNugget or a Big Mac.

"I'm not sure, sir. I think we have rice pudding."

"Rice pudding? Please give me McNuggets and Coke."

"How about some fries?" the girl asked.

"No fries," Nouhou answered politely.

Dabé ordered his food, as did Issa. They paid the young girl and walked to the van.

"Why can't I get rice?" Nouhou wondered, not being able to imagine a country in which practically no one relied on rice as a staple.

"Where do you think you are?" Dabé asked. "This is the deep bush, little brother. No rice here. In Chicago you'll get some good rice. On the road, you eat what they've got."

"We'll eat on the road?" Issa asked skeptically as they climbed into the van. For him eating was a serious business that required time and concentration.

"That's the way they do it here, Issa," Dabé said.

They drove west toward Ohio. Soon the green Poconos gave way to rolling hills, corn fields, and cows grazing in pastures. Issa enjoyed the breeze from the open windows.

"I like the bush," he said. "It's good to be out of New York. I feel free and excited."

"I felt that way when I started to drive in the bush," Dabé said. "America is vast and beautiful. Much more beautiful than Niger. Here the hills and fields are green." He took a deep breath and looked at Issa momentarily. "I've gone very far, and I'm still amazed at America's vastness. The farms never end. No wonder there is so much food here."

"Except for rice," Nouhou added.

They laughed.

"The country is not only beautiful," Dabé reiterated, "but the people are nice, too."

By the time they got to Ohio, it was early afternoon. Flat landscapes stretched to the horizon, thick bunches of trees breaking the monotony. "It will take at least four hours to cross Ohio," Dabé said. "We'll go far into Indiana and stop. I know a good place—for cheap."

Issa and Nouhou nodded their agreement and fell asleep. Around nine o'clock in the evening, Dabé pulled off the turnpike eighty miles east of Gary and registered for a room at a Motel 6. The manager, a short dark man from India, asked him to fill out a form. He didn't ask him if he was an African, where he was coming from, or where he was going. He wanted them to pay cash in advance.

"We are three," Dabé said.

"We'll bring a roller bed to your room, number fourteen, first floor."

"Thank you."

Dabé drove the van to a space just in front of the room and woke Issa and Nouhou.

"Where are we?" Nouhou asked.

"Indiana, very deep bush," Dabé answered.

"What time is it?" Issa wondered.

"Just past nine o'clock in the evening. You hungry?"

"Not me," said Nouhou.

"Me, neither," said Issa. "I'll eat in the morning."

"Good. Let's get some sleep. If we leave here after breakfast, we'll get to Chicago by mid-morning."

They slept soundly. Religious devotion, however, roused Nouhou well before dawn to recite his early morning prayers. He then woke Dabé, who wasn't a pious Muslim, and Issa, whose fatigue had overcome his piety that morning.

Dressed in their West African damask outfits, they filed out of their room and made their way across the street once again to buy a McDonald's breakfast. Having become quite fond of Egg McMuffins, Dabé ordered three of them—to go. Issa ordered a large coffee. Nouhou asked for a large cup of milk, a large coffee, and an apple Danish. They ate in the van.

"We go now," Dabé announced. "Before too long, you'll see

Chicago, little brothers. Chicago. We should get there about 10:00 A.M. We'll go directly to the place."

"What place?" Nouhou asked.

"The convention center, south of what they call the 'Loop.'"

"The Loop?" Issa wondered. "Why would there be a loop in a city?"

"You'll see."

They headed west through a flat countryside of farms and small towns that eventually gave way to the urbanscape of Gary: steel mills and chemical factories hugging the shore of Lake Michigan; warehouses with broken windows; trash-strewn streets clogged with dump trucks and tractor-trailers. To the west they saw the curve of the Lake Michigan and the Chicago skyline.

"In the name of God," Issa cried. "It is beautiful, Dabé. What a beautiful city!"

"That is Chicago?" Nouhou asked with wonder.

"Yes," Dabé proclaimed.

Soon after they paid a toll at the entrance to the Chicago Skyway, they were driving high above an unimaginable tangle of railroad tracks, diesel engines, trucks, and barges. Several freighters had docked at industrial ports. Issa and Nouhou had seen bits and pieces of New York's factories, but they had never seen so much industry from so high a vantage.

"America has power. She is very, very rich," Nouhou proclaimed. "I have never seen such wealth."

"In God's name," Issa said, "how can there be so much?"

"Little brothers," Dabé said, "Chicago is different. Black people in Harlem don't have much money. Many black people in Chicago do. They come to the Black Expo and spend very much."

Dabé pointed to the right, toward the looming Chicago skyline. "See the tall buildings?"

Issa and Nouhou nodded.

"That's the Loop."

"But I see no loop," Issa protested.

"Right," Dabé responded. "A train loops around those tall buildings. That's the real loop."

"America is a strange place," Nouhou said. "Loops, railroad cars, barges, factories."

"And no rice," Issa interjected.

They exited the Chicago Skyway and headed north on Stoney Island Avenue, a wide, eight-lane boulevard that cuts through the south side of Chicago.

"There are many McDonald's restaurants here and some cheap motels," Dabé observed. "And many poor black people." Indeed, they had just passed a group of shabbily dressed older black men chatting on one street corner. At a red light, a black woman dressed in black pushed a shopping cart across the boulevard. They soon came upon the lush greenery of Jackson Park.

"Chicago is very beautiful," Nouhou said. "There are many trees and places to walk."

Dabé took the role of tour guide. "True. There are parks all along the lake. Very beautiful."

Issa could hardly contain his excitement. "How much longer do we have to go?" he asked.

"Not long," Dabé said, taking pride in his knowledge of the city. "We go to the McCormick Convention Center. Very easy. We park and find the Black Expo registration. We get a stall, unload, and set up. Then we'll find a hotel."

"For cheap," Issa interjected, jokingly.

"For cheap," Dabé agreed, smiling.

Dabé turned onto Lake Shore Drive.

"This is a big road," Issa said. "Bigger than roads in New York."

"In Songhay," Nouhou stated, "we have no words to describe how wide this road is."

Dabé nodded, drove on, and smiled. Soon enough he exited Lake Shore Drive and turned onto a ramp leading them to the convention center, two large and long rectangular buildings, one on each side of Lake Shore Drive. Dabé parked in front of the west building. A large flag that said "Black Expo, USA" hung from its portal. "We are here," Dabé announced.

He locked the van, and the trio entered the cavernous building. Signs with arrows led them to the registration area. Everywhere they looked, they saw black people. The sudden presence of exclusively black faces contrasted strongly with the whiteness of the deep bush. Here no one stared at them. Several people, in fact, greeted them warmly.

They got in line and waited their turn to register. A tall thin woman struck up a conversation with Issa. Smooth brown skin covered her very attractive heart-shaped face. Her eyes sparkled. Like Issa, she wore African clothes: a matching top and wrap-around skirt made from black cloth embossed with white African figures—elephants, masks, warriors.

"Where are you from?" she asked in English.

"Niger," Issa replied, quite taken with the woman's beauty.

"Oh! I know where that is. You're far from home. Do you live in Chicago?"

"No. New York City. In Harlem."

"Harlem! That's great. You like it?"

"There's a lot to do there."

"How long are you in Chicago?"

"A few days. After the Black Expo, we go back."

"Well, that's good," she said. "I like your clothes." She looked into his eyes and smiled. "I have a little boutique in Hyde Park. I sell African fabrics and clothing. I make the clothes myself. I'm hoping to sell a lot here. Lots of black folks are coming, and they want to buy from people like us." She paused a moment. "What's your name, man from Niger?"

"Issa."

"I'm Keisha. I hope that we'll see one another at the expo."

"I hope so, too." Conversation had diverted his attention from the wait. He found Keisha the most attractive women he had met in America. Dabé and Nouhou both had already paid their $350 registration fees by the time Issa finally signed his form.

They went back to the van. "Get in, little brothers. We'll drive to a side entrance and unload our things. Then we'll set up," Dabé said, continuing his instructions.

The convention hall was enormous, the biggest space that Issa and Nouhou had ever seen. Accordingly, it took them some time to find their numbered spaces—on an interior row. The organizers had created two kinds of stalls: those that ringed the exterior walls of the hall—the most expensive spaces; and those that cut across the interior—spaces that sold for only $350. In their area, the trio found many Africans selling Africana: Nigerians displaying indigo print cloth and batiks; Ghanaians and Gambians selling beads;

Malians selling print cloth from Côte d'Ivoire, Benin, and Niger; Senegalese selling *djimbe* drums and African dolls. They also found African Americans selling African-Americana: multicolored quilts, dolls, a variety of clothing, silver and gold jewelry, and perfumes.

"Big brother," Nouhou wondered, "how many Africans come to these Black Expos?"

"Many come from all over. There are many Nigerians in Chicago. They come and sell. Other brothers come from Detroit and Milwaukee. Look over there," he said to Nouhou and Issa, pointing at a tall man dressed in a flowing robe. "That's Inoussa, Seyni's brother, from Wangu. He sells baseball caps."

"How long has he been here in Chicago?" Issa asked.

"Five years."

"A long time," Nouhou said.

"Yes," Dabé replied. "But he likes it. He married a woman from Chicago, got his Green Card, and has been blessed with two boys."

After completing much of his setup, Issa decided to follow his usual market pattern by taking a tour of the other vendors' displays. He greeted other African and African American vendors and wandered among the rows. He discovered a wide range of Black American enterprises that manufactured and distributed computers, cosmetics, clothing, art supplies, electrical fixtures, photographic supplies, not to exclude publishers of books and magazines.

When he returned from his excursion, he asked Dabé why so many Africans had been grouped together. "They're not trying to keep us away from the Black Americans, are they?"

"I don't think so. We don't make what we sell. Many of the Black Americans here make what they sell."

"I see."

"And, if you look around here, you'll also see some Black Americans selling the kinds of things we sell." Dabé patted Issa shoulders. "Don't worry little brother. Finish setting up. Tomorrow you're going to make much money."

Crowds had already filled the hall by the time the three arrived at the convention center the next morning.

"Not bad for a Friday, is it?" Dabé commented.

Nouhou remained skeptical. "Most of these people are vendors, not shoppers," he said.

"Sometimes vendors like to buy," Issa interjected optimistically.

"Sometimes," Nouhou frowned. "We'll see."

Wearing their damask outfits, they strolled among the aisles. Dabé greeted complete strangers, African Americans all, as if they were long-lost brothers and sisters.

"How can you be so bold?" Nouhou complained. "It is not our Songhay way to be so forward with people who do not know our language."

"True," Dabé replied, "but these people think all Africans are open and informal. So I am open and informal. It's good for business."

"Good for business," Issa repeated. "Always the business man."

"But we don't have to behave this way in Harlem," Nouhou stressed.

"True," said Dabé, "but this is the bush."

Events of the previous evening made Issa disagree with Dabé's assessment. How could anyone, even people from Harlem, think that Chicago was the bush! After setting up, they had driven south to find a hotel and a place to eat. Being a Chicago veteran, Dabé had found a room—for very cheap—near South Chicago Street. Dickerson's Hotel had been an institution in the neighborhood for many years. It stood five stories high and had single, double, and triple rooms, the doubles and triples having toilets and bathtubs— no showers. If you rented a single room, you had to use hallway toilets and baths. Two worn couches and a battered coffee table set off the lobby. The management displayed the daily and hourly room rates on a sign behind the registration desk, which had been judiciously sealed off from the public with bulletproof Lexan. Another sign read: PAYMENT IN CASH ONLY.

Dabé knew the heavyset, middle-aged African American man behind the registration desk. Leaving his compatriots in the lobby, he went to register.

"Hello," he said to the man, who seemed to be reading.

The man looked up. "Well, well, well. Hello, brother Dabé. Back again?"

"Yes. Back again, Mr. Reggie."

"You brought some of your brothers this time. Those boys look new. You best look after them, Dabé."

"I will. Nothing bad will happen."

"Sure hope so, son." Mr. Reggie had come to Chicago from Tupelo, Mississippi. The oldest of ten brothers and sisters, he took firm charge of his people, most of whom now lived in Chicago. Like the Jaguars, he saved as much as he could and sent money every month to his mother in Mississippi. "You know about the goings on around here. Best be careful. Don't be walking around too late."

Dabé gave Mr. Reggie thirty-five dollars and told him they'd be staying three nights.

"You pay me each day, okay?"

"Okay, Mr. Reggie."

Located at the back of Dickerson's fourth floor, their triple looked out over a trash-strewn alley, beyond which was a fenced schoolyard. They would sleep on three lumpy single beds. Nouhou tried the toilet; it gurgled a little but did not flush. At least the bed sheets seemed freshly laundered.

Nouhou frowned. "So this is a room—for cheap." He already missed his wife and his apartment.

"Right, little brother."

"Worry not, Nouhou," Issa said. "We are here only for three nights. It will be okay. Before you know it, you'll be home in Tamika's arms in your own comfortable apartment."

"I'm hungry," Nouhou announced. "You promised me rice."

"So I did. I know a place not far from here run by Nigerians— Igbo's. They serve rice."

Talk of African food lit Nouhou's face. "Let's go."

The restaurant comprised one-third of an Igbo grocery store, where shoppers could buy palm oil, plantain, manioc flour, dried

Paul Stoller

fish, cassava, yams, assorted hot peppers, and bitter leaves. The sharp smell of hot peppers brought a smile to Nouhou's face. As soon as the trio sat down, the owner, a short chunky man with a round face, greeted them. "Welcome brothers," he said in English. Although they were geographic neighbors in West Africa, they did not share any other language.

"My little brother Nouhou. He suffers greatly," Dabé said, pointing out his comrade. "He needs rice very much."

"We'll give you a very big bowl then. Rice, beef, and bitter-leaf sauce."

Before long the owner brought the Nigeriens three very large bowls of rice and sauce, along with spoons, a small bowl of pilli-pilli (pounded red pepper—hot, very hot), three glasses, and a pitcher of water. "Eat brothers. Eat until your stomachs fill."

Nouhou attacked his food with such ravenous ferocity, he soon called for a refill. Issa and Dabé ate more decorously.

"This is excellent sauce," Nouhou said. "What a pleasure to eat good food! The sauce reminds me of home."

Dabé and Issa agreed.

By the time they finished their food, exhaustion made their arms heavy and their legs wobbly. They paid their gracious host, thanking him heartily for his fine food, and made their way back to Dickerson's.

The trio walked up the creaky stairs to the fourth floor. The hallway stank of stale tobacco smoke, but fatigue rendered the strong odors a weak inconvenience. They stumbled into the room and fell fast asleep.

A loud knock on the door woke them in the middle of the night.

"Dabé. Dabé," said a soft female voice. "I heard you was in town. You there?"

"What the hell?" Dabé, groggy from sleep, answered in Songhay.

"Now Dabé, honey. You know I don't speak African."

Dabé professed ignorance to his countrymen.

"Dabé, this is your lady, Felice. You gonna let me in?"

Dabé got out of bed and walked to the locked door. "I have friends here. Sorry."

"You got another woman in there?" she asked with a snicker.

"No, no," Dabé whispered. "Men friends from Niger. That's all. You can't come in. Sorry."

"Okay baby," Felice said. "Maybe I'll see you around."

Nouhou stared at his older brother. "A visit in the middle of the night?"

Dabé hunched his shoulders. "You know how it is. I have friends in the bush."

"Friends who visit in the middle of the night?" Nouhou continued.

"Don't you have friends in Harlem?"

"I'm married." Nouhou answered. "Issa, however, has many friends in Harlem."

"Yes, but that's different," Issa protested. "My friends are not public women."

"Let's get back to sleep," Dabé suggested, not at all enjoying this discussion of his private affairs. "We have a big day tomorrow, do we not? Sleep is good for business."

For Issa, Chicago had become town—not bush. He liked it very much and hoped to sell well at the Expo. The expectation of good food had even convinced the ever-skeptical Nouhou of Chicago's bounties. And to make matters even more upbeat, the mid-morning crowds that streamed through the Expo's aisles made the trio quite optimistic.

The crowd quickly descended upon the Nigeriens.

"We want some kente hats," they demanded.

"Where can we get more leather boxes?" they wondered.

"These round leather hats are sooo gorgeous," they cooed.

By early afternoon, they were so busy they didn't have time to talk or leave for the bathroom. Soon their pockets bulged with cash. They changed many hundred-dollar bills and sold and sold and sold. Issa had never seen so many black people so willing to spend so much money.

Toward the dinner hour, the current of shoppers weakened, and they finally had time to exchange a few words.

"Big brother," Issa said, "am I in heaven?"

"No little brother," Dabé responded. "This is Chicago—Black Expo, USA."

Paul Stoller

And Chicago didn't disappoint them. That day, Issa took in three thousand dollars, his best day of business in the United States. Nouhou made twenty-five hundred, and Dabé sold almost his entire inventory of Asian-sewn kente hats, pulling in thirty-five hundred. After most of the shoppers had left, Keisha, the tall pretty woman who had talked to Issa the previous day, strolled by.

"How's it going, Issa?"

"Fine. We doing very good, here. We sell out tomorrow, God willing. How about you?"

"I'm doing very well, too," Keisha answered. "Could you introduce me to your friends?"

"Keisha, this is Dabé. We call him the 'Chauffeur.' And that one," he said, indicating the man who loved rice, "is Nouhou. We all come from Niger."

"Nice to meet you all," she said.

"This is Keisha," Issa added. "She sells clothes that she makes from African cloth. Her shop is here—in Chicago."

" . . . in Hyde Park," Keisha interjected with pride.

"We had very good days, all of us," Dabé stated.

"That's wonderful," she said. "Tomorrow, after business, I'm going to have a little party at my house. You wanna come? My friends would love to meet you."

"That sounds good," Dabé said. "Can you come tomorrow and tell us how to find your house?"

"Sure thing. See you tomorrow." She waved to them pleasantly and walked away.

Issa watched her longingly, wondering if he should follow her and ask her out. She had definitely shown an interest in him. Keisha's energy and enthusiasm about business deeply attracted him. Maybe he'd get a chance to be alone with her at the party.

The Black Expo remained open until 11:00 P.M., and the Jaguars vowed to remain until closing time, hoping to sell even more. They slipped off to dinner, one by one, monitoring one another's stalls. Long after the more corporate people had left the exhibition hall, the Jaguars—and others like them—remained to talk, sell, and rearrange their spaces. By closing time, fatigue streamed through Issa's lean body. Attraction to Keisha or any woman remained far from his mind, for a change.

"Older brother, we must go to sleep soon, very, very soon," he said to Dabé insistently.

"Agreed."

"And," Nouhou added, "no knocks on the door in the middle of night."

"I'll make sure she doesn't come tonight," Dabé assured them.

The Saturday crowds dwarfed those of the previous day. Hungry shoppers coursed through the hall, talking, walking, skipping, singing—and buying. They again converged on the trio's stalls. They demanded service, sales pitches, and cheap prices. Dabé and Issa, both versatile veterans of American markets, knew that smiles were good for business. By flashing their teeth at the increasingly insistent shoppers, they won many sales. Nouhou, by contrast, fared much worse, having never become comfortable with the American penchant for smiling. Even so, he sold his wares at a brisk pace. As on the previous day, they had no time to lunch or relieve themselves, which, for Dabé and Issa, made smiling all the more difficult. When the crowds thinned in the early afternoon, they spelled one another for a few minutes of relief and several moments to scarf down a hamburger-and-french-fries lunch.

Late afternoon brought another swarm of shoppers the trio's way. By the time the shoppers had left, little inventory remained in the stalls. As Dabé had promised, they had sold out. Their elation drained the fatigue from their bodies.

"I told you Chicago was sweet," Dabé proclaimed.

"By the grace of God," Nouhou interjected.

"We must be grateful and thankful for our success," Issa cautioned. "We have been blessed."

"Yes," said Dabé, "and now we can think about going to that party to celebrate our success."

"We go nowhere until we return to eat rice at the Igbo's," Nouhou proclaimed, thinking about the savory meal he had enjoyed his first night in Chicago. If he had to be far away from the comforts of wife and kitchen, he reasoned, he could at least enjoy good African food.

They returned to Dickerson's, their van empty and, for a change, their pockets filled with cash. Relaxed by the extent of their commercial successes, they dawdled in the room, bathing and readying themselves for an evening on the town. Expecting the sartorial deficiencies of his younger brothers, Dabé, who had brought extra African clothes, unpacked them and handed outfits to Nouhou and Issa.

"I don't want to wear these," Issa said. "Why wear African clothes to a party?"

"I agree," Nouhou added. "I want to wear my blue jeans and a T-shirt."

"I'm going to wear regular jeans, a T-shirt, and Air Jordans," Issa said. "It looks very cool," he added. He put on his Ray-Ban sunglasses and pranced in front of the mirror attached to the door.

"That's okay," Dabé relented. "If you two wear European, I will too. But on our trip back tomorrow, remember that it's important to dress African again."

"Agreed," said Issa, but his thoughts drifted to his cash-filled pockets. He felt elated by his success in Chicago, but worried about holding so much cash—more than five thousand dollars—in a strange city. When he took in a great deal of cash in New York, he'd immediately deposit it in his Chase Manhattan Bank account. "Do they have a safe at this hotel?" he asked Dabé.

"They do, but I've never used it."

"Then where are we supposed to put our money?" Nouhou asked.

"I usually hide mine in the room," Dabé stated.

"You're kidding," Nouhou said.

"No. I've been staying at this hotel for five years now, and I've kept thousands of dollars in cash here. Never had a problem. Never. It's more dangerous to walk around this part of Chicago with pockets filled with cash."

"I'm not leaving all of my money here," Nouhou announced.

"Neither am I," said Issa. "I'll carry all of it with me to dinner and the party. I'm glad to be wearing baggy jeans with deep pockets."

"You're taking a big chance," Dabé observed. "Suit yourselves, though. I'm leaving my money here. I know a place where thieves would never look. It's worked so far."

Dabé hid all of his money. Issa and Nouhou put cash in their pockets. They left Dickerson's and ate with gusto at Igbo's. Eating there reminded Nouhou, who ordered many bowls of rice and ground-nut stew with beef, of similar dinners in his apartment. After the meal, Nouhou, ever the pragmatist, prowled through he grocery section, buying condiments he hadn't seen in Harlem: bags of dried fish, a sack of dried bitter leaves, a carton filled with jars of red palm oil. "We cannot return to Harlem with an empty van, can we?"

The food and conversation energized the three of them. Their meal and shopping complete, they readied themselves for Keisha's party. Outside the restaurant, the orange glow of Chicago's high-intensity street lamps had transformed the streetscape of Chicago's South Side: too bright to see the stars; too dim to read unilluminated signs; too isolated to walk with safety.

They followed Keisha's directions north toward Hyde Park. Travel from the South Side proved much easier than finding a parking spot in Hyde Park. Dabé persisted and succeeded, however. "Every chauffeur," he bragged, "must have a parking charm." He pointed proudly to the little leather satchel hanging from his rear-view mirror.

When they finally parked and walked to Keisha's building, they felt a sense of accomplishment and pride.

"Dabé," Issa said, "we have done so well here in Chicago. It's not every day that you feel the pride of being a Jaguar."

"The sweetness of days like this one," Nouhou added, "should be savored."

Dabé smiled. "Brothers, we have traveled far, have seen new places, and have met our obligations to our families. Through our hard work," he continued with uncharacteristic solemnity, "we've made something of ourselves. We should be proud. Let's go and celebrate."

Keisha lived on the top floor of a three-story apartment building on East 54th Street. Dabé pushed her doorbell.

"Come in," a voice said quickly over the intercom.

The third-floor door opened to a surprisingly spacious apartment that was bigger than anything they had seen in America. The trio walked into a crowded, smoke-filled room. Keisha led them to a small kitchen filled with people and food. She told them a bit about her herself and her apartment. "I've got two bedrooms," she said. "I do my sewing in one of them."

The Nigeriens politely said nothing.

"Come on. Let me introduce you to everyone." She wore a white damask dress with butterfly sleeves and a low-cut V-neck. She had wrapped a matching white scarf around her head. As she led them to the living room/dining room, she clapped her hands, which halted ongoing conversations. "Hey everybody," she began, "listen up. I want to introduce Issa, Dabé, and Nouhou. They're brothers from Africa, from Niger. What's more, they are Songhay, descendants of great warriors."

The group made up mostly of African Americans applauded the trio and then converged upon them, offering them alcohol, which, as reasonably pious Muslims, they refused and African food, which, as fully satiated gourmands, they politely nibbled. In contrast to the Nigeriens, who tried to look European, the African Americans all wore clothing fashioned from West African print fabrics. They peppered the trio with questions about their homeland. Dabé enjoyed the attention and gave his phone number to several male and female admirers. Issa felt ambivalent about the attention, except for that of the beautiful Keisha, whom he wanted to see alone. Nouhou, who hated being an object of interest, decided that he had had enough after less than an hour.

Issa, ever the talker, had a conversation with a tall heavyset African American who called himself Abdul.

"Do you know about Kwanzaa?" he asked Issa.

Issa shook his head. "Kwan . . . wha?"

"You know," the man insisted. "Kwanzaa. Our African American celebration. We have it for seven days at Christmastime."

"That's nice," Issa remarked, trying to remember what this holiday might be about.

"We celebrate African values."

"Sounds very nice."

"Being African, you live those values."

"Yes, I do," Issa responded tentatively. In America, he occasionally found himself in confusing situations like this one. If he was one of only a few Africans at a gathering, African Americans expected him to know, understand, or explain African ideas and values that he had never heard about. In these situations his incapacity to understand these African American ideas bewildered him.

"I'm so happy to meet someone like you," the man said.

A large round woman gradually joined the conversation. "How far is Niger from Egypt?"

"Very far," said Issa.

"Can't be that far, can it?"

"I don't know."

"I mean, it's got to be kinda close. You know, all that movement from Egypt to the rest of Africa."

"That's right," the man interjected. "Egypt is the birthplace of black civilization, the Black Athena. Those pharoes were black folks just like you and me, and they left Egypt thousands of years ago and brought civilization to the rest of the world. Black folks studied the stars and practiced real medicine centuries before Whites. Way back then, black folks, who were always a kind, generous people, gave their ideas away to the Greeks. Then the Greeks stole those ideas and took credit for Western Civilization."

"That's the way it came down, brother," the round woman agreed. "Some things never change. The white man's heaven is the black man's hell. But you know what? After four hundred years of slavery, we still got our African values. And that, brother Issa, is something else."

"Yes, that's good," Issa said. "Very good."

Keisha came by. "They giving you a rap, Issa?"

"I think so. But I don't understand everything."

The African Americans laughed. "You probably understand more than you can imagine, brother Issa," the round woman said.

Meanwhile Nouhou, who wanted to leave, began to fidget. "Hey, Dabé, hey. I'll suffocate if I don't get out of here soon. I want peace and quiet."

Dabé excused himself from a conversation with three women. "What do you want now?" he asked with considerable irritation. "I'm having fun, and who knows, maybe I'll be able to go home with one of these women."

"Fine, but I want to go back, and I think Issa does also. Take us back, and you can return later."

"If that's what you want, that's what I'll do, little brother."

Issa was conflicted. Part of him wanted to leave; he was tired and a little bit overwhelmed. Part of him wanted to stay; he was enjoying the party and wanted to be alone with Keisha. But the party was too busy for good conversation with anyone. In the end his interest in and desire for Keisha compelled him to stay.

Dabé led them to the door. "Nouhou is tired," he told the partygoers. "I'll take him home, but we'll come back."

Keisha kissed Nouhou on the cheek. "Thanks for coming, Nouhou. Here's my card. I'd like it very much if you came back to Chicago."

"Thank you," said Nouhou. "Thanks for inviting me here."

"You're staying, Issa?"

"Yes," he said, deciding that Keisha was a prize worth striving for.

Appearing to sense his motives, she put her lips close to his ear. "You stay until everyone else leaves," she whispered, "and we'll have some time together."

Issa nodded with delight. "I go to take my friend home and return with Dabé."

"Good."

They left the Hyde Park apartment and walked to the van.

"Why can't you relax and have a good time?" Dabé asked Nouhou.

"I have a beautiful wife," Nouhou insisted. "I don't understand a party where you know no one. Those party women don't interest me. I just want to sleep, get up, say my prayers, and return to New York and my wife. By now she will have missed my cooking!"

Dabé shook his head. "One day you will learn how to behave, how to be an American." He turned toward Issa. "Looks like the beautiful Keisha has a thing for you, Issa."

"I don't think so," he said with false modesty.

They drove in silence until they reached Dickerson's. "Don't wait up for us," Dabé said as Nouhou got out of the van.

The next morning they looked back at the skyline of the city from the Chicago Skyway. Low clouds obscured the tallest of the sky-scrapers. Morning fog shrouded parts of Lake Michigan's coastline. Cool and moist morning air streamed through the van's open windows. Soon Gary's ever-present odor of rotten eggs fouled the air inside the vehicle. The Nigeriens grimaced, but could not close the windows—no air-conditioner in Dabé's van. In silence, they drove eastward through Gary's warehouses and factories. In their hurry to leave, they hadn't had time to put on their African clothes.

The previous night Nouhou had sunk into one of the lumpy beds and fell immediately to sleep. He slept soundly and as usual got up before dawn to prepare for the morning prayer. As he washed according to ritual, he smelled the sweet pungency of cheap perfume, which signaled Dabé's arrival. He did not greet the Chauffeur. Dabé's rumpled clothes made him look like a beggar.

"I must bathe. We must get ready to leave," Dabé said.

"Older brother," Nouhou said, "are you too tired to drive? Shouldn't you sleep before driving?"

Dabé waved his hand in the air. "I am the Chauffeur. The drive back will be nothing. You'll see." He looked around the room. "Where's Issa?"

"He didn't come back last night," Nouhou stated flatly.

"Guess he spent the night at Keisha's. Issa and his women," said Dabé, shaking his head. "I've got her phone number. I'll call her later, and we'll pick him up just before we leave town."

"You're the Chauffeur. You make our return plans," Nouhou said, eager to return to more familiar territory and his wife.

Dabé went into the bathroom and returned with his money satchel. He opened it and counted his earnings. "It's all here, Nouhou. What'd I tell you? This place is safe," Dabé said triumphantly.

After his bath Dabé recounted his evening. One of the women he met at the party had taken him back to her apartment. "I think

I made her very happy," Dabé said. "She said next time I come to Chicago, I can stay with her."

"I am not interested in your tales of women," Nouhou said.

"And that Issa," Dabé said, "he actually spent the night with Keisha! I better call soon to make sure he'll be ready when we get to her apartment."

Two hours later, after picking up a reluctant Issa, they were back on the highway. They had their first blowout, a rear tire, near the Indiana-Ohio border. Dabé pulled the van onto the shoulder of the interstate, jacked up the van, and took off the dry-rotted tire. Just then an Indiana state trooper pulled over to offer assistance. He got out of his cruiser and walked over to them.

"You guys need help?"

"We're okay, officer," Dabé said nervously.

The trooper must have disagreed because he insisted on inspecting the spent tire.

"Didn't have much tread, did it?"

"No, sir," said Dabé, who knew how to talk to power people in the bush.

"Do you have spares?"

"Yes, sir."

"Can I see them?"

"Yes, sir."

The officer, who stood tall, square, and blond in his starched uniform and Smoky the Bear hat, looked at the tires in the van's cargo bay. "You can't drive on those," he stated. "Much too dangerous."

"Yes, sir," Dabé agreed.

Inside the van, Issa and Nouhou sat stiffly and silently as they watched the spectacle.

"You all are from Africa?" the trooper asked.

"Yes, sir, from Niger."

"Where's that?"

"West Africa."

"You speak good English."

"Thank you."

"Has this van been inspected?"

"Yes, sir." Dabé pointed to the New York State inspection sticker.

The trooper shook his head as he looked at the other tires on the van's wheels. "How could they pass a vehicle with tires like these?"

"It's New York inspection, sir," Dabé added.

"That explains it." The officer paused a moment. "You know, I should give you a five-hundred-dollar fine for driving with these tires. But since you're from Africa, I'll cut you a break. Don't want you to think that folks out here in Indiana are as bad as people in New York. We're friendly out here."

"Thank you, sir."

"You must give me your word that you'll buy five new tires at the next exit. You must give me your word that you won't drive any farther on these dangerous ones."

"My word?"

"Yes."

"I give you my word. For African people, a person's word, it's very serious."

"I have heard that," said the trooper, getting back into his car.

After the trooper left, Dabé replaced the flat tire with one of his bald spares. They then drove to the next exit and found an Exxon service station.

Dabé got out of the van and walked toward the service station office. A short, square, red-faced man with blond, crew-cut hair stood in the doorway chewing on an unlit cigar. He wore a pair of grease-stained blue trousers and a blue shirt with an oval patch above the breast pocket that spelled out "Bob." He frowned as Dabé approached him.

"What you need, buddy?" he asked.

"The police," Dabé said in his accented English, "told us to buy tires."

The man pointed at the van. "That yours?"

"Yes, sir," Dabé answered. "You have five tires for it? My tires, they're all bad. That's what the police said."

The man didn't move. "Where you from?"

"Africa," Dabé said.

"That so," the man said as he walked slowly toward the garage.

Paul Stoller

"We got what you're looking for. Drive your van into the garage, and we'll put the new tires on for you and give you one spare."

"Thank you, sir."

Issa and Nouhou got out of the van, and Dabé drove it into the garage. In short order, the man mounted the new tires and placed a new spare in van's carrier. He walked over to Dabé. "Come on into the office, and I'll write you up a bill of sale."

Dabé followed him into the office.

"How you gonna pay?" he asked.

"Cash," said Dabé.

"Okay," he said handing Dabé a bill for eight hundred dollars.

"This is no good," said Dabé. "It's too much."

The man, who had sat down behind his gray desk, continued to chomp on his cigar. "That's what they cost, buddy."

"But even in New York they are cheaper. This is too much."

The man stared hard at Dabé. "This ain't New York, buddy. You gonna cause trouble?"

"No, no," Dabé said. "No trouble. I don't want trouble. I go get your money."

Dabé received the van's key in exchange for the cash, and soon they were back on the interstate, cruising along on four very expensive new tires. Dabé reflected on what had just happened.

"You know, little brothers, you always have to pay a price. Last night, I talked about not getting ripped off. I hid my money. You carried your money with you. We didn't lose a penny in Chicago. Then we come to the bush, and the police stops us and makes us buy new tires. That's okay. But that man back there stole from us. He probably thought that we're dumb Africans who don't know anything about prices. Can you imagine tires that cost eight hundred dollars in the bush! No matter what you do, you get robbed sooner or later," he said with resignation.

"Well Dabé," Issa, ever the optimist, observed, "at least he didn't ask for two thousand dollars. You still have a lot of money to take home."

"For that, I thank God," said Dabé.

Dabé's eyes concentrated on the highway. A smile creased his face. Energy and pleasure coursed through his body. And, as long as he had an audience, his mouth never stopped. Dabé might have been bitter about being ripped off for tires, but he quickly put that behind him. He wanted to talk about African Americans.

"You know," he began, "most American Blacks are very nice people—especially the ones in the bush. They have welcomed me into their homes and have been generous."

"Why is that?" asked Issa.

"Maybe because I am an African," Dabé suggested.

"Why should someone like me just because I come from Africa?" Nouhou wondered.

"Well," Dabé added, "they don't know much about Africa, do they?"

"They do have some strange ideas," Nouhou stated, "like these 'African values.' And thinking that all of us are really from Egypt. And these new celebrations, like . . . what do they call it?"

"Kwanzaa," Issa said.

"Kwanzaa. What is that? It's not African, not Muslim."

"That's true," Issa agreed. "But remember that they were slaves taken away from our lands. And remember they must deal with bad racism. Their ideas may be very strange to us. But if they are kind to us, we should show them respect, should we not?"

Nouhou agreed.

"White Americans also have strange ideas about Africans," Dabé said. "The police officer seemed like a nice man, and he let us off so easy. That's strange. Maybe he respected us because we are Africans."

"I'm not so sure," Nouhou said. "Can he really fine us for having bad tires?"

"I don't know," Issa said, "but I think so." He changed the subject. "What I'm wondering," he asked, "is why our older brother travels with such bad tires?"

"Well, little brothers, it's like this. I use a tire until it quits. I am the Chauffeur. I know what I am doing. The trooper and the tire man, that's just the price of doing business. I accept these costs like you accept theft. It happens from time to time."

"What about the danger of traveling with smooth tires?" Issa asked.

"I have no problem," Dabé proclaimed.

"Well, I do," Nouhou insisted.

Paul Stoller

"It also makes me uncomfortable," Issa said.

"Worry not, little brothers, we are on new tires now. Travel in peace."

They raced across the Ohio flatlands and careened through the hills of Western Pennsylvania. The vastness and beauty of America continued to fill Issa and Nouhou with wonder, but on the return trip their thoughts more frequently shifted to getting back home—to Harlem. Before long they cruised eastward between Central Pennsylvania's long ridges. Trees spread over the ridges like a soft green blankets. Awash in the golden dusk light, they made Issa think of Nigerien mesas—long, craggy, brown, and flat-topped, thrusting up from a flat, barren landscape.

The drone of the engine and the hum of rubber on concrete broke the silence in the van. Like a man possessed, Dabé focused on the road. Nouhou slept. Issa thoughts turned inward as he contemplated the contradictions of his life. He was man more prone to talking than to introspection, but traveling compelled him to reflect on his life. Part of him wanted to return to Niger, to the mesas that he climbed as a young boy, to the foods, smells, and conversations of his past. These memories made him ache for Khadija and his family. He could make a fine living for himself in Tarma, farming rice and millet and trading in dry goods. But an increasingly more substantial part of him wanted to remain in New York. He loved the brotherly camaraderie among the Jaguars there. Among them, amity rather than obligation charged their friendships. The absence of never-ending familial obligations triggered feelings of expansive freedom, unlimited possibility, and boundless desire. Issa also liked Harlem. He liked the young women who seemed attracted to him. And now that he had tasted the bush, he already yearned to return to Chicago. Keisha's company and body excited him much more than the other women he had been seeing. Her similarity to Khadija increased his attraction to her. He wanted to see her, talk with her, and especially sleep with her again—and soon. These contradictions troubled him. In truth, he did not yet know where his path might lead him.

They reached the Lincoln Tunnel at ten o'clock in the evening. On the trip to Chicago, Dabé had talked incessantly, as if he'd been released from the solitary confinement of New York City. On the trip back to New York, his determination to drive eventually sealed him off from his compatriots. At last, he broke his silence and said, "We are home."

Groggy with sleep, Nouhou said, "It will be a long time before I return to the bush. I enjoyed myself, but I prefer Harlem."

"You are unadventurous, Nouhou," Issa complained. "I, for one, will return to Chicago and other places in the bush. What do you say, Dabé? Can I travel with you again?"

"I say you can come with me anytime." Dabé felt quite proud of himself. He had introduced Issa and Nouhou to the bush and his way of life. He looked forward to new comradeship on the road. He liked Issa's talk, and it was always better to travel with someone like Issa, who learned quickly the ways of the bush.

NIGER

chapter 23

In May the Nigerien air can be searingly hot. When the Harmattan blows, the air fills with a fine dust that clogs pores and irritates sinuses. When the desert wind abates, the dust settles, the air clears. On one such rare May morning, Khadija stood behind the counter of her new shop in Niamey. After much hard work, some infusions of Issa's American dollars, and the generous credit of her friend Yusef, the shop was already well stocked with canned goods, soaps, kerosene, peanut oil, spices, Chinese green tea, candy and chewing gum, mosquito nets, pots and pans, and Nigerien homespun cloth. So far sales had been so brisk that she had already restocked her peanut oil and kerosene. That morning she expected a shipment of dates.

The shop was not only larger, but had many more shelves and much more storage capacity than the one in Tarma. In fact, the storage area, a separate room behind the counter, was so big that Khadija had put a bed in it in case she wanted to remain in the shop for her siesta. The depth and width of the floor space left enough room between the counter and the door for browsing. Khadija had quickly realized the potential of the expanded space. Based on her observations of successful shops in Abidjan, she placed display tables at strategic points in the shop and covered them in matching print cloth—a dark blue with swirling white designs. She arranged her pots in arrays that looked like pyramids and folded her cloth in dynamic patterns. She decorated her whitewashed walls with

Nigerien checkerboard blankets and bright strips of Malian home-spun cloth. Before long her efforts had paid off; curious customers flocked to the shop as much to see Khadija's displays as to buy her products.

Khadija heard the clap of hands outside her door announcing a visit. A teenager dressed in long, faded blue robes and a black turban stood at the shop's threshold.

"I have brought dates, fresh and dried, from Yusef," the boy said.

"Good. I have some tea brewing. Come in and drink some before you unload the dates." Khadija, like most traders in Niger, attempted to be gracious to all the people who came into her shop.

"Thank you, madame."

She led him to a corner of the shop where she had stationed two director's chairs. Between them stood a low, round table with a tooled brass surface. To one side of the table, charcoal glowed red in a brazier. Bubbles of tea frothed from the spout of a small porcelain teapot. Khadija liked to offer tea to her customers. "Sit and relax," she said. "I will go and get sugar and tea glasses." Moments later she brought a large cone of sugar, one large glass for tea mixing, and two small shot glasses for drinking. "The tea has boiled. Why don't you mix it?"

"Is this the first boil?" he asked.

"Yes," she answered, "you'll need to add quite a bit sugar." Most people in Niger used the same measure of tea for three boils. By the third boil, the less-concentrated tea requires less sugar.

He nodded and went to work. In Niger men, not women, usually prepare tea. The boy used the edge of the large glass to break off a chunk from the sugar cone, then gingerly opened the hot lid of the teapot and put the sugar inside. After waiting a few minutes for the sugar to dissolve, he used a small piece of cardboard to hold the teapot handle and lifted the pot high over the mixing glass. As he tilted the pot, a long thin stream of tea emerged like a waterfall, slowly filling the large glass. He poured the glass of tea back into the pot and repeated the same sequence twice more. Finally, he poured tea into the small drinking glasses. He and Khadija settled back in their director's chairs and sipped the strong, sweet liquid.

Paul Stoller

"How do you know Yusef?" Khadija asked, wanting to know more about her generous, but still mysterious, Arab friend.

"He's my cousin," the boy answered. "I am Jamal. Yusef has told me much about you. He admires you very much. Even though you're a woman, he thinks you are very good at trading."

"That is very kind," Khadija said, laughing.

"Please do not tell him I said this. He will not like me telling you what he has said . . . about you, I mean."

"Understood, Jamal. Our talk is between us."

Jamal smiled. He was tall and lanky. Clusters of pimples broke the smooth contour of his coppery face. "I will unload the dates now."

He got up as they finished their tea and went to work. Jamal hauled the cart in front of the door and began to carry the sacks into the shop.

People liked Khadija's place. A small group of regulars had already formed—women from nearby neighborhoods. Ramatu often stopped by. Khadija's proud mother, happy to get a touch of the trading life, occasionally visited, too. In Niger women often spent hot afternoons together sitting and talking. The regulars found Khadija full of life, a woman whom they could trust like a sister. During the week, they'd pass hours talking, sipping—and buying. New customers discovered Khadija's every day. She greeted them warmly, and if they spent some time in the shop, she offered them tea and introduced them to one or two regulars already sitting in the parlor.

Suppliers had also discovered Khadija. Yusef sent some of them over to the shop; others heard about her through word of mouth.

The previous week, a tall, thick, round Senegalese man had entered the shop carrying a leather attaché case. He looked around approvingly and greeted the three women who were seated around the low brass-topped table. "Good morning ladies, which of you is Khadija?"

Khadija stood up and walked slowly toward the man, who towered over her. He had a jowly face rendered square by prominent cheekbones. "What brings you to my shop?"

"I am Abdu Gueye, madame, and I come to see if you'd like to buy silver jewelry from me."

"Perhaps, sir. Let's see what you've brought." She walked to her counter and motioned for him to open his case.

Gueye remained silent while Khadija let her eyes feast on an array of silver rings and necklaces. The filigreed rings had been smithed with elegant delicacy. The Tuareg silver necklaces, which were attached to beaded strings, bore the irregularities of a less sophisticated forge, but were beautiful all the same.

"I'd like to try the Tuareg silver. I don't think my shoppers will go for the rings. I will pick out ten necklaces."

She picked out the smallest of the samples.

"A good choice, madame," said Gueye, admiring her choices.

Khadija knew that local women preferred the smaller pieces, the shapes of which had been inspired by the Southern Cross constellation. "My people will like these Agadez crosses."

"Since this is our first business," Gueye said, "I'll give you a good price—a thousand francs each. Just take the samples and see how they do. You can pay me later, or if it doesn't work out, you can give them back to me."

"Very good, Monsieur Gueye. A pleasure to do business with you."

Kareem, the international courier, also visited her shop a few days after it opened. Already a corpulent man, he seemed to have expanded exponentially during his last sojourn in the United States. Several days before his departure from New York, Issa had told him of the new shop. When Kareem saw it for himself, he seemed quite impressed.

"Hey, Khadija, hey. Your shop is wonderful. May God bring it much success."

"I thank God for your visit and am grateful for my good fortune, Kareem. Come in. Come in. Have some tea and meet my friends."

"A Songhay man who lives in New York?" one of the regulars asked Khadija.

"He has an import-export business," said Khadija.

"In the name of God," another of the regulars exclaimed, extending her hand in Kareem's direction.

"Khadija," Kareem said, looking over her displays. "you're walking your path—and in full stride."

"It feels very good to be here, Kareem. I'm never at a loss for company. I'm thankful for much progress. And your business?"

"Business is okay. I now supply Jaguars up and down the east coast of America. I'm always at the post office sending packages."

"And your family in America?"

"They are in good health. Thank you. My son Issaka has started school. He's very smart. Last year, the school gave him an award as the best student in his grade," Kareem beamed. "I'm very proud of him. When he gets older, I hope to send him to a private school here so he can learn French."

"May God will it," Khadija said.

"If Issaka has French, English, and Songhay, he'll be able to work in any country."

"And when he becomes older and prosperous," Khadija interjected, "he'll look after his papa. He'll become a citizen of the world."

"May God will it," Kareem proclaimed.

"You live in America?" one of the regulars asked.

Kareem explained that he had two families: one in New York and one in Niamey.

"I hear that New York is beyond the ocean," the same woman stated. "It is almost noon here. What time is it there?"

"The sun will be rising now."

"In the name of God! That is very, very far." Like many people in Niger, the woman marveled at the immensity of a world where it could be noon in one locale and dawn in another. "Your son may become a citizen of the world," she added, having overheard the conversation between Kareem and Khadija, "but you're one right now."

This comment made the Kareem smile with great pleasure as he took his leave of Khadija and her companions.

chapter 24

In her new shop Khadija seemed, as they say in Niger, comfortable in her skin. But the path to this satisfying point had been steep and cluttered with debris. She had left Tarma burdened by sadness. Despite her efforts, her in-laws had not accepted her. Rumors spread by townspeople deepened her sorrow. She was disloyal and disrespectful. She went to Niamey not for business, but to visit her lovers. However outrageous these rumors had been, they still weighed heavy in Khadija's heart.

For Khadija, however, melancholy never sapped her resilience. She ignored many of the townspeople's narrowed-eyed glances and stares. During her last few days in Tarma, Khadija had focused her energy on moving. First she sold the remaining inventory in her shop. To her surprise, the town merchants bought her goods at cost, a very kind gesture during a liquidation sale. Her shop's liquidation complete, Khadija packed her personal items: clothes, jewelry, wedding blankets, sheets, a bed frame and mattress, pots, pans, and dishes. No one in the compound talked to her as she worked. She hadn't expected conversation; incessant activity helped her to bury her sorrow. On the day of her departure, the old cart driver brought his vehicle to the compound. Young men in his employ loaded Khadija's things. The family gathered and silently watched them work.

Wanting to leave the house with her pride intact, Khadija dressed in her most beautiful outfit—a shining black-on-black, cotton wrap-around skirt and a white, long-sleeved silk top embroidered in gold around the neck and cuffs. She smiled at Issa's family.

"I wish you well. May God protect you."

The family responded with silent stares.

She left the compound with her entourage. As the cart lumbered up the mesa to the taxi depot, Khadija felt a progression of emotions: pride, sorrow, fear. She had stood up to Issa's mother. And yet, she had failed to convince his family of her resourcefulness and that made her sad. She also wondered what would become of her marriage; that thought still frightened her. What if Issa took a second wife, perhaps an American? Would she still be married to Issa in five years? Even though many Songhay men and women married five or six times in their lives, Khadija thought that it would better to be without a husband than to be one of two wives. But she found the idea of losing Issa altogether unthinkable. She still wanted to have a child, and she missed and wanted the comfort of a man who loved her. But love and comfort alone, she realized, could no longer completely satisfy her. She had enjoyed running her own shop in Tarma. And she seemed quite a good trader, perhaps as skillful as Issa. She understood that she could never again completely relinquish her independence for the sake of a man.

The bush-taxi driver, a customer of Khadija's, demonstrated concern for her by looking after his client's comfort on the trip from Tarma to Niamey. He insisted that she sit with him in the more comfortable cabin of the Toyota Minibus. When he dropped off passengers along the way, he bought her fruit and soft drinks to bolster her spirits. After depositing passengers at Niamey's taxi depot, he drove her directly to her mother's compound and moved her things into her childhood home.

Khadija's mother, Fatima, invited the driver to lunch, but he graciously declined. In Fatima's neighborhood, people often talked about the old woman's graciousness, kindness, and resourcefulness, and especially her resolve. She had been a beautiful young woman, slight, copper-skinned, and bright-eyed—the daughter of traders. As a teenager she married a handsome and robust farmer, Hamani, who energetically cultivated his family's lands. Hamani's zeal for farming produced extraordinarily high yields. They prospered in Niamey and soon had a small family of four children. One day as Hamani weeded one of his millet fields, lightening struck him and he died. Left a widow, Fatima quickly learned to fend for herself. She first sold cooked foods and then later opened a spice business in Niamey's central market. She never complained about her sorrowful fate and taught her children to be like her—proud and tough. In time, grace and generosity complemented her resolve. Age had drained the beauty from her body, but had left her a handsome woman. However slight she might be, Fatima nonetheless projected inestimable strength. People took notice and paid her deference. Although her children lived far away from Niamey, she remained close to them. And so her daughter's homecoming made her soar with happiness.

Niamey had become a densely populated city, and the cramped living conditions constricted the space in Fatima's compound. Surrounded on three sides by other families also living in compressed spaces, Fatima's home consisted of two small, rectangular mudbrick structures, perhaps ten by twenty feet each, and a smaller dwelling half that size. She lived in the one of larger houses and used the second for guests and storage. She cooked in a small enclosure near the dirt compound's center, where an acacia tree grew. Assortments of cast-iron pots, wooden and metal cooking spoons, and porcelain basins filled with soapy water lay scattered across the compound's yard.

Khadija moved into the second mudbrick house. During her time with Issa's family in Tarma, she had forgotten the noises of the city: babies crying, children screaming, and adults arguing in the next compound; mobylettes puttering and trucks growling on the busy street outside. She wondered how she could sleep amid such ongoing commotion.

Fatima clapped outside of Khadija's door. "My daughter, welcome home. I am so happy to have you with me."

They sat down on canvas chairs in the center of the compound. "Thank you, my mother." Although Khadija had always been formal with her mother, she also harbored great affection for her. Fatima had been both a father and mother to her.

On previous visits Khadija had explained her difficulties with Issa's family—especially with her mother-in-law. At that time, Fatima had been empathetic but had advised perseverance. She had said that it was important to maintain a marriage, even if it entailed great personal sacrifices. During Khadija's residence in Tarma, her mother's view had never wavered. When Khadija's resolve weakened, Fatima had urged forbearance. She had fully supported Khadija's decision to open a dry goods shop—a way, she had suggested, of dealing with the considerable social difficulties of life in Tarma. Because of her own sense of pride and forbearance, Khadija had followed her mother's advice.

Paul Stoller

"What finally made you chose to leave?" her mother asked her now.

"I could no longer bear to live where I wasn't wanted. Those people loathed me, my mother. How can anyone live under those conditions?"

"My daughter," Fatima said, "don't fret anymore. You have made your decision. Here you are loved; you are home."

"Thank you, my mother," Khadija said. "You have always looked after us, encouraged us." Tears streamed down her cheeks. "That is why I couldn't bear to remain in Tarma."

"And your husband? What does he say?"

"He has not said much."

Fatima liked and respected Issa a great deal. She found him a hardworking and attractive man who reminded her of her own husband. She thought it courageous for a noble like him to marry a commoner like Khadija.

At that moment, Khadija wanted her marriage to work despite its many difficulties. She longed for the modern marriage that she and Issa had discussed in Abidjan. She envisioned a large villa in Niamey filled with laughing children, friends, and family. And yet, seated in her mother's compound, those visions seemed so dreamlike, so unreal and unrealizable.

"If Issa is truly angry about your leaving," Fatima said, "you may lose him, and that will be a great pity. Such a fine young man." Fatima took a deep breath. "But I also want you to know that you are my flesh and blood. I do not understand the ways of young people. No matter. You are first in my heart. Whatever you decide to do, it will be good for me."

Khadija held her mother's hand. "Thank you, my mother." She looked skyward. "Times have changed. Before, it would not have been possible for me, a young woman, to run my own shop. Before, a husband might go away, but at least he would return to plant his fields. Now Issa is in America, and it has been a long time since I've seen him. Before, a woman might sacrifice her life for her husband's family. But no longer, my mother. There must be another way, don't you think?"

"Of this, I know little."

"I think there is another way. You gave me your tenacity and courage. Now I will use what you taught me to make my way in the world."

Fatima smiled at her daughter for a long moment and then returned to her own house. They never again discussed the subject.

A few days later Khadija heard the ring of the telephone in her mother's house. Fatima's brother, a prosperous trader, had it installed a few years earlier so that he could make business calls in the relative privacy of his sister's compound.

"Hey, Khadija, hey," her mother called. "They are calling you from America." Fatima, of course, meant that Issa had phoned, but in Songhay, in-laws rarely refer to one another by name. "They are calling you from America."

Khadija entered her mother's small room, picked up the phone, and sat on a three-legged wooden stool.

"How is your health, Issa?" she asked, beginning the conversation with the customary greetings.

"Praise God. And yours, Khadija?"

"I have health and good spirits."

"I am calling," Issa began, "to see how you are. I have spoken to my mother. She called and said the family is suffering—too little food that is not properly cooked."

"I am truly sorry for the suffering of your family." Khadija said.

"My heart is heavy for my family," Issa said.

"If your heart is so heavy, why not return? Why not come back to Niger so you can personally look after them? If you come back, I will join you again."

"You know that I can't do that right now," Issa said tensely. "I haven't made enough money to return with honor."

"Then you'll continue to send them money. Maybe you can tell them to hire a good cook or someone to run the household. With the money you send, they can do it, can they not?"

They both felt uncomfortable and avoided confronting the subject of Khadija's departure. Instead, they talked a bit about their respective businesses. Issa did ask her if she might continue to look after the family.

"I'll ask some people to look in on them. Don't worry," she assured him, "they'll be looked after."

After this first conversation, Issa continued to phone almost every week. He talked sparingly about his business fortunes and his life in New York City, though he did complain about the doldrums of the winter market in Harlem. He continued to avoid asking her to return to his family. She tried hard to talk to him enthusiastically, for she still wanted her husband to return to her. But she also knew that Issa no longer understood her needs and desires. Her dreams of a life with him became more and more distant.

Khadija's economic ambitions soon overpowered her personal sorrows. She started the difficult path of building a business in Niamey. She'd have to start small and save her money before she could open another dry goods shop. She used some of the proceeds of her liquidation sale in Tarma to purchase spices, buy a table, and rent a space in the central market. A few weeks after her arrival in Niamey, Khadija stood behind a colorful table filled with fresh and dried red peppers, peanut cakes, tamarind, ginger, and garlic. She also sold sesame and had found a rare delicacy, *gensi* (wild grass seed), which attracted throngs of shoppers.

She enjoyed the spirited banter of the market, which made her feel more alive than she had in years. Frequently, she would lunch with her cousins or with her friend, Ramatu. Seated behind their tables, they would eat ravenously the various rice dishes that market women prepared. Afterward, they'd drink water, sip tea, and recount stories. Whenever Ramatu and Khadija ate together, laughter erupted, especially when Ramatu told outrageous stories about fat, limp Songhay men or about the misadventures of one of her various husbands.

"I've had enough of these men."

"Really," Khadija would say, egging on her friend, wanting her to recount more steamy stories of romance, an item that had been absent from her own life for far too long.

"Let me tell you about Issifi, the strong soldier," Ramatu would begin. "He had thick arms, a beautiful chest, and the face of a king."

"And?"

"And . . . nothing. A large frame. Empty inside. The box was beautifully wrapped, but when you opened it, nothing inside. Sooo small, hah!"

"True?"

"True," Ramatu said. "What of Issa?" she asked.

"Issa doesn't have that problem, my friend," Khadija responded. After their laughter died down, Khadija's smiled faded. "I think America has changed him," she told Ramatu, to whom she could express her deep-seated fears. "When I talk to him, he seems like a different person. He still says that he wants me, but the words are empty of feeling."

"Maybe he doesn't want to return to Niger. Maybe he likes his life in New York. Maybe, my friend, he is killing his money on other women."

"He probably is," Khadija admitted. "But he also feels responsibility toward his family. Maybe he's confused."

"Like most men," Ramatu said, "he's confused about painful or inconvenient responsibilities, but not about his personal pleasures."

"I give Issa more credit than that," Khadija said. "He does send money to me and to his family. He writes. He phones."

"Do you want to visit him in New York? Do you really want him to come back to Niger?"

"I don't know." Khadija missed Issa, but now she deeply enjoyed her life with friends and family.

"Even in the most modern marriages," Ramatu stated, "it's always the woman who has to sacrifice the most. If Issa returns, you'd have to limit your business." Though expressed with good humor and generosity of spirit, Ramatu's opinions had always been laced with pragmatism.

Before long Khadija was successful enough to contribute food to her mother's household and even to save some money. Fatima, who had for years lived apart from her children, took great pleasure in preparing sumptuous sauces for her daughter. And Khadija liked living with her mother. Fatima might disagree with her about many issues, but no disagreement weakened the bonds of their relationship, which seemed to grow closer and closer. They very much admired one another. In the evenings Fatima would invite her friends and family to visit. They would invariably compliment Khadija on her will to succeed. Some of them expressed pride in her independent spirit; others expressed criticism of her decisions, but did so with affection. Many of them said that she took after her mother. Bedtime, however, remained difficult for Khadija. She still missed

Paul Stoller

the intimacy of marriage and the wonderful sex she'd shared with Issa. She often thought about the attractive men she noticed or talked to in the market. In Niger it was hard for a woman to live without a man. Men often married several women and enjoyed cavorting with consorts. Women, by contrast, married one husband. And if they took lovers, even if their husbands had been absent for long periods of time, they usually faced a fusillade of disapproval. At least Khadija had her friends and family, for which she was grateful.

Winter gave way to spring, the hot season in Niger. Khadija had been judiciously saving money for several months. Then one hot day in early April she visited her friend Yusef. As always, he stood tall and wiry behind the counter of his shop, the white of his long shirt contrasting sharply with the copper skin of his angular face. When he looked up to see Khadija, his face softened. He smiled.

"Ah, Khadija, come in and sit down. Have some tea," he said, gesturing toward the unoccupied chairs positioned next to a low brass table. "I was just about ready to drink my second pot. Join me."

"With pleasure, Yusef." She felt herself drawn to him immediately. His open and kind smile chased away thoughts of her troubles and frustrations.

They sat down, and Yusef poured tea into the glasses.

"It is a pleasure to see you on this hot day. It has been more than two weeks since your last visit. How goes the market?"

"It goes well, Yusef. Very well."

"Allah be praised," he said. "People come to your table to buy. They like you. And you supply special items. So I have heard," he added, not wanting her know the extent of his interest in her affairs.

"Exaggerations, Yusef. People come to me because they get good value for good spices. I try to be pleasant, and if they like me, I am very grateful."

"I hope that your business continues to thrive."

"So do I." Khadija shifted in her seat and sipped the tea. She fingered the gold embroidered sleeve of her black caftan. "Can you advise me about something?"

"By all means."

"I want to open a dry goods shop in this section of Niamey. I have saved money, but I'll need to find a good location and will need to know good suppliers."

"I'll be honored to help you. I'll ask around about shop space, and once we've located a place that you like, I'll introduce you to a group of suppliers. In this way, you will be able, with God's blessing, to move forward." Her trust in him made his heart soar, but he hid his emotions from her.

"I am very grateful for your advice and help, Yusef."

"The pleasure is all mine. You are my friend, and so I will do what I can. May God will your success."

They conversed politely, formally, even though they felt drawn to one another.

Yusef's eager help proved invaluable. He quickly found a fine space for a reasonable rent. He then introduced Khadija to several other Arab suppliers, who guaranteed cheap rates for their products. Before the end of April, Khadija had shut down her spice table in the central market, ordered supplies, and designed her product displays. In early May, Khadija was able to open her shop. On that day, she thanked God for giving her strength and for bringing shoppers. She thanked Yusef for his help and the credit he had extended her. Her friends and family celebrated with her. They drank tea, told stories, and recounted how good it was to be a trader. Yusef came by and congratulated his friend. As always, a long white shirt framed his lanky build. He carried an ornate brass platter, his gift to Khadija to bring good luck to her new enterprise.

"I wish you much success, Khadija," he said upon seeing how she had fixed up the space. "You have a good eye and a head for business. He extended the brass platter toward her. "A gift. Use it to serve tea to your customers," he said almost shyly.

"Thank you, Yusef. Thank you," she said, quite moved.

On that day Khadija felt that she had become a Jaguar.

HARLEM

Many months before Khadija had opened her shop, Issa gazed at the cloudless autumn sky above Harlem. Although it had been a good business year so far, today only a few shoppers strolled down the sidewalk. Perhaps it was too early in the day? Most of the other Jaguars had not yet arrived.

He stared at the office supply shop across from his table and felt the weight of having been in New York for long time. He'd lived downtown and uptown. He'd been to the American bush, having traveled to Chicago, Detroit, Milwaukee, Indianapolis, Philadelphia, and Atlanta. Like the Jaguars of old times, he had learned much from his varied experiences. This precious knowledge had been transformed into ever-increasing profits. He had used his money to support his family and to invest in inventory. Sometimes he thought about what people in his village might say about their distant son. He knew that they'd say he had honored his family by meeting his obligations. They'd say that courage had become his friend, for he had walked unknown, potentially dangerous paths and like the jaguar had emerged not only unscathed, but stronger. Perhaps they'd even say that he had become a wise man because the one who travels broadens his experience. Experience, as the elders say, is the fertile soil in which wisdom grows. Even if he went home now, they'd visit him and ask him to recount the story of his life and experiences in America. They'd seek him out for advice: personal and commercial. He'd receive his admirers in a large compound filled with the laughter of his family's children. The beguiling power of these images prompted Issa to pinch himself and shake his head. Reality slowly glided his thoughts back to the ground. Did he really want to return to a tranquil but staid life in Tarma? And what of Khadija? He continued to sleep with other women, but he still wanted her as his wife. If possible, he wanted her to be the mother of his children. As a Muslim, of course, he could have as many as four wives. There was no shortage of candidates both in Niger and America.

He had seen a good deal of Keisha, the woman he met the previous year at the Black Expo in Chicago. She was the first African American woman with whom he felt an emotional bond. Such beauty! Such kindness! Such resourcefulness! He admired her a great deal. When he went with Dabé to Chicago, he stayed in her Hyde Park apartment. Keisha's various sexual contortions, which had been unknown to him before he'd come to America, inspired him to make love to her throughout the night. When he got out of her bed in the morning, his legs buckled. He had never experienced such thrilling sexual intensity. The more time he spent with Keisha, the more he wanted her. Every other month, she'd come to New York to stay with him. The last time she'd been to New York, Keisha said that she wanted to marry Issa.

"One day," she said, "I want to see your village and meet your family. Maybe one day, I'll live there with you."

"Life's hard there" is all that Issa said, thinking it unlikely that Keisha would ever travel to Niger. He still wasn't sure if he wanted to get married again—especially to an independent American woman, however attractive, appealing, and sensual. By the same token, he didn't want to lose Keisha.

"That's what everyone says," Keisha said, trying not to reveal her own concerns. She loved Issa deeply but wondered if he'd be able to make a commitment to her. She knew that he already had a wife in Niger whom he liked and admired; she knew that Issa spoke to his wife every week. She also realized that she could not bear to share Issa with another woman. And yet Khadija's existence did not completely threaten her, for Issa had not seen his wife in almost four years.

The boldness of American women continued to shock Issa. He often wished that they'd be a little more like African women. Keisha's

Paul Stoller

forwardness forced Issa to think seriously about the course of his life. Perhaps taking a new wife would be a solution to his dilemma?

Nouhou's arrival jolted Issa from his reveries.

"What do you think of having more than one wife, Nouhou?"

"I'm against it. Living with one wife is hard enough, my friend. Why complicate matters with two or three? I remember my paternal uncle. He had four wives and led a miserable life."

"How so?"

"He said to me: 'Nouhou, just take one wife. Two wives means much noise. Three wives means constant argument. And four wives! With four wives only death can bring you peace.'"

They laughed.

"Are you thinking about marrying Keisha?"

"Not now. But she's putting pressure on me."

"What would Khadija do if you took a second wife?"

"I don't know. She'd probably divorce me if I announced a new wife."

"She might," Nouhou agreed.

"She has always talked about modern marriage. You know, one wife, one husband."

"And so did you, my friend."

"Things are different when one is alone in America," he said flatly.

A rare, tense moment of silence filled the space between them.

"I heard on the television," Nouhou said, cutting through silence, "that the mayor will shut down this market next week."

"I expected it," Issa said with resignation. "We should meet and discuss our options. We have to act quickly and decisively—like Jaguars."

"That's true. Perhaps we can meet tonight at my house. I'll cook a big meal. One cannot discuss important matters on an empty stomach."

"One cannot," Issa agreed, smiling at his friend's culinary view of the world.

The clear autumn sky masked the cloudiness that New York City politics had brought to Harlem. For more than a year, most of New York City's elected officials had been vowing to remove the street vendors from 125th Street. They had circulated plans to move them to an open air lot at 126th Street and St. Nicholas Avenue. Later in the year, the Masjid Malcolm Shabazz, the mosque founded by Malcolm X, offered to bring the market to their vacant lots on 116th and 117th at Lenox Avenue. Throughout the year, arguments erupted between vendors and store owners, elected officials and local residents, Africans and African Americans. Discussions about the fate of the market permeated the Jaguars' daily conversations.

The summer business had been brisk. Issa and Nouhou sold hats and bags from their tables four to five days a week. Issa also had managed to travel widely that summer, going to Chicago, Indianapolis, Kansas City, and Detroit. On each trip good fortune had lined his way with money, much of which he reinvested in inventory. He also spent a great deal of time with Keisha. Toward the end of the summer, the market space question resolved itself when the Jaguars learned that the mayor had decided to move the market to the space owned by Malcolm X's mosque.

Acrimonious debates disrupted business-as-usual on 125th Street. Harlem residents complained that the Africans left the streets strewn with garbage. A large proportion of African American and Asian store owners applauded the mayor's decision, saying that it removed the unfair competition. They believed that without the presence of hundreds of street vendors, business would improve. Many people, though, condemned the mayor's decision. Some of the store owners wanted the vendors to remain. Many of the African American vendors condemned the mayor's plan as a racist plot to transform Harlem into a haven for white people. People lost their tempers, calling one another "pig" or "traitor" or "Uncle Tom." Emotions ran high. Everyone feared that violence might erupt at any moment, especially if the police had to move in to disperse the market.

That summer, though, nothing happened. People said that police would stampede onto 125th Street to beat and arrest black people. They said that street vendors would sabotage White- and Asian-owned stores. They said that the immigration people would sweep through the market to catch unregistered aliens and deport all "illegals" back to Africa. None of these things came to pass. News of the African market's imminent demise, in fact, spurred business. By late August business boomed on 125th Street. Expecting that their favorite vendors might soon depart, people swarmed through the market buying baseball caps, T-shirts, handbags, jewelry, and Africana. Tourists from Norway, France, Germany, Japan, California, Ohio, and New Jersey came to experience "Africa-in-Harlem" before its demise.

"We're so sorry that the market will be gone. We really love it," a young woman told Issa. She tried on a straw hat and examined herself in the mirror Issa had handed to her. "Where are you going to go when the market closes?" she asked.

"I don't know. We're talking about it."

"Why not come to my town, Toledo? People would love your stuff."

"Maybe. Who knows where we'll end up?"

By the time Issa arrived that evening at Nouhou's apartment, the others had already gathered. On crossing the threshold, he smiled to himself, for at Nouhou's he felt like he was in Niger. Aromatic cooking odors blended with the lingering redolence of oil-based perfumes and incense. Sounds of Songhay reverberated in his ears.

The Jaguars sat at Nouhou's dinner table. Ayel, the tailor, was there as well as street-savvy Seyni, Dabé, Tamika (who had by now learned to speak Songhay—with a decidedly American accent), and Mounkaila, a tall, barrel-chested man, who sold scarves and baseball caps on Canal Street in Lower Manhattan. Nouhou stood over them, ladle in hand.

"Serve yourselves the rice, and I will give you sauce and meat."

"What kind of sauce is it?" asked Mounkaila.

"It is tomato-based baobab sauce, my friend. Eat until you burst. It will make your big troubles seem small."

Everyone laughed.

Nouhou looked up at Issa, who had been watching from the threshold. "Are you not hungry, little brother?" Nouhou asked. "Sit and eat."

Because the other men had already started to eat, they did not greet Issa. Issa sat down, and Nouhou served him. They ate in silence.

Mounkaila finished first and belched loudly. "Praise be to God," he proclaimed. "I've eaten well. No place is left for more."

Nouhou nodded. The others continued to eat. Some of them

asked for water. Others, like Mounkaila, belched, which among Nigeriens signifies the greatest expression of culinary satisfaction.

Their stomachs satiated with the fine Nigerien food, their lungs filled with the odors of home, the Jaguars readied themselves for serious talk, for New York City politics would soon drastically alter their lives.

"Brothers, we must talk about what to do," Nouhou proclaimed. "We are being removed from the market. What must we do? How do we act?"

"I understand something of the politics here," Seyni stated. "It seems that right now everyone hates one another. The Farrakhan people hate the Malcolm X people. Rich black people hate poor black people. Black people hate the Spanish and the Asian people. White people hate and fear black people. Black people hate and fear white people. And the black people call us 'brother,' but they really don't know us. Some of them even think that we are the ones who sold them into slavery. Life can be very confusing."

"It is a pity," Tamika said, adding her voice to a West African palaver in which all conversationalists voice their frustrations before deciding how to resolve a problem, "but what Seyni says has some truth. Many of my people know little about Africa, and it makes me very sad. But there are others who know quite a bit and respect Africans."

"We are still powerless," Seyni continued. "We pay no taxes. We don't vote. Who will support us? Who will listen to our complaints?"

"No one," Ayel said. "No one at all. This city is terrible. I want to leave it."

"Where will you go?" Issa asked.

"Greensboro, North Carolina. I've asked for papers, and I am told that I'll soon get them. Once I have them, I'll go. Business is very good there. I'll make clothes for many new clients. Life will be sweet, Inshallah."

The response stung Issa, who had tried for more than two years to obtain papers—without success. He expected to hear from immigration any day about his most recent request.

"May God be with you," Issa said, with no small measure of envy.

Paul Stoller

"That is one way to act," Seyni noted. "For myself, I'm a trader. I can do nothing else. We must act like true Jaguars. We must adapt."

"I agree, but how do we do that?" Dabé asked.

"We must not be part of their politics," Seyni said. "That will land us in trouble. It's like drug dealers on the streets. They're going to deal drugs every day, no matter what. But, if you leave them alone, they leave you alone."

"So what will you do?" Mounkaila from Canal Street asked.

"I will peacefully rent space from the Malcolm X people on 116th Street."

"That will never work," Issa stated. "No one will go there. Too many drug houses and not enough business. You'll be lost there."

"I'm not so sure," Seyni said. "I'll try it and see what happens."

"Why not go to the malls?" Nouhou wondered.

"Too expensive," Tamika stated. "It'll cost you a thousand a month, and who knows how much you'd sell."

"I don't know," Nouhou countered. "I've been to White Plains Mall. There are many, many people there, and they buy all the time. And I saw vendors there."

"What must you do to sell there?" Issa asked.

"I don't know. Does anyone know?" Nouhou asked.

His question prompted silence. No one had yet understood the workings of brightly lit American malls.

"I think you'll find it to be very expensive," Seyni said, agreeing with Tamika. "I've heard that they have many, many rules, also. You won't like it."

"There are so many malls, though," Issa said. "I've seen the ones in White Plains and in Brooklyn. And they sell things in the skyscrapers in Midtown."

"In the lobbies?" Nouhou asked.

"Yes," Issa said. "I wonder how much they make in a week?"

Ayel shifted anxiously in his chair. "I'm glad I'm a tailor. It's all too difficult for me. New York is too big and difficult. I'd rather work in the bush—in peace."

"Where will you sew?" Issa asked.

"I don't know. There are many possibilities. If they don't work out, I'll work in a factory. There's much work in Greensboro."

"For me," Issa stated, "I want to be Jaguar here in New York."

"Yes, but being a Jaguar here," Ayel countered, "is different than being one in Africa. Aren't you tired of trading in America?"

"I must always be a Jaguar," Nouhou asserted. "I'm proud to be a trader, to be in control of my life and living. I can't work in McDonald's or in a factory. There's no freedom doing that."

"I'd never encourage him to work in a factory," Tamika added, who understood how trading gave Nouhou's life a solid foundation. "He's a Jaguar. He's good at what he does, and I support him."

"Praise God," said Mounkaila. "Nouhou, you have a fine woman."

"I thank God for her," Nouhou said. He and Tamika felt quite happy together, a rare occurrence given the disparities between their life experiences, languages, and cultures.

"Being here," Ayel continued, "has changed me. I don't like the Jaguar life anymore—too many problems and too little respect."

"Yes. There is too little respect here," Mounkaila agreed.

"Mounkaila," Issa asked, "how much does it cost to be on Canal Street?"

"It costs eight hundred a month for two shelves of space in the front of a shop. If you want more space, it costs three thousand a month."

The Jaguars gasped.

"That much!" Issa exclaimed.

"In the name of God," said Nouhou. "How do you manage?"

"We have many people who pass by, and there are many tourists all the time. They don't buy African things, so we sell them hats, gloves, scarves, and T-shirts."

"Is there space downtown?" Issa asked.

"Yes. If you come and visit, I'll introduce you to people, and they can find you space. Maybe you can rent shelves or a table. Maybe you'll find a storefront with a window."

"Or maybe you'll come with me to the bush?" Dabé interjected.

"I'll take my business to the Malcolm X market," Seyni stated confidently.

"You speak with great confidence," Issa said. "How can a market work in such a bad place?"

"In time," Seyni countered. "In time."

Paul Stoller

"But how long can one suffer?" Nouhou wondered. "I'll try to seek business downtown."

"I'll try downtown but will also go with Dabé more and more," Issa said.

"And I," Ayel said, "refuse this crazy life in New York. I'll wait for my papers and work in the bush."

"I hear that the Black American traders will march when the police come on Monday," Issa stated.

"It's true," Seyni said. "Will any of you march with them?"

"I'll stay at home and take a day off," Issa proclaimed.

"So will I," Nouhou said.

"I'll remain on Canal Street," Mounkaila said.

"And I," Dabé said, "will be in Indianapolis."

"If the march begins," Seyni advised, "we should be sure to remain far from the police as well as the crowds. When there are many people, the bandits come out and do terrible things."

Everyone nodded.

Although the Jaguars had formed a kind of brotherhood, each walked his own path. Wherever they might be, however, they'd make regular payments to a kitty, a kind of informal insurance fund, which could be tapped when one of them suffered an illness or a theft. They'd also hold periodic palavers to discuss economic and political issues. And yet, once they'd made personal decisions, they acted as individual entrepreneurs, each taking the path that best suited his particular situation.

That night each of the Jaguars thought he had made the best choice, and yet, each of them respected the decisions of the others. They wished one another the best of luck. No one knew what would become of their enterprises, but each of them had the personal resilience to adapt to situations that shifted sometimes unexpectedly, sometimes violently. As Jaguars they knew that somehow they'd carry on. In their hearts, each of them knew the bare truth of Issa's saying: There is always a way. That maxim had guided them for many generations.

chapter 26

A few weeks later, Issa and Nouhou huddled near the electric space heater in the corner of their unheated storefront, which they shared with Luis and Maria, from Ecuador. The December air carried a bone-chilling dampness, which made them shiver—even inside their newly rented space. The Nigeriens displayed hats, scarves, baseball hats, and gloves on two tables near the window. Handbags and Nigerien leather bags hung from hooks on the walls. They positioned a mirror on the front wall. The Ecuadorans folded their hand-woven wool sweaters on one table near a partition that divided the store space into two halves—used and unused. The mustiness of the cracked walls gave the store a stale odor, which mixed with the smell of damp wool.

The store had been a greeting card shop that catered to business people who worked near Broadway and Canal Street in Lower Manhattan. When City Hall began its seemingly interminable repair of the subway, right in front of the store entrance, the owners relocated and rented the space to Issa, Nouhou, and the Ecuadorans. The owners had made a wise decision, for subway repair is usually quite bad for business. From the beginning the rattling pulsations of the jackhammer made Issa's head ache. Construction dust clogged Nouhou's sinuses. To make matters even more precipitous, the city closed off much of the sidewalk in front of the shop, making it difficult for people to walk by and look at the merchandise in the window—let alone enter the store and buy something.

A short Asian man bundled up in a military fatigue jacket stepped across the store's threshold. "Hello, Issa," he said in heavily accented English.

Issa, who wore a black leather jacket over two sweaters, looked up from his seat next to the space heater. "Yo, Park," he said trying to imitate the street talk of Harlem. "Wassup?"

The man smiled at him. "You not come in yesterday."

"Yeah. Took the day off."

"Ah, Issa, you stay at home and make babies."

Paul Stoller

Issa laughed. "Right," he said trying to mimic the Korean's speech. "I stay home yesterday and make babies."

Park wagged his finger at Issa. "You bad, bad boy. You not work hard enough. Too busy making babies."

Issa said to Nouhou in Songhay. "What do these people think?"

"They think that we spend all our spare moments 'making babies.' God give me patience. Some people are so ignorant," Nouhou observed.

Issa turned toward the Korean, who worked as the super of the apartment building next to the store. "Park, you spend more time making babies than me. You got more time, and you got more babies."

Laughter rocked the man's body. He shook his head and walked out.

Issa and Nouhou sipped on the coffee they had purchased from the Salvadoran cafeteria near their store. A woman dressed in a long wool coat and a knit hat came in and looked at the handbags displayed on one of the walls. Issa stood up.

"Yes? Can I help you?"

"Yes . . . no English," she said.

Issa surmised that she was a tourist from Latin America. He tried to speak to her in what little Spanish he had learned. "What you want?"

"No . . . Spanish," the woman replied. "Portuguese."

Issa caught the eye of Maria, his Ecuadoran space-mate, who sat next to her folded sweaters. "Maria," he asked in English, "you can speak to her?"

"I don't speak Portuguese, Issa. Sorry."

The woman fingered a "Gucci" bag. Issa took it down, and the woman inspected it. "Good."

"You want?" Issa asked in English.

The woman pointed at other bags: A brown and maroon "Dooney & Bourke," and a black "Coach."

"You like these?" Issa asked.

"Yes."

"You Spanish?" Nouhou asked.

"Brazilian," the woman answered.

"Which one you like?"

The woman pointed to the Dooney & Bourke. "How much?"

Issa wrote $45 on a small writing pad and showed it to the Brazilian woman.

"Okay." She gave him the money and took her new bag.

A short round man with thinning white hair and a florid face walked in with his arm around a woman, equally short and round, but with olive skin and black hair.

"Issa," he said loudly. "How are you today? How are all the people of Africa?"

"The people of Africa are fine today. Thank you."

Issa liked this man, who liked to bring them coffee and bagels in the morning. He occasionally brought Issa and Nouhou Vietnamese food, which they liked almost as much as African dishes.

"How's business?" the man asked.

"We thank God," said Nouhou. "Do you buy today?"

"No," the man said pleasantly. "My wife and I just came by to say hello and give you some coffee."

"That's right," the woman said, smiling and nodding yes. "Some coffee and bagels."

"We like your bread, the bagel," Issa said. "It is very good."

"Thank you," said the man. "We should go now."

"He is a good man," Nouhou said in Songhay as the man and his wife left. "He is kind and generous and not boastful. He'd make a good Muslim."

"But he's Jewish."

"Anybody can become a Muslim," Nouhou said. "He'd be a good candidate."

"He is a lot nicer than some of the Chinese, Arabs, and other Jews around here. They all charge too much for space," Issa said.

Nouhou laughed. "Any why shouldn't they? We all have the same problems. Many of us have no papers. None of us have power, anyway. Besides, we have little choice. Where are we going to sell our things? They have space that we need, so they take much money from us. Wouldn't you do the same thing?"

"No, I would not, Nouhou," Issa retorted. "I like making

money, but I don't like making it through another person's pain and suffering."

"Neither do I, really. It's not the Jaguar way," Nouhou admitted.

"That's true, but some of our brothers let money swell their heads, and they lose their way and become greedy."

"True. True."

A tall burly black man dressed in a long wool coat and a red, black, and green wool cap walked into the shop carrying a bolt of brown cloth. "Mind if I set it down?" he asked.

"R. J., wassup?" Issa greeted him.

R. J. sat down on a metal chair. "Christmas will be here soon. Let's hope that Santa takes good care of everybody."

"I see you bought Mali cloth," Nouhou observed, pointing to the brown-and-black print cloth based upon traditional Malian mudcloth designs.

"Yeah. It's Mali cloth, but it's not made from cotton. It's polyester, man, and made in Cameroon. Much cheaper."

"What you do with it?" Issa asked.

"I'll mix it with black nylon to make bags like the ones that come from your homeland. You want to buy some, Issa?"

"Yeah. They will sell."

"Good. I can come back next week. How many you want?"

"Maybe ten or fifteen."

"Try fifteen and see how they sell. You can pay me later."

"How much you make this year?" Issa asked.

"About eighty thousand."

"Eighty thousand dollars?" Issa said with wonder.

"That's right."

"You pay tax?" Nouhou asked.

R. J. laughed. "You kiddin'? I never pay taxes. How 'bout you guys? You having a good year?"

"It's bad here, R. J.," Issa said.

"Yeah. We too far off the street," Nouhou said. "We need permit for street. How we can get one?"

"They're hard to get, but I've got friends who rent them. If you want, I'll telephone one of them and see what his rates are."

"That's good," Nouhou said.

"I'll give you the number next time I stop by, okay?"

"Yeah."

R. J. stood up. "Got to go uptown and then on to Brooklyn. Long day today. See you brothers later."

Issa and Nouhou had been in the Broadway storefront shop for little more than a month. Being downtown changed their routines. In Harlem, Saturdays and Sundays proved to be the busiest and most profitable days. Downtown, weekends meant tourist time, and tourists rarely ventured into the shop, preferring to stroll along Canal Street. In Harlem, Issa attended to errands or visited his Asian suppliers on Mondays or Tuesdays. Downtown, they would sometimes close their unheated shop on Saturdays and Sundays.

As time passed, frustration mounted. Their monthly rent—twenty-five hundred dollars—had not yet been offset by increased volume. Issa let his phone bill lapse, and in short order the phone company disconnected his service. Phoneless, he asked friends and associates to call his beeper, which he kept attached to his belt, and used pay phones to return their calls.

Downtown, they usually sold a good deal of merchandise during weekday lunch hours. On a good day they might take in seven hundred dollars between 11:30 A.M. and 2:00 P.M. Boyfriends bought their girlfriends scarves. Girlfriends bought their boyfriends gloves or baseball caps. Husbands bought their wives handbags or wool caps. Wives bought their husbands Nigerien leather attaché cases. Women bought themselves "Gucci" or "Polo" handbags. If this pace could only be maintained, Issa thought, he'd make it downtown. Invariably, though, the pace slackened by mid-afternoon, a fact that depressed the usually irrepressible Issa.

"It's no good," he told Nouhou. "How can we go on like this? I have no phone, and I can't send money home."

"What can we do?" Nouhou wondered, who also felt frustrated.

"We can go up to 116th Street."

"I don't know if I can go there. I still have pride, and I don't want to give money to those people at the Mosque."

"But how will you get by?"

"I will give this space a bit more time and then try to find another space, maybe back in Harlem."

"I also have pride, but I will not let pride get in the way of my responsibilities. I must provide for my family."

"As we all must," Nouhou said soberly.

"How can we make a life here, Nouhou? America is crazy, is it not?" At that moment homesickness swept into his being. Thinking of home, he compared his current misfortune to Khadija's considerable success. He realized that although he took great personal pride in his Jaguar capacities, he would have to become more successful if he was to stay married to his wife. His present difficulties had also strained his relationships with American women—even with Keisha. At least his forays with Dabé provided encouraging measures of pride and cash. "Nouhou," he continued, returning to the subject under discussion, "people here have little pride or responsibility. The American Blacks don't have it. The Spanish don't have it. The Whites don't have it. It is always Look out for yourself." He paused a moment. "This," he said, "is not our way."

"Yes. It's Look out for yourself," Nouhou repeated glumly.

"Just like that drought in Niger ten years ago," Issa said. "They called it the Look Out for Yourself Drought. You remember?"

"It was a hard time," Nouhou said, thinking back.

"There was little food that year," Issa stated, "and people who had food didn't want to share it with anybody. That was a low moment for us. We used to share what nourishment we had with people who had no food. That is the Muslim way, is it not?"

"Yes, it is, brother," Nouhou agreed wholeheartedly.

"In America, every day is like the Look Out for Yourself Drought."

"America has changed me," Nouhou reflected with sadness in his voice. "It has probably changed you, too, Issa. Do you think you'd ever again be happy living in Tarma, or Niamey?"

"I don't know. America is crazy, but I still like it. So many opportunities. With the right array of papers, I could make so much money and live very well. Soon I'll have my papers and my problems will be solved," he added with more customary enthusiasm.

"Exactly. We must be patient, Issa. Things will work out. Remember our Songhay proverb: An old man's talk may appear to be twisted, but in the end, it works itself out."

"I've always liked that one," Issa said.

"With patience, Issa, you may become one of those international Jaguars like Kareem who travel between Africa and America, importing and exporting, making lots a money and having two families, one in Africa and one in New York. That, my friend, would be a good life, would it not?"

"It's what I hope for myself."

"With patience, Issa, it may come to pass."

"May God will it."

Their conversation had made them feel a bit more upbeat as they kept the cold at bay by huddling over the space heater.

chapter 27

A few months later, Issa and Dabé stood by the battered van just as a group of uniformed children marched into the Catholic elementary school on 117th Street and Lenox Avenue. A tall chain-link fence separated the school playground from the street. Dabé had parked his road-weary vehicle across the street from the school next to the 117th Street entrance of the Malcolm Shabazz Harlem Market—a large blacktopped square, also enclosed by an imposing chain-link fence. The market had become the economic home to 240 street vendors—mostly West African.

The bright sun hung low in the morning sky. Issa still felt a trace of winter's chill, but the scent of spring now permeated the air. He sipped coffee as Dabé, Nouhou, and Seyni loaded the van for a journey to Pittsburgh. For this trip they packed Africana only: bright striped Ghanaian reproductions of kente cloth; red leather sacks and bags from Niger, black-and-white mudcloth from Mali, round-headed wooden Akwaba dolls from Ghana, and the ever-popular "Colon," wooden statues depicting colonial caricatures, carved in Côte d'Ivoire. Because Dabé, as usual, wanted to get an early start, Issa and his crew had come to the market at sunrise. The loading complete, they prepared to leave.

As Issa sat down in the van, he thought about how much had

Paul Stoller

changed during the past several months. He and Nouhou had finally given up their space on Broadway. The only way to make one's way downtown, they concluded, would be to rent an expensive shelf or table directly on Canal Street, where shopper volume remained continuously heavy. Although their shop had stood only fifty meters uptown from Canal Street, that distance put them at a great economic disadvantage. Tending to be timid explorers, most tourists followed the crowds, which rarely walked by their shop. Worse yet, the City of New York had failed to complete its subway work, which filled the space with construction noise and kept the flow of shoppers to a trickle.

Modest sales and immodest rents compelled them to try something else. Nouhou looked for store space on 125th Street, but found the rents too high. Eventually, he reluctantly rented a stall at the Malcolm Shabazz Harlem Market, where he sold baseball caps, gloves, and scarves. The Masjid Malcolm Shabazz ran the market with competent efficiency, and a daily rent of seven dollars made the space quite affordable. And yet, the pace of business seemed slow. Many of the Jaguars complained that the fence enclosing the 116th Street space made it look more like a prison than a market. But, as shoppers gradually discovered the new market, business picked up.

Despite the significant downturn in their fortunes, many of the Jaguars stoically adapted themselves to their altered economic situation. Seyni rented two stalls under one of two large, striped tents set up by the market management. There he displayed his selections of African clothing: baggy pants, loose-fitting shirts, and djelabahs—all fashioned from colorful West African print fabrics. Seyni had become quite careful about his money, which he now marshaled with great determination. "I must not waste my money," he told Nouhou. "I want to return to Niger to marry a woman from my village. Then I'll bring my wife here to study a trade that will help us both here and at home. We will stay for a few years, and then I will return to Niger and grow potatoes. I don't want to stay here for a long time. I still want to make a life for myself at home."

There were other men from Niger at the new market. One sold counterfeit watches: Rolex, Cartier, Benrus. Some of his lower-end novelty watches looked like small pistols. Moving the "barrel" revealed the watch's face.

The shift in market space did not affect Kareem. Just as his appetite for good food swelled his belly, so is appetite for commerce expanded the profitability of his import-export business. In Africa, he supplied Nigerien markets with North American electronics. In North America, he provided Nigerien leather and textiles to vendors and shops throughout the eastern third of the United States. Since Kareem's American wife was proud of his African heritage, she agreed to send their children to Niger for their secondary-school education. They both agreed that life as African American teenagers in the Bronx would soon corrupt the sense of discipline and respect they had taught their children.

Dabé, the Chauffeur, continued his unrelenting tour of the American bush: Chicago, Indianapolis, Oklahoma City, Memphis, New Orleans, Dallas, Santa Fe. With zest, he drove through rain and snow, howling wind gusts and thick fog—all to bring his cargo and passengers to their destinations. One thing differed, however, for now Dabé had a partner in the chauffeur business: Issa.

Mounkaila, who had helped Issa and Nouhou find commercial space in Lower Manhattan, continued to sell baseball caps, scarves, and gloves along Canal Street. Volume remained high—so high, in fact, that he asked his oldest son, a man in his twenties, to come to New York to help him. Once his oldest son acclimated to New York, Mounkaila would return to his wife in Niger. But the right time had not yet arrived for his return. He once told Issa that he was getting too old to remain for long in New York. "It is a town for young men. I am ready to return to my village. I'm an elder now, and I want to rest."

That morning, Dabé joined Issa in the van and started the engine. As usual they drove down West End Avenue, crawling through the always clogged Lincoln Tunnel. At the junction of the New Jersey Turnpike, they headed south toward the Pennsylvania Turnpike, where they'd turn west toward Pittsburgh and an African American cultural festival. "Many dollars to be gathered there," Dabé remarked.

"May God will it," Issa said.

By now Issa had accustomed himself to the routine of the road: the drone of the van's engine; the whistle and whir of the wind thrashing the windshield; the hypnotic thumps created by the contact of tires and highway seams; the panoramic vistas of seemingly endless farmland; the antiseptic blandness of fast food restaurants; the dim seediness of cheap roadside motels. Being on the road excited Issa. He felt like an adventurer. Even now the sheen of exploration hadn't worn off. Travel along the interstate prompted states of dreaminess that charged his imagination. Although he and Dabé traveled thousands of road miles in silence, there seemed no end to Issa's internal conversations. By now Issa had developed the habit of conducting internal dialogues—something he hadn't done in Africa. The one who had always talked now explored the depths of his emotional being. He thought endlessly about the vast economic potential that America held for him and wondered how he might better capitalize on American opportunity. He well understood the American penchant for trademarks—real or fake. For four years he had bought all sorts of handbags, all of them manufactured by Chinese and Koreans. The bags all displayed prestigious trademarks: Gucci, Polo, Dooney & Bourke. The shoppers on 125th Street, locals and tourists alike, bought tens of thousands of dollars of merchandise from him. But no matter his entrepreneurial skill, Issa's powerlessness limited his options. In the end he had decided to team up with Dabé. His decision had so far proven to be a good one.

From the outset, however, Issa knew that he couldn't blindly follow Dabé's path. On the one hand, Issa like seeing new places and meeting new women. On the other hand, he sensed that he needed more stability in his life. Unlike Dabé, he didn't want a hotel to be his home address. He didn't want to sleep in a different bed every other night or suffer a regular diet of tasteless hamburgers and greasy french fries. He also missed the emotional and physical comfort of family. How long would it be until he established his own household, until he fathered children? Jaguars, as Issa knew well, did not live lives of regret. If they encountered dead ends on their various paths, they turned around and sought other paths to their destinations. Issa felt that he had reached a crossroads on his path. He sensed that soon he would have to choose a new direction. If he took the path to the left, he'd continue to make money by traveling with Dabé. He'd send some of it home, reinvest some, and spend the rest of it buying clothes, seeing films, and entertaining women. He admitted that such a path was exciting, but had no real destination. In his three months of almost continuous travel, he'd been back to Keisha's four times. She was the only woman in America who had held his interest. She continued to remind him of Khadija. Through her resourcefulness and passion, she had taught him about American sexuality, which he found every exciting.

On remote stretches of the interstate in Pennsylvania or Kentucky, he would sometimes close his eyes and see himself walking on an immense rock-strewn plain. Completely lost, he would pray to Allah to show him a way out. Then he'd open his eyes and see yet another farmscape. He continued to feel that his legal status stood between him and Jaguar fame and fortune. If only he had papers. He had tried to obtain a work authorization permit. He had reapplied and had been rejected again and again. Seyni had told him that he had little chance of being granted asylum. "The politics for immigration are bad now," he said. "The only way you'll get a work authorization card is if you marry an American citizen."

Issa had avoided this option, for he did not yet want to take a second wife. He had enjoyed his freedom in the U.S. and knew that even though Nouhou was happily married to an American woman, such a union was quite demanding. Furthermore, Issa's ongoing infidelities in America hadn't diminished his love for and obligation to Khadija. When they had lived together, the thought of taking a second wife hadn't entered his mind. He remembered that when they married, Issa and Khadija both believed that changing times and economic circumstances had made polygamy an outmoded practice. Khadija had stated that she'd have a difficult time living in a household of Songhay co-wives. Issa also admitted to himself that he'd be hard pressed to manage a polygamous household. And then there was the cultural problem. How would Issa find an American woman who could understand him, let alone his other wife? Issa decided not to reapply for asylum for now. Having spent almost a thousand dollars in legal and bondsman fees, he realized the futility of his quest. He'd have to continue his trading without papers. He'd manage, he told himself.

As they crossed the Delaware River and collected their ticket for the Pennsylvania Turnpike, Dabé's voice ended Issa's reverie. "We'll be in Pittsburgh in five hours," Dabé said. "We'll go to the Civic Center first."

Paul Stoller

"Will it be very beautiful in the mountains this time of year?" Issa asked, having learned to appreciate the vast beauty of the American countryside.

"I don't know."

"Maybe the trees will be flowering?"

"Maybe. I don't notice things like that. Too busy driving."

Light traffic meant that they made good time. Before long they had climbed the gentle hills the of Pennsylvania Dutch country. In the distance smooth mountains rose like loaves of dark bread.

NIGER

While Issa took in the blooming wild flowers in the mountains of Central Pennsylvania, Khadija felt the stickiness of sweltering Nigerien heat amid the mountains of canned goods stacked in her shop. Sweat rolled down her cheeks and trickled along her backbone. The sides of her blouse stuck to her skin in patches. For relief, she rubbed her forehead, arched her back, and daydreamed of a cool dip in the Niger River. For her, the months that Europeans called "spring" had simply brought on incessant, energy-depleting heat.

However difficult these climatic discomforts may have been, they had little effect on Khadija's zest for her new business. To compensate for the heat, she shifted her hours of operation, opening at dawn instead of 7:00 A.M. and closing around 9:00 P.M. instead of sunset. At midday, she closed the shop and went home to lunch, sleep, and bathe before returning at 4:00 P.M. Although the heat compelled Nigeriens to operate at a slower, more deliberate pace, they still managed to go about their business—and, much to Khadija's delight, continued to buy dry goods at her shop.

This day, however, had been particularly trying. The Harmattan had been howling since mid-morning, transforming Khadija's shop into a hot, stuffy, and gritty vault. Although she now paid for electricity in the shop and had purchased a large fan and a cooler, these conveniences had also become inconveniences. The fan had stopped working the day before—too much dust and dirt in the motor. And to make matters even worse, the electricity had been cut for several hours, making her cooler rather hot.

One of Khadija's regulars, a woman well into her forties, lumbered into the shop. "It's too hot today, sister. The sun is now lower in the sky, but the wind, it still blows very hot."

"We all suffer, do we not? But with patience," Khadija said formulaically, "we will get by."

"That is true. But we'd get by a bit easier if your fan worked."

Khadija smiled and agreed.

Late afternoon customers gradually drifted into the shop. One woman bought some Dutch Wax cloth. Another woman bought soap and laundry detergent. Another bought kerosene, peanut oil, and a small bag of dried dates. A tall, slim, middle-aged man dressed in a white boubou and baggy pants strolled in. Despite the heat's persistence, he looked cool and comfortable.

"Good afternoon," he said, greeting Khadija.

Khadija replied with her usual graciousness.

"I've heard, madame," he said, "that you have silver jewelry at very good prices."

"I do have silver jewelry. I will leave it to you, sir, to say if I'm selling them at good prices."

The man smiled. "I want to buy my wife a gift."

Khadija led him to a locked glass case in which she had arranged her silver and gold jewelry.

"You have very good taste. May I see the large Agadez cross?"

"By all means." Khadija opened the case and gave him the necklace.

"It is very beautiful and well crafted."

"I think so, too. It will make a very fine gift, sir."

"How much?"

"Since you're such a fine gentleman," Khadija said. "I'll make you a special offer: five thousand francs."

"That is a very good price for such silver, madame, but I must make a counteroffer: three thousand," the man replied, as Khadija expected. At market, a patron or client who didn't bargain would lose face.

"How about four thousand?" Khadija asked.

The man beamed. "Agreed, madame. It is a pleasure to shop

Paul Stoller

here. I will tell my wife and friends to come and buy products from you."

"Thank you. Your words bring me honor."

"The honor is well deserved," he said graciously, leaving the shop with his purchase.

Later in the day, Yusef's young cousin Jamal walked in.

"Hey, Khadija, hey. How is your late afternoon?"

"I am in health and good spirits, Jamal. And yours?"

"I praise God for my well-being."

Khadija pulled a bottle of Coca-Cola from the large clay pot that sat on the floor and gave it to Jamal.

"It's cool," he stated with gratitude.

"Yes. When they cut the current, I put some bottles in the 'African refrigerator,'" she said, pointing to the clay plot.

Jamal smiled. He opened the bottle against the edge of the shop counter and took a swig of the Coke. "I come with a message from Yusef. He'd like you to have dinner with us tonight."

"But I will not close until later. You will have to wait too long to eat."

"We'll wait for you. We eat late on hot evenings."

As Khadija's business had expanded, her friendship with Yusef deepened. He continued to extend her credit, introduced her to the most reasonable wholesale suppliers, and helped her to build display cases and shelves. Khadija wondered why Yusef, who had two wives and seven children, expended so much of his energy on a married woman. "Why do you do these things for me?" she asked him when he was fashioning her jewelry display case.

"Among my people, friends extend themselves to one another," he replied.

"But I have given nothing to you," Khadija protested.

"Oh yes you have," Yusef said. "I've watched you closely, and you've taught me much about selling products to customers. You and I offer the same kinds of products, but your sales have already outdistanced mine. Why? It's the way you deal with people. I've watched you and learned from you, and my sales are increasing." He paused and looked intently at her. "And I have much more to learn from you."

Khadija had never met a man who accorded her so much respect. She knew that Yusef liked her. She also thought he might be attracted to her. But what made the respect sweeter still was that Yusef seemed genuinely interested in her friendship. He didn't want to be her economic rival or take over her business. And so far, at least, he had been quite reserved and respectable. Such reserve and respectability did not resonate with what she had heard about Arab male behavior toward women. And yet, Yusef seemed exceptional. He'd invite her to his compound, where they'd eat meals prepared by one of his two wives, neither of whom he had yet introduced to Khadija. Among the Songhay it is rare for men and women to share meals; it is almost unheard of among Arabs. During these meals they'd talk about subjects that men rarely discuss with women: business trends, political policies, traditional social customs, changing religious practices. Khadija enjoyed these discussions. She had much to say about business practices and traditional social customs. And she listened intently when Yusef, a man well read in Islamic philosophy, talked about society and religion.

"Why do you talk to a woman about these matters?" Khadija once asked him.

"Because you are astute in business and are very intelligent."

That night she closed her shop a bit earlier and walked the short distance to Yusef's. Children played tag in the darkened streets. The murmur of evening talk breezed through the night air. She heard the crackle of radios tuned to evening news broadcasts. Young men as tall and dark as Niger river grass whisped by on their way to their evening assignations. A woman appeared briefly in the shadows of a compound portal like a snake emerging from its nest. She threw a basin of dirty water into the dirt road and disappeared back into her home. At an intersection, the stench of a rotting pile of garbage saturated the air.

She soon reached the door to Yusef's villa, where she clapped her hands three times to announce her arrival. Jamal, who was waiting for her, opened the door.

"Yusef is waiting for you. I hope you're hungry. There is much cous-cous and mutton, and a spicy harissa."

Jamal led Khadija into a large compound, a rectangular space the size of a basketball court, lined by shallow, single-story cement rooms, whose stark uniformity reminded one of barracks. One small mudbrick structure, the cooking house, stood to one side of the compound, next to a well. Yusef, looking cool and lanky in a his loose-fitting white tunic and baggy white pants, sat at a small table under a tree in the middle of the compound. His wives and children could be neither seen nor heard. Jamal left Khadija and retired to one of the rooms situated along the compound's long back wall.

"Sit down. The food is ready," Yusef said, pointing to two covered enamel bowls. He gave Khadija a glass plate and a wooden spoon. "May I serve you?"

"Shouldn't I serve you?"

"You are my guest."

"True." Because she wanted to meet Yusef's wives, she asked, "Why doesn't one of your wives serve us?"

"Ahh," said Yusef, who didn't seem at all perturbed by such a potentially impertinent question. "They made the food. Is that not enough? Besides, it gives me pleasure to serve good food."

"But I would very much like to meet your wives," Khadija persisted.

Yusef served the cous-cous and sauce. His copper skin glowed in the lantern light. "In our tradition, family life is very, very private. Our women are extraordinary people, but in our compounds, people who are not family do not often see them."

"Not even friends?"

"Not if the friends are males."

"And what of me? I am your female friend."

"For which I am grateful."

"Then why haven't I met them?"

"In time, I hope that you will. They are remarkable women. They have seen you and heard your words. They have much respect for you."

"Do you insist that they wear veils and remain behind your compound's walls?"

"I do not insist. They do not wear veils in the compound, and, of course, they often leave the compound, both day and night, to visit their female friends. They cover themselves when they leave. That is our custom. They are very beautiful women. This way, young men treat them with respect. That is important to my wives—and to me."

Khadija thought about the limitations of such a traditional household. She felt that she could never accept such social restriction. She ate in silence. The creaking of insects filled the night air. As people strolled by, the murmur of their conversations intensified then faded away in the distance. Thousands of stars filled the inky blue sky above the compound, which was illuminated by the dull yellow glow of a single lantern. The dim light intensified Yusef's features, which Khadija studied as she ate.

"Among the Songhay," Khadija said, breaking the silence, "women run the household, but we are also free to work. We also believe in modesty, but we never wear veils."

"I like this," Yusef confessed. "I like your spirit of independence." Yusef shifted in his chair and looked intently at Khadija. "Let me ask you something."

"Yes?"

"Did your father have more than one wife?"

"No. My father died when I was a child. My mother raised me. She is a proud-hearted and generous woman."

"And your husband?"

"His father had three wives. His mother is still alive, but both his father and the co-wives are dead."

"What do you think of a man having more than one wife?" Yusef asked.

"I don't like it. I've seen what that has done to my mother's brother. He has three wives and many girlfriends. He's not able to pay attention to his children or to his wives. His compound is filled with resentment. Seeing that, I told myself that I would never be someone's second or third wife."

"But you know," Yusef added, "there can be much peace and happiness in a household with several wives. There is in mine. The burden of household work is divided, as is child care. And if the co-wives respect one another, sharing the chores gives them a sense of freedom. Even we Arabs recognize that the world is different today. I know of some households where one or two wives stay at home while the third one works outside of the house. They all have children and respect one another—like sisters—and are loved and respected by their husband."

Paul Stoller

"That sounds interesting. But it's hard to believe that it really works. Don't your wives get jealous of one another?"

"Sometimes, but not often. They respect one another."

Khadija again lapsed into silence to think about Yusef's statements.

This time it was Yusef who broke the silence. "And your husband? Would he want to take a second wife?"

"When we married, we agreed to maintain a modern marriage."

"What do you mean?"

"We agreed that Issa wouldn't take another wife and that we'd remain faithful to one another."

"And?"

"I have been faithful to him, even though I haven't seen him in almost five years. It is difficult."

"You, then, are a fine woman." Yusef paused and took a deep breath. "And your husband? What of him?"

"I don't know," she said, pausing briefly. "I doubt that he has remained faithful. I do know that he has not taken a second wife."

"When will he return?"

"I don't know."

"Will you go to see him in America?"

"Once I wanted to. But he's made no effort to bring me there. Now that I have the shop, I don't want to leave Niger."

"Forgive me for saying so," Yusef said softly, "but your life is difficult. It's filled with sorrow: the death of your father; the pain of living with your husband's family in Tarma; the absence of your husband; the emptiness of a house without children."

However much Khadija tried to conceal her emotions, her expression betrayed her deep sadness. Yusef sensed her despair. He leaned toward her and touched her hand lightly. "Please forgive me for saying this, Khadija, but as your friend I must: How can you live like this?"

Khadija stared up at the starry sky. "My shop gives me strength. I have my family here and my friends." Khadija fought back tears. "I would very much like to meet your wives," she said again. Her conversation with Yusef had increased her desire to know the people in his family.

"But it's late, and they have no time to get themselves ready."

"That doesn't matter to me. I wouldn't want to put them to any trouble," she said gently.

"Very well. I'll get them." Yusef stood up.

Moments later he led his wives, Zeinab and Lila, into the compound. Dressed in black robes redolent of perfume, their movement into the compound reminded Khadija of a gentle, fragrant breeze. Lila's smooth brown skin stretched with her broad but shy smile. She was short and thin with a round face offset by bright hazel eyes. Zeinab, by contrast, was quite tall. Her green eyes, which glistened in the pale light, softened a face whose angular features made it look hard.

They extended their hands to Khadija.

"How are you?" Lila asked in Arabic.

"How goes the night?" Zeinab asked, also in Arabic.

"Praise be to God," Khadija responded, using one of the few phrases she knew in Arabic.

As Lila began to speak in a velvety voice, Yusef translated. "We are very pleased to meet you. We have heard your voice and have seen you walk. We like the way you talk and move. We respect your work and think you are a handsome woman with a beautiful spirit. This we feel very strongly."

"Thank you," Khadija said, again through Yusef. "You are very kind."

"There's more," Zeinab continued. "We want you to know that you're always welcome in our house. We welcome you as our sister. We've been asking our husband to bring you around, but he felt it was bad manners to do so. We're happy that you insisted on meeting us."

"In our tradition," Lila continued, "a person learns much by listening to the way others talk, by watching the way they move, by understanding their faces. We've had time to listen to your words and watch your movements, and now we've understood your face."

After a few moments, Khadija got up to take her leave of Yusef and his two lovely wives.

"We hope you will visit us again soon," they said as she left the compound.

Paul Stoller

The "spring" heat continued to sap the vitality of the increasingly barren landscape. Grasses shriveled and dried. Fields became parcels of sand and millet stumps. Baked relentlessly by the sun, the muddy bottoms of ponds, now waterless, looked like plains of old, cracked leather. Spring brought not the fresh green fragrance of renewal, but the pungent smell of death. In the bush vultures circled the swollen carcasses of dead cows and donkeys. In the city the stench of rotting garbage mixed with the mustiness of dust—a carrier of deadly meningitis.

As spring progressed the humidity of the approaching rains compounded the heat's discomfort. In late May humidity during the day increased the heat's intensity. In the evening sultriness robbed the night air of its cool relief. The hot humid days and stuffy sultry nights continued until the *kursol,* the Songhay term for the time of the first, unalterably violent dust storms. Sometimes these storms blew dry and gritty; sometimes downpours followed the wind and dust.

Khadija prayed that the rains would come soon. During May she would rise well before dawn to savor a few cool breezes that wafted into the compound. At first light the air's moisture made the sky hazy. She would walk to her shop and notice puffy cumulus clouds building up to the south and west. The fleecy white clouds would soon puff their way across the sky, promising yet another day of unwavering heat and humidity.

When walking to the shop on an afternoon in early June, however, she noticed a band of dark gray clouds on the eastern horizon. Suddenly, the breeze changed directions, now blowing from the east. In short order, the breeze stiffened, carrying the strong smell of dust mixed with the faint scent of rain. Would it rain or not?

As the cloud bank built higher in the eastern sky, its color gradually changed from dark gray to light brown—perhaps the sign of an impending dust storm. Khadija quickened her pace and reached her shop before the storm hit. She paused outside the door to watch the mountainous cloud of dust move in on Niamey.

The storm's approach triggered a frenzy of activity in the neighborhood. Boys tethered their stray animals. Men closed window shutters. Women gathered their children off the street. Just before the dust cloud, which looked like a giant brown wave about to break upon a beach, came crashing down on Niamey, Khadija enjoyed a few moments of eerie silence, the kind of quiet calm that sometimes accompanies the unleashing of nature's raw power. She breathed deeply, sensing the cool proximity of moisture. The rumble of thunder, which soon shattered this rare moment of silent pleasure, jolted her into action. She rushed into her shop and frantically closed her shutters and door. She grabbed a length of cloth and wrapped it around her head and face, in the manner of desert nomads, to filter the dust and grit.

The wind's thump against the side of the shop announced the dust wave's arrival, which quickly blotted out the sun. The temperature plummeted. Rivulets of wind streamed through the cracks around Khadija's windows and door, thickening the shop air with dust. Khadija tried to turn on her lights, but the electricity was out. She found a flashlight. A shaft of light illumined air as thick as fog. Outside, the howling wind lifted poorly secured roofs off their foundations and flapped unfastened window shutters and doors. As the thunder came closer, the smell of rain grew more pungent.

At first large droplets of rain splattered sporadically on the daub roof and dappled the dirt road in the front of the shop. The thunder, much closer now, seemed to bring on the rain, which whooshed into Niamey in wind-swept sheets. The sound of the downpour on neighboring tin roofs sounded like a stampede of cattle. Khadija wondered if her unimproved roof could withstand such natural fury.

She soon had her answer. The first leak sprang in the shop's back corner. Mud flowed down the whitewashed wall, gushing over her blanket and fabric displays. The second leak appeared in the roof's middle, allowing a narrow waterfall of mud to cascade onto the jewelry display box. The intensity of the downpour increased. More leaks appeared—indeed, so many leaks that Khadija could do little to protect her goods. With resignation she sat near her counter and glumly watched mud stream down all of the shop's walls. She had been so preoccupied that spring that she had neither the time nor the funds to repair the roof. And now she would have to spend considerable sums to repair the roof and replace damaged goods, for surely this would be the first of many rains during the season.

Somehow she'd get beyond this setback, she said to herself. These thoughts of resilience, however, had little effect on the storm, which mercilessly lashed into her leaky shop. Splattered by mud, she moved her chair to the most protected corner of the shop and shivered in the darkness, waiting for the storm to abate. After almost two hours, she looked up and saw Yusef standing in her doorway. Having secured his own shop, he had been on his way to visit his compatriot's shop when he noticed the state of Khadija's roof. He walked toward Khadija's slumped figure and picked her up very slowly. Before she realized what she was doing, she had wrapped her arms around him. They embraced one another, first very slowly and then with great abandon. She led him to the cot in her storage room. They quickly shed their wet clothes and let their passion sweep over them much like the storm swept over Niamey. The beauty of their lovemaking amazed Khadija. It had been such a long time since she had been intimate with a man. She wondered how she had been able to get along without this marvelous and necessary aspect of life. For some reason she felt no guilt about taking pleasure from a man other than Issa. She also harbored little concern about how this passionate interlude might affect her friendship with Yusef. For her, fate had gloriously intervened in her life.

chapter 30

Two months later, well into the rainy season, Khadija walked home after closing her shop for the evening. The dirt streets glimmered in the bright moonlight. The full moon danced among scattered clouds. From behind the high walls and closed doors that the lined the road, she heard a baby's cry, the murmur of conversations, the din of cassette music.

Business was still very good. She had recovered from the first rainstorm's devastation. Yusef had helped her rebuild the roof and rearrange her shop. She replaced items that had been ruined or spoiled by mud and water. She had a new tin roof installed. Although the fury of subsequent storms rivaled that of the first one, rain posed no further threat to her goods. Khadija felt good about the decisive way she had acted in the face of adversity. Issa had long ago taught her that no matter one's circumstance, a trader must demonstrate decisiveness and strength.

Her friendship with Yusef had continued, as did their intimacy. For now they enjoyed one another and avoided the topic of where their passion might lead. This avoidance didn't bother Khadija because she felt good about her life now. Her business success had made her beam with pride. She enjoyed the good natured banter with friends and family that took place in her shop. And she savored the sex she shared with Yusef. He'd visit her after hours in her shop. They'd drink tea, talk, make love slowly—sometimes for as long as several hours. Then they'd both return to their respective homes.

As she walked into her mother's compound that evening, the aroma of peanut sauce infused the air. Her mother greeted her warmly, as did two of her cousins and her old friend, Ramatu, who visited frequently in the evenings.

"Come daughter," her mother said. "Sit and eat in your house."

"Sit little sister," Ramatu said. "After you eat, we want to hear about your day."

The dying cooking fire crackled. A donkey brayed. The din of conversation echoed in the thin night air. Khadija's thoughts drifted to Issa. She knew that uncertainty charted the course of their future. Perhaps he'd stay in America for many years or even settle there permanently. Perhaps he'd split his time between Niger and New York City. America had changed the man she'd married; she worried that he'd never again be happy just living in Niger. And yet she didn't want to ask him for a divorce. She still loved him and wanted to have his children. If Issa could only have a business like Kareem's and split his time between Africa and America, she'd be able to have children while maintaining her independence. She felt blessed by a circle of friends and family who loved and respected her. In time, she reasoned, she'd either reconnect with Issa or marry

Paul Stoller

someone else and, with God's blessing, have children. For now, she had come to terms with her life. Life triggered in her a deep sense of satisfaction. Even though she hadn't followed the traditional path of Nigerien women, she had become an independent, modern person. Against all odds, she had become a Jaguar.

Khadija sipped more water, finished her meal, and then told her family and friends the story of her day.

THE AMERICAN BUSH

As Khadija closed her shop in Niamey and walked home for an evening of food and conversation, Issa sat at a picnic table at a rest stop on the interstate near Indianapolis and stared at a cluster of trees in the distance. The summer sky above had been blanched by the noon sun. The air was thick with the smell of exhaust. There was no breeze, and it was hot and sticky. He was once again wearing baggy jeans, a white T-shirt, and Air Jordans, having given up wearing African clothes when he traveled in the bush with Dabé.

Seated at the table next to him was a large family having a picnic. A heavy-set older man, dressed in a blue baseball cap, blue T-shirt, and white shorts, sat at the edge that table. He carefully cut a hamburger into bite-sized morsels and put some of them on a young child's plate.

"Thank you, Grandpa," the little girl said.

"You make sure to eat it all, Becky," he replied.

At the far end of the table a large woman and another little girl were eating their hamburgers and fries. "I like being on vacation, Mommy. When will we get to the lake?"

"Soon, dear," the large woman said as she ate. "Very soon." But after looking at her daughter's half-eaten hamburger, she added, "Jenny, we're not going anywhere until you finish your lunch."

Americans never ceased to amaze Issa. How many times had he seen parents coaxing their children to finish their meals? More often than not the parents failed, and large amounts of food had to be thrown away. In Niger, children often went hungry and so ate every scrap of food offered to them.

Families streamed by Issa's table headed for a meal at Pizza Hut or Roy Rogers. Dabé had gone to use the telephone and had left Issa alone with his Coke and his half-eaten Roy Rogers hamburger. Issa didn't like the hamburger but was determined to finish it—as a matter of principle. A bee buzzed over the open lid of Issa's soda. He felt invisible, a common experience for him in America.

Issa and Dabé had been on the road for more than two weeks now and were finally returning to New York, their van empty, their pockets bulging with cash. As a traveling Jaguar, Issa had made more money than he could have ever imagined. He had been able to send lots of it to his family in Tarma, who, he had heard, sang his praises in the streets of the village. They said that Issa was a great Jaguar who had explored the farthest reaches of the American bush. They said that he owned large cars and big houses. They've said many things, Issa thought to himself, sighing quietly.

Issa might have conquered the American bush, but he felt somewhat deflated by his success. He spent more time on the road than in Harlem, and he missed his friends. Although Issa was always surrounded by people—the crowds at convention centers, outdoor festivals, hotel lobbies, and highway rest stops—he felt increasingly alone. Citizens of the world, he realized, rarely feel completely comfortable and at home. Having no kin in America, he missed his family in Niger. Alone at night in some highway hotel room, his thoughts drifted to Khadija. He would see her face and imagine her, with no small measure of pride, tending her shop. During such moments, he longed to smell the aroma of roasting mutton, to taste the zest of Tarma sauces, to listen to old men's evening stories, to breathe the air of his homeland. And yet, he realized that if he settled in Tarma, life would quickly bore him. Young Jaguars like him, he told himself, need change, challenge, and adventure.

Out of the corner of his eye, he saw Dabé slowly walking toward him and wondered if he would ever want to return home. Sometimes it's hard, Issa said to himself, to be an African in America.

In July 1977, when after a year's residence it was time for me to leave the Songhay village of Mehanna, an elder said to me, "ni go g'iri fagaandi," which literally means, "you will bring boredom to us." In stating this typical Songhay farewell, the elder was implying that he would miss my talk. Among most Songhay, silence usually results in a state of social boredom. Talk provides the foundation for the social personality of the Songhay of the Republic of Niger. It is through external expression rather than internal dialogue that a person constructs the composite of his or her social self. It is through external expression that lessons are learned, that history is told, that change is understood. For most Songhay people and for many other Africans, spoken words are sacred and stories are treasured. This is evident in the works of such celebrated African writers as Chinué Achebe, Amos Tutuola, and N'gugi wa Thiong, whose novels feature more external than internal dialogue.

As an anthropologist, my implication in things African has compelled me write anthropological works that contain many narratives and much dialogue. This effort has been my humble attempt to maintain a representational fidelity to African ways of talking social life—the charge, as it were, of the African griot. By the same token, I have also attempted to maintain representational fidelity to anthropological ways of writing social life, which means that in my ethnographic works narrative has been—with varying degrees of success—juxtaposed with or embedded in theoretical ruminations and social analysis. I am at work, for example, on an ethnography, *Money Has No Smell*, that analyzes in detail the social forces that have affected the social lives and economic practices of West African street traders in New York City. This professional challenge, which I have been proud to undertake, has some representational limitations. The ethnographic writing style sometimes muffles the drama of social life as it is lived. This tendency pulls the reader away from the excitement and trauma of lived reality and limits the depth of characterization. The people in ethnographies, who are sometimes called informants, are often portrayed as unidimensional. In telling the story of *Jaguar*, I wanted to write a text in which the drama of social life was presented in the foreground, in which the personalities of characters were developed through inner reflection and, more important, through outward expression—in words and action. I therefore chose to write a work of fiction. This decision gave me the license to talk social life, to explore the tribulations of contemporary African men and women who struggle with issues of love, desire, regret, and social obligation—ethnographic issues well suited to fiction.

The story of *Jaguar* did not come to me out of thin air; it is based upon a thirty-year association with West African peoples in the Republic of Niger and in New York City. Had I not been conducting ethnographic fieldwork there, this book could not have been written; however, *Jaguar* is not simply an attempt to use fiction to enliven the sometimes staid genre of ethnography. It is also an exploration—through narrative, montage, and characterization—of the social lives of men and women caught in the vortex of global change. It is a story of triumph and disappointment, fidelity and betrayal, courage and timidity, tradition and change. The characters are composites of the men and women I have encountered in Niger and in New York City. Some of the incidents in the book, like the police action to disperse the African market on 125th Street in Harlem in October 1994, did take place and were witnessed by me. Other events in the book, both in Niger and in New York City, are the products of my ethnographically inspired imagination.

Much of this book was written during the 1994–95 academic year, while I was a Guggenheim Fellow. I thank the John Simon Guggenheim Memorial Foundation and West Chester University

Paul Stoller

of Pennsylvania for providing the funds to free me from a year of teaching in order to concentrate on writing projects. As previously mentioned, *Jaguar* is partly a result of ethnographic fieldwork in New York City, conducted between 1992 and 1998, that was graciously supported by research grants from the Wenner-Gren Foundation for Anthropological Research and the National Science Foundation (Law and Social Behavior Program).

I am indebted to many people. For ongoing support and encouragement, I owe deep gratitude to Robert Rosenberg, Lisa Ruggeri, and Allen Feldman, whose hospitality in New York City has been much appreciated. I want to thank my friends David Napier, John Homiak, Jean-Paul Dumont, Elli Dumont, Alma Gottlieb, Philip Graham, Kirin Narayan, Marina Roseman, Patricia Smith, and Dan Rose for their ongoing encouragement and critical insight. I am grateful to my brother Mitchell Stoller and his family, Sheri, Betsy, and Lauren Stoller, for being a part of my life. Sidney and Goldie Stoller, my parents, taught me to appreciate human decency and to savor the wonders of life. For that lesson, I am profoundly indebted. Adamu Jenitongo, my Songhay father, instructed me in the difficult lessons of humility and respect. I struggle to follow his existential path. Jean Rouch, ethnographer extraordinaire, tried to cultivate in me a sense of intellectual bravado and artistic daring. His work has been an inspiration. With a rare and deeply appreciated fidelity, T. David Brent, executive editor at the University of Chicago Press, supported the publication of *Jaguar* from the beginning. I thank him for his friendship. I also thank my good friend John Miller Chernoff for reading the manuscript with his uncanny sensitivity to things African. Jasmin Tahmaseb McConatha was the first person to urge me to write *Jaguar*. I am not only grateful for her four years of unflagging encouragement, but also for her insightful comments that guided my revisions in draft after draft of the text. Her insights are reflected on every page of the book. Last, I must thank the community of West African traders in New York City for graciously inviting me into their lives. Given the difficult circumstances of their everyday struggles in a culturally, socially, and politically alien environment, the daring, creativity, generosity, and humility they embody is quite simply inspirational. It is a privilege to know such people.